MURDER IN NICE

BOOK 6 OF THE MAGGIE NEWBERRY MYSTERIES

SUSAN KIERNAN-LEWIS

SAN MARCO PRESS

Murder in Nice. Book 6 of the Maggie Newberry Mysteries.
Copyright 2014 by Susan Kiernan-Lewis. All rights reserved.

Books by Susan Kiernan-Lewis
The Maggie Newberry Mysteries
Murder in the South of France
Murder à la Carte
Murder in Provence
Murder in Paris
Murder in Aix
Murder in Nice
Murder in the Latin Quarter
Murder in the Abbey
Murder in the Bistro
Murder in Cannes
Murder in Grenoble
Murder in the Vineyard
Murder in Arles
A Provençal Christmas: A Short Story

The Stranded in Provence Mysteries
Parlez-Vous Murder?
Crime and Croissants
Accent on Murder
A Bad Éclair Day
Croak, Monsieur!
Death du Jour
Murder Très Gauche
Wined and Died
A French Country Christmas

The Irish End Games
Free Falling
Going Gone

Heading Home
Blind Sided
Rising Tides
Cold Comfort
Never Never
Wit's End
Dead On
White Out
Black Out

The Mia Kazmaroff Mysteries
Reckless
Shameless
Breathless
Heartless
Clueless
Ruthless

Ella Out of Time
Swept Away
Carried Away
Stolen Away

The French Women's Diet

PROLOGUE

Lanie sipped her glass of red wine. The majestic Hotel Negresco filled the view from her small balcony at the Soho Hotel that faced the busy *Promenade des Anglais*.

She noticed the familiar silhouette of the Negresco even before taking in the curve of the brilliantly blue Mediterranean as it outlined the dramatic stretch of umbrella-dotted beach. To be sure, she thought, the view must be every bit as remarkable from the Negresco—that grand dame of luxury and British superiority. But, as she'd asked Bob last spring when they'd booked the tour: *would you rather stay in a landmark or gaze upon it?*

In the end she'd gotten her way, but not because the idiot cared one way or the other. She shook her head. How the man had risen to become the preeminent travel guru of the Western world she would never understand.

The truth was, the man wouldn't know a *pourboire* from a po'boy. Lanie retreated from the balcony.

If one more person comes simpering up to me to say how nice Nice is, I shall vomit on their Louis Vuittons. She dropped her robe on the carpeted floor before walking to the bathroom, where she gave her appearance in the bathroom mirror a quick, satisfied look before turning off the water cascading into the bathtub. She poured herself another glass of wine, set the bottle on the floor next to the tub, and slipped into the soothing, fragrant hot water.

After the tour's recent drive through Provence, Lanie was officially sick of the smell of lavender, but if she wanted bubbles in her tub tonight she would have to endure it.

God, the French think they invented the stuff...and everything else decent. She made a face as she leaned back into the tub and tried to get comfortable.

As the tension left her shoulders she had to admit it hadn't been a terrible trip so far. Bob had promised her the bulk of the presentations and he'd been true to his word—even without having to sleep with him. The thought was disgusting. Bob Randall was heavyset and continually flushed. She couldn't imagine how they managed to color correct his face in post-production.

She noticed, however, none of it stopped that whore Dee-Dee from coming on to him.

The fact was, this trip to the south of France was critical to all of them—three travel guides vying for one slot as co-anchor on Randall's crazy-successful video travelogue series, *Americans Love Europe.* The ten-day trip along the Côte d'Azur was the audition that would launch one of them—her, Dee-Dee or that skank Frog, Desiree—into the most coveted, career-making position in travel reporting.

She took a sip of her wine and let out a sigh. Maybe she *would* sleep with Randall. With everything at stake, now was probably not the best time to get all moral and pure. If she was careful, Olivier need never know...

She heard a sound from the bedroom.

She held her breath and looked at the closed bathroom door, wine glass still in hand. What was it she heard? A muted creak from a floorboard giving way to a stealthy footstep? The sound of one of the pigeons venturing from the balcony into the room in search of crumbs? Did these old hotels creak and groan for no reason? She strained to listen, but the sound didn't repeat. What was it Bob had said? There had been a recent upswing in attacks against tourists in Nice. Just enough to make her a little edgy... and ruin a perfectly nice bath. After a moment, she let out the breath she was holding. She likely hadn't heard anything at all, she reasoned.

When she heard the sound again, it registered in her brain as a definite creak...coming from the bedroom. She sat up straight in the tub. As she listened to the accelerated drubbing of her heart pounding in her ears, Lanie suddenly remembered she had given Bob a key. But was this the sort of thing he would do? Just enter her room without calling first?

She stared at the closed bathroom door. There had been no reason to lock it. Frankly, she was surprised she had even bothered to shut it. Could she have imagined the sound a second time? Perhaps it was the noise from the street?

She saw the doorknob of the bathroom door begin to slowly turn.

"Hello?" she called, hearing the panic in her voice. "Who's there?"

When the door opened a dark figure filled the space, backlit against the balcony door.

"Oh, it's you," Lanie said with a sigh. "Did you get lost?"

The dark shape lunged at her. Lanie scrambled to stand up in the slick, soapy water and collided with her attacker, falling backward with a splash.

She gasped and tried to gain purchase in the slippery interior, slick with soap. She clutched at the figure's jacket. Her legs slipped out from under her and strong arms pushed Lanie backward. She tried again to get to her knees, but an explosion of pain slammed into her head. Bright vibrating stars obliterated her vision. They faded slowly to black, taking all sound with them. All, that is, but the soft popping of the lavender bubbles.

1

"He needs a hat, Laurent." Maggie stood on the threshold of the French doors, her arms crossed, and watched her husband read the newspaper on the patio while jiggling the baby absentmindedly on his knee.

"He's fine," Laurent said without looking up.

"It's too hot out here for him." Maggie frowned and took a step onto the patio from the coolness of the house. As she often told her friends back home in Atlanta, summer in Provence alternated between blazing hot and so-hot-you-could-die.

"*Bon*," Laurent said, depositing the baby on the slate flooring under the table. "He is in the shade now."

"Laurent, no!" Maggie yelped as she ran to the baby and scooped him up off the ground. "There's God knows what under there. Scorpions, rat droppings..."

Laurent had yet to look away from his newspaper. "As you wish."

Maggie brushed the baby's chubby knees in case any hint of sand or dirt had attached. She snuggled him close and kissed his neck, which prompted the nine-month-old to giggle.

"Besides, you know he wouldn't stay put," she said, speaking more to little Jean-Michael, or *Jem* as Laurent had begun calling him. "*Would* you? He would be in the *potager* in a flash ripping up all your precious radishes and potatoes."

"I do not grow potatoes in the *potager*," Laurent said, turning the page of his newspaper.

"Well, whatever you grow in there."

"Besides, Monsieur Jem is more than welcome to help his papa in the *potager*. Even ripping up radishes would be more attention than his *maman* has paid it."

Laurent's *potager*—parsley and English thyme interspersed with radicchio, beets, spinach and radishes—was planted at the door leading into the house, ready to be plucked as quickly as it took the grill to get hot.

"Gardening is not my thing," Maggie said, kissing Jem's head and bouncing him on her hip.

Laurent finally looked up at her and grinned. "I love to see the two of you *c'est ça*." He dropped the paper and held out his arms and Maggie moved to perch on his knee, baby still in her arms.

She loved the smell of the two of them—her two men, she thought with a happy sigh. Laurent was citrus and tobacco—although she rarely saw him smoke—and little Jem had that indefinable baby-smell that made it impossible not to kiss his sweet head whenever he was in her arms.

"Happy, *chérie*?" Laurent murmured into her neck.

She felt a spasm of warmth race up her spine as his hands stroked her back through her thin blouse. "You know I am," she whispered.

It was true. She loved it here. But she hadn't always. There had been many adjustments to living in a three-hundred-year-old house, not the least of which were the antiquated bathrooms.

She smiled remembering how hard she'd lobbied for central air when she first arrived before accepting that closing the shutters during the hottest part of the day in summer typically cooled the house sufficiently.

It had been a long and difficult adjustment, with all profits from the vineyard going back into the vineyard.

"Hi, you two. I hope I'm not interrupting anything."

Maggie and Laurent looked up to see their friend and houseguest, Grace Van Sant, standing in the open French doors. Every time Maggie saw Grace she was amazed at her friend's cool beauty. Grace once joked that her mother named her after Grace Kelly, but to see her now, impeccably dressed, languid in her blonde elegance and poise, it was no joke.

Fact was, Grace's mother had nailed it.

Laurent stood up, slowly sliding Maggie to her feet. He was six foot four, a big man with a gentle touch and a silent tread. More than once, Maggie had marveled at how his grace and stealth belied his size.

"If Grace is back," Laurent said, gathering up his newspaper, "it must be time for lunch."

Grace walked onto the patio. "Glad I can serve as such a reliable timepiece for you, Laurent," she said, smiling. "Is Zouzou still napping?"

Laurent went into the house as Maggie pulled the portable baby monitor out of the pocket of her slacks and flipped it on. The sounds of the toddler's snores competed with the static of the device.

"Kind of defeats the purpose if you keep it turned off," Grace remarked wryly.

"Totally defeats the purpose of having a little peace and quiet," Maggie said, handing the monitor to Grace, "if you have to listen to every breath and gurgle as they sleep. No offense, Grace. I assure you Zouzou's snorts are more adorable than most."

Grace laughed and snapped the monitor off. "I take your point, darling." She gently tweaked Jem's plump cheek. "How's this little one? Did he sleep at all?"

Maggie sat down at the outdoor table Laurent had just left. "No, and it's driving me crazy. Why won't he sleep?"

Grace sat down. "Well, I've heard the smart ones don't."

"Are you serious?"

"Just what I've read."

Maggie looked into Jem's bright blue eyes. When he saw he had her attention, his toothless grin widened and drool crept down the corner of his mouth.

"Plenty of time to be an overachiever," she said to him. "Take the opportunity of a nap when it's offered."

"Good luck with that," Grace said, leaning back into the cane chair, a tired smile on her lips.

Maggie knew Grace was working hard to keep her spirits up and her mood bright. The divorce from Windsor was finalized the week before, and although Grace was the one who had pushed for it, it had been a long, hard spring while she coped with what the breakup truly meant for her and her little family of four. When Maggie and Laurent offered refuge for her and Zouzou at their home in Provence, Grace had gratefully accepted.

"How's the business coming?" Maggie asked. Grace was attempting to create an online children's clothing boutique using Provençal and Parisian wares.

"Oh, it's a long way from coming. I guess I thought I'd just spend my days shopping for adorable clothes for Zouzou and Jemmy, clue in the rest of the world through Facebook or something, take my middle-man cut, and go back to having a life."

"And it's not like that?"

"I don't know what it's like, dearest," Grace said wearily. "I've never had to work before and I don't think I like it."

"A startup is the most work of all," Maggie said.

"Thanks, precious. You always know just what to say."

"Oh, here comes Laurent with the wine."

"Case in point," Grace said with a smile.

Laurent set down a tray of filled wine glasses and a bowl of olives.

"One of yours, Laurent?" Grace asked as she took the wine glass he handed her.

"*Non*," he said. "Better."

"No way," Maggie said, sipping from her glass. "Mmm-mm, but whoever made it, it's good."

"Lunch in ten minutes," Laurent said before leaving them again.

"He is a man of few words, your papa," Grace said to the baby.

"That's for sure." Maggie let the dry fruitiness of the rosé fill her nostrils before taking the next sip. Laurent was trying to fine-tune her palate when it came to wine. She began coughing, the light tickle of the aroma overwhelming her.

"You okay, sweetie? Choke on an olive pit?"

"Very funny," Maggie said, her eyes watering as she gained control of the coughing.

"Well, how about *your* business?" Grace asked. "Selling any books?"

Maggie shrugged and reached for one of the olives from the stoneware dish filled with olive oil. This one had a tiny ceramic cicada perched on the rim of it. "I think I sold one. No, make that two. I sold two last week."

"That many?"

"Well, I won't find out for sure until quarterly royalties come in, but my agent has told me not to get my hopes up."

"Is that because you haven't earned out your advance yet?"

"What advance? No, it's because I haven't sold any books yet."

"Well, that's disappointing."

"Tell me about it."

"Are you not promoting it enough?"

"I don't know, Grace, I was thinking of changing my name to rhyme with Rowling, but Laurent thinks it sounds desperate."

Grace laughed. "What does your publicist say?"

"Oh, dear, dear Grace," Maggie said, shaking her head. "She

says the same thing Santa and the tooth fairy say: *if only I existed I could really do things.*"

"You don't have a publicist?"

"It may surprise you to know that Stephen King and I are not one and the same."

"For that you may be thankful," Grace said.

"Nobody has a publicist unless they're a well-known author, or unless they hire one themselves."

"Well, why not hire one?"

Maggie scooted her chair closer to the table and looked over Grace's shoulder at the door to the house. "Can I ask you to do something for me, Grace?"

"Why do I get the idea this *something* has to do with not letting Laurent know?"

"Because I don't want Laurent to know."

Grace sighed. "Keeping secrets from Laurent never ends well. When will you learn that?"

"I need you to find out something for me."

"Darling, when it comes to winkling information out of your husband, I would imagine *you* were in the best position to do that."

"You'd think so, but he can always tell when I'm up to something. He won't suspect you."

"Thank you for giving me the opportunity to damage my relationship with the one man besides my father who is still speaking to me."

"I really need your help with this, Grace."

"If you're worried about another woman, Maggie, let me stop you right there, because if you don't know that darling hunk of a man by now and how crazy he is about you—"

"That's not it."

"I should think not."

"I need you to find out..." Maggie dropped her voice and

glanced again toward the house. Grace leaned in closer to catch her words.

"...if we are having money troubles."

Grace frowned and leaned back in her chair. "That's it?"

"You don't know the French if you think that is not a very big deal. And a very private deal."

"Even from you?"

Maggie looked beyond the terrace in the direction of their vineyard. A platoon of olive and fig trees lined a pebbled path from the terrace leading to the fields. From there, the truffle oaks, thyme bushes and cypresses created a virtual park, framing the forty hectares of grape fields and emphatically demarcating the property.

The vineyard was cut into four quadrants by two narrow dirt roads. The larger of the two—often used for tractors—sliced down the center of the vineyard past an ancient shed with an abandoned well at its threshold. It was a beautiful walk, Maggie mused, especially at sunset, and she and Laurent often enjoyed taking it with the dogs before dinner, when the final rays of sunlight draped the vineyard in a soft glow.

"Laurent never talks about money," Maggie said, turning back to Grace. "I have no idea where our money comes from or how."

"Seriously?"

"And because of how he made his money before we met..." Maggie raised her eyebrows to indicate that Grace should feel free to fill in the blanks.

"You know he doesn't do that sort of thing any more," Grace said. She was bouncing the baby, who was becoming more and more agitated, on her knee.

"I know it's in him to cut corners, grease a palm here and there, take advantage of a situation. Did I ever tell you he once told me he couldn't promise not to lie to me because he might have to sometime?"

"That's actually kind of honest."

"Laurent has his pride. I haven't brought a single solitary euro into the family coffers since we moved to France. It's been all him."

"And now you think there's a problem with money?"

"That's just it. I don't know."

"And he won't tell you?"

"He brushes aside my questions, or worse, gets annoyed with me for even asking."

"I see."

"I really wish he'd confide in me, you know? We're in this together but he's such a...sexist he doesn't see that. Just find out for me, Grace. If there's a problem I can always go to my dad for money."

"That's probably the last thing Laurent would want."

"*What* is the last thing I would want?" Laurent asked as he joined them on the patio, a tray of dishes in his hands.

Maggie mouthed the words to Grace: *hearing like a bat*. "For Grace to have a piece of chewing gum before lunch," she said sweetly.

"*Sacré bleu!*" Laurent turned to look at Grace with horror. "You are chewing gum?"

"No, of course not, Laurent," Grace said. "I just asked Maggie if she wanted a stick for later and she said—"

"Chewing gum obliterates the purity of the taste experience," Maggie said, as if reciting it from memory. "Oh, warm goat cheese on mesclun! Here, hand me Jem, Grace. He adores the rosemary balsamic reduction that Laurent makes."

"That looks amazing, Laurent," Grace said as Laurent placed a goat cheese cake on a bed of greens and set it in front of her.

"It's nothing," he said, but Maggie could tell he was pleased.

"Laurent," Maggie said, spearing a chunk of goat cheese, "I told you about my brother and his wife coming next weekend, right?"

"*Bien sûr.*"

"Your brother is coming to France?" Grace asked as Laurent refilled her glass of rosé.

"He's actually already here. Haley talked him into taking this Côte d'Azur tour. You've heard of the Bob Randall show? The travelogue guy who goes around Europe?"

"Of course. Your brother's traveling with Randall's tour?"

"It's supposed to be a trial tour of some kind for the television show. Haley and I went to school with one of the tour guides, Lanie Morrison. Lanie told Haley they needed a couple of people to play tourists on the trip so Haley and Ben got to come for next to nothing."

"Where are they now?"

"I'm not sure. They were coming down through the Luberon."

"They didn't stop?"

"No, they wanted to do the whole tour and come see us after it was over."

"Has Ben ever visited you and Laurent before?"

"Nope."

"Are you guys not close?"

"Not a bit."

"Oh. Sorry."

Maggie waited until Laurent had retreated back into the house for the next course. "Ben is a big hotshot lawyer back in Atlanta. Laurent and I have, like, zero in common with him."

"What about his wife?"

"Haley's sweet. I love her to pieces, but because of Ben I never saw much of her when I lived in Atlanta."

"He's that bad?"

Maggie shrugged. "Not Lex Luthor evil. Just kind of a low-grade douche."

"Yikes. Your own brother. So why is he coming to see you now?"

"I have no idea. My parents are excited about it because they think this means he's going to reach out more to the family, but I think it's just going to be awkward as hell. Might be a good time for you to take a little shopping trip to Paris. Maybe I'll go with you."

"Not on your life. While I adore how utterly stress-free and serene life at Domaine St-Buvard is with you and Laurent, frankly I could use the stimulation." Grace sipped her wine. "So is your school chum, the tour guide, coming to visit too?"

"No. I thought about inviting her for like a nanosecond, but we're not really friends any more."

"Some dramatic reason why not, I hope?"

Maggie laughed. "No, we just drifted apart. I heard she got married and then divorced, and the one occasion I saw her in the last ten years she spent most of the time riffing on how much she hates men."

"Well, we have that in common."

"It's weird, because when we used to hang out I was actually closer to her mom."

"That *is* weird."

"She was a very cool mom. Always laughing and ready to share a secret. Every time I came over to Lanie's house, I ended up talking to her mom for hours. And yet Lanie treated her like she was a hideous bore, and stupid beside."

"Exactly as wee Jemmy will treat you when his time comes."

"Shut up. He never will. Will you, muffin?" Maggie kissed the baby's ear and squeezed him tight. He reached for her with fingers sticky with goat cheese.

"*Allo*, Zouzou is ready for her lunch," Laurent announced as he came back out to the patio, this time with a three-year-old girl in his arms, her face creased from her nap.

Grace stood up and took her from Laurent. "*Merci, Oncle Laurent*," she said. "Are you hungry, petal?"

"You have cheese in your hair," Laurent said to Maggie as he reached for Jem.

"I know. My lover finds it particularly alluring."

"*Oui*," Laurent said, his eyes glittering with meaning. "He does."

"Come on, join us, Laurent," Grace said. "Oh, my goodness, is that fried calamari? Wherever did you get it?"

"Try the lemon pepper *aioli*," Maggie said, scooping a small fritter into the golden sauce. "It's the reason I married him, I kid you not."

"We need more wine," Laurent said, scanning the table with a frown.

"We have plenty," Maggie said. "Come and sit down. Tell us all about how plump and sweet our grapes are at the moment."

"I see you are being witty," Laurent said, pouring himself a glass of wine.

Grace laughed. "Yes, tell us, Laurent. Maggie says the harvest looks awesome this year. I don't know ripe grapes from tennis balls, but they do look pretty on the hills surrounding the house."

Laurent sat down and Maggie couldn't help notice that his usual zeal for talking endlessly about the vineyard seemed to be lacking. She knew for a fact the harvest was better than it had ever been. Something wasn't right if Laurent wasn't clapping his hands together in delight, ready to recount every minute detail of the vines' growth pattern.

"It will be a good harvest this year," he said simply, sipping his wine.

"Yay," Maggie said, leaning over and taking Jemmy's hands and making them clap together. "A 'good harvest' means many trips to Paris for Mommy and a nice private *école maternelle* in Aix for Jemmy." She shot a covert glance at Laurent to see his reaction but, not surprisingly, his expression was impossible to read.

"That's great, Laurent," Grace said. "It's earlier this year than last, isn't it? Or am I imagining that?"

Maggie watched Laurent's eyes and for a moment she thought she saw a shadow pass across his face. An earlier ripening generally meant a better quality product. So why did the thought of it seem to make him solemn?

"*Non*," he said. "It's true. We will harvest sooner this year."

Maggie exchanged a look with Grace. Something was definitely not right.

2

"Will you call her? What will you say?" Haley Newberry glanced at her husband from where she sat on the bed. He seemed tired, as if he hadn't shaken off his jet lag, although they'd been in France for over week already.

"The truth," Ben said. He stood at the balcony overlooking the *Promenade des Anglais*. "That we're coming earlier than planned."

"I hope you'll at least present it as a request," Haley said.

He turned to look at her. "Why? They sit on a farm counting their money and watching the grapes grow. How could our coming a week early possibly be a problem?"

She hated seeing him like this. Tense. Distracted. Hard.

"You're right," she said. "It probably won't be. You've never met her husband, have you?"

Ben turned away again. "You know I haven't. What was the point?"

Right, Haley thought sadly. *Because it's not like you cared about deepening the relationship with your sister.*

"Does she think it odd that we're visiting now?"

Ben went to the dresser and picked up his cell phone. "I have no idea what she thinks."

"She was good friends with Lanie, you know."

"A thousand years ago." He punched in a number and turned back to the balcony view.

Haley waited. It was hard to imagine death in the midst of such intense beauty. The azure-blue of the Mediterranean seemed to frame everything around it with a storybook semblance that belied everyday woes like hangnails or indigestion...or death.

"Hello, Maggie. This is your brother, Ben. I hope I'm not catching you at a bad time."

Haley allowed herself one more glimpse of the sea over Ben's shoulder and then retreated to the bathroom for her shower.

MAGGIE WAVED her hand to command quiet from Laurent and Grace in the kitchen where they were feeding the children their breakfast. She handed a spoon of stewed apricots to Laurent and settled on a barstool.

"Hey, Ben," she said, "we're really looking forward to your visit next week."

"That's why I'm calling. There's been a change of plans."

"Oh?"

Maggie was surprised to realize the thought that he might be canceling prompted a surge of relief. She looked at Laurent, who was studying her over Jem's head.

"Yes, there's been an accident here on the tour," Ben said. "Haley and I are having to drop out."

"An accident?" Maggie focused her full attention to the phone call, but still saw Grace out of the corner of her eye turn her body toward Maggie.

"Actually you know her," Ben said. "Lanie Morrison? I think

Haley mentioned in her email to you that she was one of the tour guides?"

"Lanie had an accident?"

Maggie detected the brief hesitation before her brother answered. "She did," he said. "She was found this morning. She was...unresponsive."

Maggie stood up. "She's *dead*?"

Laurent tapped Maggie on the wrist to get her attention. He mouthed *qui?*

"Lanie Morrison," Maggie said to him. "The one I went to school with. Ben says she was found dead this morning."

"And so of course the remainder of the tour is cancelled," Ben said on the line. "Haley and I were hoping we might come to Domaine St-Buvard earlier than planned."

"Yes, of course," Maggie said, trying to process this news. "How did she die?"

"I really don't know."

"Well, how did you find out about it?"

"Maggie, I'm happy to answer any questions you have when Haley and I arrive, which, if it's all the same to you, will be tomorrow evening."

"Is her mother coming over?"

"Pardon?"

"Lanie's mother. Ann Morrison. I assume she's coming to Nice to bring...Lanie home?"

"I don't know about any of that. Will you or someone meet us at the train station? And is Arles the closest one?"

"What? Oh, yeah. Arles. Call us when you're about an hour out and one of us will be there with the car."

"Very good." He hung up.

Maggie sat and stared at her phone. "God, he's a jerk."

"Lanie died?" Grace asked, holding Zouzou on her hip, a spoon in one of the child's chubby fists.

"That's what he said." Maggie shook her head. "She was only

thirty-five. How did she die, I wonder?" She looked at Laurent. "As I understood it from Haley, this was Lanie's chance to earn a permanent slot on Bob Randall's television show."

"Maybe she had health issues?" Grace asked.

"Maybe." Maggie looked around the kitchen. "Can you guys finish up breakfast without me?"

"Why?" Laurent asked, frowning.

"I just want to look at something on the Internet," Maggie said as she gave Jem a quick kiss and hurried into the living room where her laptop was. Booting up quickly, she typed in the name *Ann Morrison* and found the phone number she was looking for.

IF IT HAD BEEN tricky finding reasons to leave Domaine St-Buvard *before* Jem was born, it was positively onerous now, Maggie thought as she accelerated on the A8 heading toward Nice and the coast. Unlike Laurent, she needed a break from time to time from the constant monotony of rural life. Having Grace live with them helped immensely. *But even a glass of wine and your best girlfriend is no substitute for a weekend shopping trip to Paris*, she thought with a smile.

Maggie reviewed her conversation yesterday with Lanie's mother. Annie Morrison had been distraught, of course, but her relief was palpable over the phone line when Maggie offered to meet her at the Nice Côte d'Azur airport. Maggie had never met Lanie's father. He and Annie had divorced years ago and he'd long since passed away. For reasons she couldn't put her finger on, Maggie wasn't surprised to hear that Annie had never remarried.

It took three hours to drive to the coast from Domaine St-Buvard, and as Maggie drove she reran the tapes in her head of her efforts to convince Laurent that she needed to go. Not surprisingly, he resisted the idea. She knew he didn't mind taking care of

Jem. *That* little duty he embraced with enthusiasm. Maggie was lucky to pry the child out of Laurent's arms. Her husband had always begun his day patrolling his vineyards, only now he did it with Jem tucked in one arm. Thinking of the image of Laurent and Jem outlined against the horizon this morning as they returned from their vineyard walk reopened a kernel of worry in Maggie.

There was definitely something going on with the vineyard and with Laurent. Normally, he would return from his walk with a spring in his step. He used to say it was like visiting a special lover—you always felt great afterward.

Maggie shook her head and grinned in spite of herself. *The French.*

But lately there had been no spring in anybody's step and no cheerful mood spreading into the late morning and the afternoon. Lately there had just been motions being gone through and items ticked off a vast to-do list.

Not at all Laurent's style.

Maybe Grace would have some luck finding out what was up, Maggie thought. This was actually a perfect opportunity for her to use her quiet skills to find out those things Laurent worked to keep hidden—Laurent, who was the most closed, private and secretive of men. But then, Maggie thought with a smile, he'd never really been up against a true Southern belle in her prime before.

She took the airport exit and parked the car, focusing on the task at hand. She hoped Lanie's mother would lean on her. Annie admitted on the phone that she spoke no French, had in fact never been to France. Maggie hurried to the receiving line of the incoming flight from Atlanta and scanned the crowd for sight of her, wondering if she'd have trouble recognizing her. The last time she'd seen her, nearly eleven years ago now, the woman had been seriously overweight.

Annie was easy to pick out in the crowd, and Maggie realized with a sinking heart it was not because Annie was heavy. While everyone else was moving quickly—to locate luggage, greet loved ones, find ground transportation—one woman was trudging, head down, through the throng as if looking for something on the ground. Maggie'd had plenty of time on the drive over to imagine the horror of losing your only child. Now that she was a mother herself, the thought was especially harrowing. She couldn't imagine what Annie was going through. And she didn't want to.

"Annie!" she called to the heavyset woman walking toward her. Annie lifted her head, her face flushed for a moment, but the light that flickered in her eyes quickly extinguished when she saw Maggie.

For a moment she thought it might be...

Maggie moved to her side and put her arms around her. As soon as she did, Annie began to weep, her shoulders shaking in Maggie's embrace. Seeing the naked pain of Annie's grief was almost unbearable. But when Maggie reminded herself of what Annie was attempting to bear, she held her tighter and let her cry as long as she needed to.

An hour later, they were driving up the coast to Nice. Annie spoke very little. When Maggie's hand wasn't on the gearshift, Annie was reaching for it.

"Where did you book?" Maggie asked gently.

"I...Lanie's hotel," Annie said, her voice raspy and hoarse from hours of crying.

"The Soho," Maggie said. "Do you want to check in first?"

Annie shook her head. "No. I want to see my baby."

Her words raked a chord of pain across Maggie's heart. *They'll always be our babies*, she thought as she pictured Jem laughing and clapping his hands; her gut twisted painfully.

She drove to the *Bureau du Coroner* off the *Rue de la Prèfecture* and parked in the public parking lot. Hand in hand, she and Annie walked into the police morgue where Lanie awaited them.

After giving their details to the officer at the front desk, Inspecteur Alphonse Massar met them in the lobby. Maggie was surprised to see he was elderly. In fact, he looked to be nearing retirement. A tall man with grey hair and a tightly trimmed, grey pencil mustache, he entered the lobby and bowed curtly to both women. He had such a strong military bearing about him that Maggie half expected him to click his boot heels together. He glanced at her, but without much interest. If Maggie had been expecting him to reach out to Annie with words of comfort or solace, she was disappointed. She held Annie's hand tightly and stayed close.

This next part was not going to be easy.

They followed Massar down a long hall of offices. Maggie was surprised to see Massar's name on one of the doors. It made sense, she reasoned, for the police to share real estate with the bodies they collected from the city. It was certainly tidier and more convenient that way. Something about his office door bothered her, but she pushed the feeling to the back of her mind. She needed to be present in every sense of the word for Annie.

Massar led them into an elevator, which took them two floors below the main entrance. There, the temperature dropped significantly. Maggie had the sense that they were literally entering a catacombs of graves buried deep beneath the city's vibrant and pulsing core. Perhaps Annie did too, for her hand clutched tightly at Maggie's.

Massar opened a door to a large room, for which Maggie was grateful. She was already having trouble breathing just thinking of how far below the surface they were. She didn't think she could handle a small room at this point.

A table was set off to the side against the wall, a draped body on it and a large overhead lamp poised over it. Massar strode to the table and waited for Maggie and Annie to catch up to him. He turned on the light and, once they were standing next to him, jerked back the drape to reveal the corpse. Annie sank to the floor without a sound and Maggie, momentarily stunned, failed to move fast enough to catch her. Massar whipped the drape back over Lanie and knelt next to Annie. Maggie took a step back and felt her stomach lurch.

In the background of her mind she heard Massar talking to Annie in French. The words didn't matter. The voice was kind. Maggie stared at the draped body and a series of images burst into her head: Lanie in her cheerleading outfit; Lanie lip-syncing to a Backstreet Boys song in her mother's living room; Lanie drinking her first beer and laughing when most of it ended up down her shirt front.

And underneath it all was the niggling memory of what she'd seen on the walk down to this terrible place—the door with Massar's name on it and the plaque under it that read *Enquêteur Homicides*.

Homicide detective.

3

"They think she was murdered," Maggie said to Grace on the phone that evening after she and Annie had checked into the Soho—Annie had begged her to stay with her. After her afternoon, Annie promptly took two sleeping pills and went to bed. Maggie spoke on the phone from the balcony, the door open in case Annie needed her.

"You're kidding. Why?"

"I don't know but I intend to find out."

"Does Lanie's mother know yet?"

"No. She's so upset about it all that she hasn't really asked any questions about how Lanie died. Just the fact that she did is occupying all her mental abilities at the moment."

"I can imagine."

"I know. Me too. It's awful, Grace. Just terrible to think of one of our own little dears..."

"I know, dearest, so shut up. I don't want to think of it."

"But the point is, the cops are looking at this as a homicide. If Annie asks them, they'll have to give her answers."

"Because that strategy has worked out so well for us in the past."

"Problem is, I don't think she wants to ask too many questions."

"Well, she probably would if she was told the truth about how Lanie died, don't you think?"

"Maybe. But I'm not sure she can take much more. And telling her that her daughter is not only dead but was murdered definitely qualifies as *much more*."

The sound of the hair dryer falling to the carpeted floor made Maggie whirl around to see Annie standing not four feet from her, her eyes wide with horror, mouth open.

"Oh, shit," Maggie said into the phone.

THE CAFÉ FACED the *Quai des Etats-Unis* and the brilliant blue of the sea beyond. Only in Nice did the café chairs face the street rather than the table, Maggie noted as she poured her bottled water into a glass. It was the dinner hour but neither she nor Annie had done anything but pick at their meals—omelets with *pommes frites* and the omnipresent bowls of citrus olives.

"I didn't know how to tell you," Maggie said. "I thought you'd had enough for one day."

Annie looked like she'd aged twenty years since Maggie had seen her last. She wasn't sure part of that hadn't happened just since she picked her up at the airport today. After her unsuccessful attempt at napping, Annie had agreed to go out with Maggie to talk about what the new information meant.

"You think Lanie was murdered."

"It's the only obvious explanation as to why her case is being handled by a homicide detective," Maggie admitted. "You haven't talked to anyone about how she died?"

Annie looked around the street helplessly, as if expecting to find someone to answer the question for her. She looked at her hands in her lap. "No. I heard all that mattered. I came."

"I understand," Maggie said. "Of course. But now that you know it was not an accident..." She waited until she thought Annie could handle the rest of her sentence before proceeding. "You'll want to talk to Inspecteur Massar about what he knows."

"Of course. Although..." Annie looked up and squinted in the direction of the Mediterranean. "It won't bring her back."

"No," Maggie said slowly. "That's true."

"Will you go with me?"

"Of course."

"Will you call him for me and ask him to see me?"

"First thing tomorrow."

"Will it make a difference in my being able to...take her home, do you know?"

Maggie leaned across the table and took Annie's hand and squeezed it.

"Let's take it one step at a time, Annie. Okay?"

Annie nodded bravely, her eyes straying once more to the impossibly beautiful, intensely blue sea that seemed to fill the horizon.

That night, Maggie was relieved to see that Annie was exhausted enough to finally sleep. Once she was sure Annie was asleep, Maggie slipped into the hallway of the hotel. She'd gotten Ben's room number from the concierge when she'd checked in. His room faced the front of the hotel, one flight up.

Maggie took the elevator and quickly found his room. She knocked and heard all conversation in the room cease when she did. Light footsteps moved to the door and it opened just a crack. Maggie recognized her sister-in-law, Haley, peering out at her.

"Maggie!" The door jerked fully open and Haley stepped into the hall, her arms instantly around Maggie. "We wondered if we'd see you tonight. Come in, come in."

Her brother's wife was a statuesque blonde. Even at thirty-six, Maggie still saw the bouncy cheerleader in Haley. The athletic thighs that had bounded to the tops of human pyramids now regularly lunged across the clay courts of Atlanta's ALTA tennis tournaments.

"Hey, Haley," Maggie said. "I just wanted to touch base with you. I haven't had a chance before now."

Over Haley's shoulder, Maggie saw her brother lounging on the couch in the inner room. He didn't bother getting up or removing his legs from the coffee table. She saw an open wine bottle on the table.

"How is Lanie's mother?" Haley asked, her hand still on Maggie's arm. "She must be devastated."

"She is, yeah. She finally went to sleep." Maggie stepped into the living area of the room and her brother lifted a glass to her as she entered. She wondered for a moment if he might be drunk.

"*Bonsoir*, little sis," Ben said. "Welcome to Nice. The crappiest city in paradise."

"Don't listen to him," Haley said. "We're all just so shaken up about this."

"Did you know she was murdered?" Maggie said to her brother. She hadn't seen him in over two years and was surprised to see that he'd aged. In her mind, he always remained the same: tall, athletic, thick brown hair and riveting blue eyes. Handsome, of course. All the Newberry men were good-looking in that bland, Anglo-Saxon way. Now that she really looked at Ben, his mouth seemed to have taken on a permanent twist to it. Like a sneer that just stayed.

"Who said it was murder?" Ben said, slurring his words and putting to rest any doubt Maggie had about his condition.

"I found out today that the city's homicide department is handling her death."

"Well, there you are. My sister, the supersleuth. Dad would be proud," Ben said sarcastically.

"We're all so upset," Haley said. "The police talked to us, not that I had anything to say. I'd taken a sleeping pill and gone to bed early with one of my headaches."

"Yeah, thanks bunches by the way for the iron-clad alibi, Haley," Ben said. "Good to know you can be counted on to be unconscious when it counts."

"They don't suspect you, Ben," Haley said, her voice tinged with the slightest of plaintive whines.

"Okay, well, anyway, I just wanted to check in," Maggie said, turning away. "And to tell you guys to go on to Domaine St-Buvard without me. I'll follow along tomorrow or the next day."

"You're staying in Nice?" Haley asked. "Whatever for?"

"God, don't encourage her, Haley," Ben said from the couch. "Will what's-his-name pick us up? I know how the French are when it comes to time. I'm not waiting in a circa World War II train station for him to finally remember what time it is."

"Ben, stop it," Haley said. "You're embarrassing me."

"What else is new," Ben said in a low voice as Maggie slipped out into the hallway.

"I am so sorry, Maggie," Haley said. "He has been under unbelievable strain lately for a couple of different reasons. Please don't listen to him."

"Don't worry, Haley," Maggie said, leaning in to kiss her sister-in-law's cheek. "I never have."

THE NEXT MORNING, Annie insisted on meeting the rest of the tour group at breakfast.

"These were Lanie's colleagues," she said as Maggie locked their hotel room door. "And her boyfriend, Olivier. He was on the tour too. Oh, he must be devastated."

"Lanie was traveling with her boyfriend?"

"Well, they didn't room together, but they were definitely an item. He's the videographer on the tour. Olivier Tatois. I met him briefly last winter when he came to Atlanta with Lanie."

They took the elevator downstairs to the hotel breakfast

room. Maggie wasn't at all sure what to expect, but she could tell Annie was eager to meet these people.

When you've lost everything, even the faintest wisps of the person you lost counted for something, Maggie thought sadly. Perhaps Annie was hoping to get a little piece of her daughter back in the memories and joint affection of these people. The minute they walked into the room, Maggie sensed that was not going to be possible.

She recognized Bob Randall immediately. His travel show was syndicated, and had been for several years. He was considered the ultimate authority in European travel-on-a-budget for the average American. His affable downhome style translated well in his television series, and while he'd been doing it for at least a decade Maggie was surprised to see he didn't look a day older than when he'd first started.

A tall man, Randall broke away from the group gathered around a large round table and strode to where Maggie and Annie stood hesitating in the café entrance.

"Mrs. Morrison," he said, his hand outstretched to take Annie's. "I am so sorry to meet you under these circumstances. Every one of us here loved Lanie dearly."

Annie's eyes fill with tears. "Thank you, Mr. Randall," she said hoarsely.

"Please call me Bob, and come meet the others on our tour." He tucked Annie's arm in his and pulled her away from Maggie toward the table. Maggie followed. She noticed her brother and Haley remained seated. Haley smiled wanly at her but Ben scowled into his coffee and did not look up.

"Everyone, this is Lanie's mother..."

"Annie," Annie said softly as she nodded at the two couples and two single women at the table.

"Annie," Randall said. "Move over, Anderson," he said to the distinguished looking man seated next to a hatchet-faced woman in her mid-fifties with a brand new face-lift. "Annie, this is Jim and Janet Anderson. They were playing the part of the tourists for our little experiment. And there's Ben and Haley Newberry across there. You may have already met them." Maggie noticed Ben still didn't look up.

"To my left is Mademoiselle Desiree Badeaux, and to her left, Miss Dee-Dee Bell, both of whom worked with your daughter on this tour."

"*Competed*, he means," Dee-Dee said as she smiled at Annie. She looked a little plain to Maggie, even dumpy. "We were all going after the same prize. I really admired your daughter, Mrs. Morrison. She was a total ballbuster, but I mean that in the nicest way."

Maggie noticed Annie's look of confusion as she turned from Dee-Dee to the French woman next to her that Randall had introduced as Mademoiselle Desiree Badeaux, although Maggie did think it had been many years since the woman could honestly claim *that* title.

"Madame," Desiree said, nodding curtly at Annie. Pencil thin and wearing a bone-hugging knit dress, Desiree clearly cared very much about her appearance. Maggie guessed she was mid-forties. Her dark hair was bobbed and offset high cheekbones and full lips.

"We are all just so upset at what happened to our darling Lanie," Randall said. "My mind is still blown. I cannot adjust to what happened." He grinned as if this were an endearing trait they should all enjoy knowing. Maggie winced. Celebrities were a special case unto themselves, she thought.

He pulled a chair out for Annie and Maggie slipped into a free one next to Haley.

"Thank you all," Annie said as Randall poured her a cup of coffee from a pot on the table. "I wanted to meet you because you were all important to Lanie." She looked around the table, her eyes resting on Maggie as her touchstone.

"I was hoping to see Olivier this morning," she said, an attempt at a smile trembling on her lips.

"Oh, my gosh, didn't you hear?" Dee-Dee stopped in the middle of applying lip gloss. "He's gone."

"Gone? Gone where?" Annie looked at Maggie as if she might possibly know.

"They arrested him, I heard," Dee-Dee said, snapping her purse shut loudly. "He found the body, you know."

What an ass you are, Maggie couldn't help think.

"Arrested Olivier?" Annie looked around the table, bewildered. "But Olivier *loved* Lanie. That's impossible."

"Well, you know the French," Dee-Dee said with a grimace. "*Cherchez la femme*. Or in this case, I guess it would be *l'homme*. Anyway, they wouldn't have taken him away if they didn't know something we don't know."

Maggie watched Desiree's reaction to Dee-Dee's words. The look that Desiree gave Dee-Dee was one of undiluted loathing.

"That can't be," Annie said to the group. "I know Olivier. He would never hurt Lanie."

"Love makes you do strange things," Dee-Dee said.

"What would you know of love?" Desiree sneered. "From what you see on television soap operas?"

"You French think you own the whole love and passion thing," Dee-Dee said, turning in her seat to face the Frenchwoman.

"I imagine anyone might own it more than a woman who has never known a man's touch," Desiree said.

Whoa! Score one for Team France, Maggie thought as Dee-Dee's face blushed deep red.

"All right, ladies," Randall said. "We have company. Let's try not to bicker, shall we?" He turned to Annie. "And yes, losing Olivier will put a considerable crimp in our taping abilities for the remainder of the tour but I feel sure we—"

Maggie spoke up. "You're continuing the tour?" She glanced at her brother and Haley. "I was told you were canceling it."

"Of course we're continuing the tour," he said. "I mean, it's horrifying and all that but I've got a production schedule back home and we need to get this co-anchor question decided."

"When are you leaving?" Maggie asked.

Randall shrugged. "The police have Olivier as their man and they see no reason why the rest of us need to remain in Nice. We leave for Cannes early tomorrow morning. Desiree will be presenting on our first stop on the Côte d'Azur. I'm not counting Nice as part of the test because of Lanie dying and all."

Maggie saw Annie swallow hard. *God! These people were insensitive.* She looked at her brother but he was studiously working not to look at her.

"I understand Ben and Haley Newberry are dropping out of the tour?" Maggie said.

Ben snapped his head up when she spoke.

"Yes, unfortunately," Randall said. "They have other business in France. They were never scheduled for the coastal part of the tour in any case. Just Provence to Nice."

Oh, really? Her brother returned her steady gaze. Caught in a bold-faced lie in front of half a dozen people and he stared at her as coolly as if it had never happened.

"I'm sorry," Randall said, looking at Maggie now. "I didn't catch your name. You are a relative of Lanie's?"

"A friend of the family," Maggie said. She couldn't resist glancing back at Ben when she said that and was rewarded with a look of disgust as he rolled his eyes and directed his attention back to his coffee.

∼

"Mademoiselle Morrison drowned to death in her bath," Inspector Massar said, intoning the words as if passing sentence.

He spoke no English, and as Maggie sat in front of him, Annie at her side, she couldn't help but be amazed that she had come so far in her linguistic abilities that she was actually serving as translator.

But how the hell was she going to translate that?

"Then why do you believe she was murdered?"

"The body suffered blunt force trauma to the upper cranium," he said, pointing to his own head. Annie followed his hand motions with her eyes. Maggie was grateful she couldn't understand what he was saying.

"Do you have the murder weapon?"

Massar fidgeted in his chair. "Not at this time."

"Then are you sure it's murder? Isn't it possible she could have slipped and fallen?"

"There was a word written on her forehead, Madame," Massar said abruptly.

A burning sensation formed in the pit of Maggie's stomach. Any hope she'd held out that it might truly be an accident evaporated immediately.

"May I ask what word?"

His eyes flickered to Annie and Maggie instinctively clenched her stomach muscles. The word must be a bad one. And one that Annie might recognize.

"Slut," he said. "The killer wrote the word *slut* across the body's forehead."

Annie reacted by turning to Maggie and gripping her arm. "What's he saying? Why is saying that word?"

"He...he's trying to explain to me why he believes Lanie was murdered and didn't accidentally drown in her bath." Maggie felt Annie's nails dig into her arm and she forced herself not to pull away.

"Why is he saying that word?"

"It's a little confusing," Maggie lied. "I'm not sure what word he's really saying. I'm sorry. My French is still a little spotty."

She heard the air come out of Annie in a long sigh, as if she'd been holding her breath.

Maggie turned back to Massar. "That's an English word."

"*C'est ça.*"

"Well, why do you have a Frenchman in custody? If it was him, wouldn't he have written *salope* or *prostituée*?"

"*Slut* is shorter," the detective said with a shrug.

"Do you have any other evidence that makes you believe it was Olivier Tatois?"

"We can prove that the key used to gain access to Mademoiselle Morrison's room that night was used by Monsieur Tatois."

"Really?"

"It was found in his possession."

"But that wouldn't be unusual, right? Since they were sleeping together?"

"That is true."

Maggie couldn't believe how impervious the man was to her questions. He not only didn't seem to hold back information from her, he didn't act as if he cared one way or the other.

Maybe he was close to retirement or something.

"May I ask you if the body...if Mademoiselle Morrison was wearing face makeup?"

Massar frowned. "Of course not. She was in the process of taking a bath."

"If she wasn't wearing makeup," Maggie said, "why do you think she was expecting her lover?"

His eyes darted away, as if considering this. He was too French not to see the logic in it. In the end, though, it didn't matter. He shrugged—that maddening, classic Gallic gesture that ended all conversations without satisfaction or resolution.

Laurent did it all the time.

"Monsieur Tatois has no alibi for the time in question," he said.

Well, jeez, neither do you and somehow you're not in a holding cell facing a charge of murder.

"Will that be all, Madame Dernier?" Massar said, standing, effectively ensuring that it was, in fact, all. Maggie stood and so did Annie.

"When will you release the body to her mother?"

"The autopsy will be finished tomorrow. Madame Morrison may make arrangements to have the body shipped to the United States by Friday." He held out a hand for Annie to shake and then offered his hand to Maggie before escorting them out of his office and down the long hall to the lobby of the police department.

As the two stood on the street corner, Maggie put her arm around Annie.

"Come on, Annie," she said. "Let's find a quiet place to talk." She glanced down the long pedestrian shopping street studded with multi-colored and striped umbrellas over café tables and was about to move toward the closest one when she noticed a familiar form sitting at one of the tables.

Desiree sat facing her, smoking feverishly, focused on her companion, to whom she was gesticulating wildly. The Frenchwoman's face was contorted into a heavy sneer, the force of which nearly made Maggie gasp for how instantly it transformed Desiree's features into something ugly and raw. *Whatever she was saying, Annie didn't need to be anywhere near it*, Maggie decided.

As she tugged Annie away in the opposite direction, Maggie heard the same cawing bray of laughter coming from Desiree's companion that Maggie remembered hearing at breakfast when Bob Randall had shown his amusement over some trivial thing.

4

It looked more like the opening act for a circus than one of the world's most famous beachfronts.

Maggie watched a long line of joggers, cyclists, roller skaters and even a few acrobats walk, ride and roll two deep past the café table where she sat with Annie. Add the odd Segway and baby stroller, she marveled, and you'd have a parade of the strangest collection of narcissists and showoffs to rival Venice Beach.

Doesn't anybody in Nice own a computer? Maggie had seen tourists with their noses stuck in tablets and smartphones in as gorgeous and remote hideaways as Mürren, Switzerland, and yet here in the middle of civilization it seemed the *Niçois* wanted nothing more than to prance along the boardwalk, to see and be seen.

Strike that, Maggie thought wryly as a mime danced by, his hands climbing nonexistent walls as he moved. *Nobody cares that much about seeing. They all just want to be seen.*

The waiter brought the carafe of rosé Maggie ordered, but Annie put her hand over her wineglass and asked for bottled water.

"I'm afraid I haven't been entirely honest with you, Maggie," she said.

Maggie frowned, dragging her attention away from the circus of people and vehicles along the Promenade des Anglais. "What do you mean?"

Annie sighed. "Lanie and I were estranged. Had been for years."

"I'm sorry to hear that."

"I'm afraid the reason for it involves you."

"Me?"

"Even now, I'm ashamed to say it. I've tried for years to redeem myself to Lanie. But she wouldn't listen."

"I don't understand. What happened? I remember you were the coolest mom I knew. You understood me better than my own mother did. I can't tell you how fondly I remember our talks around your kitchen table."

"That was right after the divorce. I wasn't doing very well at all."

"I thought you were awesome."

"Well, I wasn't. In fact, what I was mostly was drunk. Lanie and I were fighting daily. She blamed me for her father leaving. She was probably right. Once...no, more than once, I told her I wished her father had gotten custody of her but I needed the child support money so that's why she was with me."

"Annie, don't do this to yourself. It was a bad time for you. I'm sure Lanie understood that when she became an adult."

"I told her I wished *you* were my daughter."

"Oh."

"Not just once. Several times. Whenever you came over, you and I would talk—just as I imagined in my fantasies that Lanie and I might some day."

"I...I had no idea."

"No, you wouldn't. The more I drank, the more I began to

think that *you* were the daughter I really deserved, and Lanie was just part of my punishment. I was messed up. Eventually I got help and kicked the booze, but by then the damage to Lanie was done."

"She must have hated me."

"No, she hated herself for not *being* you. For failing me. For failing her father."

"I can't believe this. My friendship with Lanie did end abruptly, and I never knew why."

"Well, now you do. You probably also never knew how important you were to me during that time, did you?"

Maggie shook her head, stunned at Annie's confession.

"You are the last person to owe me anything," Annie said. "I ruined my relationship with my only child, and her friendship with you—a friendship she could have really used during that time."

"It was a terrible time for both of you," Maggie said numbly.

"I need you to find the person who did this to Lanie," Annie said. "I can't believe I'm asking but I have to know and I need *you* to be the one to do it. I used you to hurt Lanie and I never fixed that in her lifetime."

Annie grabbed a tissue and held it to her face, her eyes squeezed shut until the moment of intense grief passed.

"Can you see why I need you to step in now and set this right? It's not even your mess to clean up. And it's too late for me and Lanie. I know that. But she's been gone three whole days and I still haven't reached for a drink. There may be some hope for me to survive this, but if there is...I'm begging you, Maggie, if you ever cared for Lanie—or for me—find out who did this to her. Help me finally do right by her."

∼

Janet rapped sharply on the hotel room door. It was late afternoon; a good time to catch people in, as it was a good time to take a nap and escape the heat of the day. Although she was sure *some people* weren't bothering with sleep.

The door opened a crack and Janet felt a tightness in her jaw. Did he think she would try to force her way in?

"I need a minute of your time," she said tersely. "If you're alone, that is."

"As a matter of fact, I'm not," Randall said, his eyes droopy and veined with red. "What do you want?"

"I want," Janet hissed, trying to keep her voice low, "to remind you that Jim and I are not the only ones to be hurt by loose lips."

"Jesus, Janet," Randall said, "spit it out before I shut the door."

"You told Lanie about me and Jim."

She dared him to deny it. She literally quivered with anticipation. A part of her wanted him to try.

"I didn't, as it happens, but so what? Nobody cares but you."

"Oh, believe me, Bob, you're wrong about that. Jim cares a great deal."

"Well, he should have thought of that then shouldn't he?" Randall began to push the door shut and she surprised herself by stepping a foot into the room and wedging it against the door.

"I wish the rest of the world knew you the way I do," she said in a loud whisper. "I wish your *little friend* knew what you were capable of."

"Funny, Janet, I was going to say the same thing about you."

She saw by the way his eyes went suddenly blank that he didn't care who he hurt. Especially her. For a moment, the stark look startled her because she hadn't expected that kind of honesty from him. She pulled her foot back just in time as he slammed the door in her face. She stood there for a moment, hearing her own breath, the sound of the door echoing softly in her head, until she realized one of her fingernails had been too close to the door jamb.

A thread of blood traced down her finger to her wrist.

∾

Maggie walked Annie to their hotel room and closed the drapes while Annie took a sleeping pill and a bottle of water to bed. It occurred to Maggie as she slipped out of the room that Annie was in prime position to swap one addiction for another if she wasn't careful. Maggie rode down in the elevator and found a large wing chair in the lobby with a view of the Mediterranean. She dialed home and closed her eyes, willing herself to sound calm and nonchalant when he answered.

"*Allo,*" Laurent said. "Are you on your way, *chérie*?"

"No, I'm *not* on my way, Laurent," she said, already feeling defensive and hoping she didn't sound it. "This is a very tense business. A woman has lost her only child. I'm doing what I can to smooth things over and take some of the horror out of it for her, but it's not an easy or fast process."

"When are you coming home?"

"Would you please listen to me? Lanie's mom is really upset and I'm helping her sort out all the bureaucratic red tape in getting Lanie's body shipped home. I did tell you they're calling it a suspicious death, right?"

"You are not needed for that."

"I'm needed to be with *her*, Laurent. She has no one."

"Why have I not heard of this person before now if she is so important to you?"

"That is a very interesting story and I'm going to tell you as soon as I get home."

"I have time now."

"Well, okay. Let's see...I guess it's not so much that she was important to me as the other way around. Without knowing it, I was used as a sort of wedge between her and Lanie when...look, it doesn't matter, Laurent. Why can't you take my word for the fact that she needs me?"

"*Incroyable*! Your *child* needs you."

"Jemmy has *you*—he's probably sitting on your lap right this minute—and I'm only talking about another twenty-four hours. Annie has no one."

"If you tell me you have agreed to investigate this woman's death, I am putting Jem in his car seat and driving to Nice tonight to bring you home."

"Jeez, Laurent, way to overreact. Did I say I was investigating it? Did I even hint at that? The police have someone in custody that they are very happy with and I have no reason to doubt their choice."

"So this is just about helping your friend's mother navigate the red tape?"

"Yes, that is it. Almost completely."

"Almost?"

"Completely."

There was a pause. "Twenty-four hours?"

"I promise. Put the baby on the phone; I'll promise him, too."

"He isn't old enough to know your ways yet."

"Laurent Dernier, you take that back."

He made a sound of disgust.

"Oh, I meant to mention that my brother and Haley are on their way. He said he'd call you when he's an hour out from Arles. Okay?"

Laurent grunted, which Maggie decided to take as an affirmative.

"Meanwhile, can you tell me what cute thing Jemmy's done since I've been gone?"

AN HOUR LATER, Maggie hurried up the broad stone steps of the Soho lobby to the front desk. It was after three in the afternoon but there were no guests in the lobby or standing by the desk. The concierge, a tall man with a long jaw and small eyes that missed nothing, watched her approach from under heavy eyebrows.

"Excuse me," Maggie said to him in French. "I'm in Room 205."

The man didn't respond.

So it's like that, is it? It had been a long time since Maggie had bumped up against an imperious or outright rude service person in France. Even in Paris, most of them nowadays seemed to know on which side their *beignet* was buttered. And the south of France especially was usually a little more accommodating to tourists and foreigners.

"Mademoiselle Morrison died in your hotel two days ago," Maggie said bluntly. If she expected the man to blanch or soften, she was disappointed. He continued to wait for her to get to the point. "A glass of wine was found in her room. Did she order it through room service that night?"

The man smiled faintly, surprising Maggie. It was the look from a man wondering how long before someone asked him the million-dollar question.

"*Oui,*" he said.

"And did she order just a glass or did she order a bottle?"

"A bottle," he said. "A Côtes du Rhône."

"No bottle was found in her room."

He shrugged. "The valet did not wait for her to drink the whole bottle."

"So is that your smart-ass way of telling me he delivered the bottle and left it with her?"

"As you wish, Madame."

"You've been a peach," Maggie said, turning away abruptly. "Thanks."

So Lanie had been bashed in the head with her own wine bottle. Maggie took the elevator to the second floor, her mind racing. That meant whoever had interrupted Lanie in her bath had probably not come there intending to kill her but somehow things escalated and the killer used whatever weapon he could find.

In this case, a bottle of killer Côtes du Rhône.

Where was the bottle? Surely the cops had gone through all the rubbish bins and garbage cans around the hotel. Would they think to look at a wine bottle as the weapon? Maggie sighed. There must be a hundred bottles a day tossed in the hotel garbage, not even counting the ones the guests brought in themselves.

As Maggie turned the corner from the elevator, she slowed and then stopped. She could easily see the room she shared with Annie at the end of the hall. And she could also see a woman kneeling in front of the keyhole.

At first she thought the person was attempting to spring the lock on the door, but as she stood there she saw the woman was trying to peer through the ancient keyhole into the room. Maggie took several quiet steps on the balls of her feet until she was close by and then cleared her throat.

The woman jumped to her feet and whirled around to face Maggie.

It was Dee-Dee Bell. Even in the semi-darkened hallway, Maggie saw that the woman's blouse was food-stained and her hair had yet to be combed that day.

"Oh, my goodness, you startled me!" Dee-Dee said, her hand to her throat. Maggie was close enough to smell her breath. She took an involuntary step back.

"Did you drop something, Miss Bell?" she said sharply, her irritation ratcheting up as she waited for an explanation.

"What? Oh! Yes, I did. I dropped my room key but, well, here it is! I found it."

"Okay, that's bullshit. You were trying to look inside my room. What's going on?"

"I don't know what you're talking about. I dropped my key."

"Where is it, then?" Maggie peered at the woman's hands.

Dee-Dee scowled at Maggie and took a step toward her. "I made a mistake, okay? Give me a break. I thought this was Desiree's room. Hers is right next door. Okay?"

"How is that any better than you trying to peek inside my room?"

"Well, it's better, Miss whoever you are—and I don't really know why I'm answering your questions—because I have a reason for looking in Desiree's room."

"A reason."

"Yes, if you must know, I thought I saw a man go in here."

Maggie's key was in her hand and in the lock within seconds. "Who?" she asked, her voice tight with concern.

A man came to visit Annie? Annie was asleep. Wasn't she?

"Well, I didn't get a good look." Dee-Dee said, glancing down the hall as if contemplating making a run for it.

Maggie stepped into the darkened room, confirmed snores were coming from Annie in the bed, and returned to the hallway. "What man?" she asked again. "Why would you care if a man was in Desiree's room?"

"I'd care plenty if it was Bob Randall," Dee-Dee said in a taunting tone.

"Bob Randall and Desiree are an item?"

"Not in any imaginable universe," Dee-Dee said. "But I'm sure she *wishes* they were."

Maggie hesitated and then pulled the room door shut. She turned to Dee-Dee and nodded toward the elevator. "Why don't we take this conversation downstairs so Mrs. Morrison can sleep undisturbed? Say, the hotel bar?" Maggie forced herself to smile and was rewarded by what appeared to be a genuine smile back.

THE WAITER BROUGHT two glasses of white wine and retreated to the mahogany-encased vestibule leading to the kitchen. The bar at the Soho was elegant. A small plaque indicated the hotel had been built in the late seventeen hundreds by an intrepid pair of Brits sick of the English winters but wanting to retain as many touches of home as possible. The bar looked like it could be easily transplanted back to the interior of any one of many elegant hotel bars in London.

"I think we were all surprised the police didn't ask more questions," Dee-Dee said, sipping her wine. Maggie couldn't help think that even the tiniest hint of blush would do wonders in perking up the woman's sallow complexion. *Did she not have a mother? Girlfriends? A mirror?*

"Bob said it was because they didn't have a decent translator and none of us speak French. Except Desiree, of course."

"Lanie didn't speak French?"

"No, she hated the French. Regaled us all for hours with anti-France jokes. Some of them were pretty funny."

"Is it strange that she gave tours in France?"

"Not at all."

"What about you? You're not here because you love France?"

"Oh, hell, no." Dee-Dee laughed. "I'm here for the job. We could be in Helsinki for all I care."

"Don't you feel your delivery will lack empathy or...depth if you're not passionate about the places you're going to?"

"Yeah, I can see how you'd think that. Most people do. But this is a business, and more than that, it's entertainment. It's got nothing to do with the place."

"That's too bad."

"If you say so."

"When I came upon you in the hallway, you seemed concerned that Bob Randall and Desiree might be together in the room."

"Yeah, but now that I really think about it, that's ridiculous."

"Are you and Bob together?"

"I guess you picked up on that, huh?" Dee-Dee simpered.

"Did Lanie know about it?"

Dee-Dee's smile evaporated. "She knew," she said slowly, as if processing the information herself, "but it's not like she wanted him. Bob said they'd nearly gotten together a couple of times but nothing happened."

"Did Bob want something to happen?"

Dee-Dee snorted. "More like *Lanie* wanted something to happen."

"Because of the co-anchor slot."

"Hey, that is *not* why Bob and I are together."

"Sure. I believe you."

"Besides, Lanie was with someone."

"You mean her boyfriend, Olivier?"

"Now, you see, that was always hard for me to believe that she and Olivier were together. Have you met him? The camera guy? He is seriously hot. No, because she and Jim hooked up at the beginning of the tour."

Maggie's face must have looked confused because Dee-Dee added, "Jim Anderson? The old rich dude? The old *married* rich dude?"

"Lanie was sleeping with him?"

"Well, he *is* rich."

If what Dee-Dee said was true, Maggie had to admit it qualified as a pretty solid motive for Olivier.

"Are you sure?" Maggie asked.

"Ask anybody. Three days after we started the tour his old ball and chain throws a major hissy at breakfast saying Lanie's a whore and not to ever come near her old man again. I'm not even kidding. It was serious gonzo stuff. You can dress those old broads up but they're still raw ore underneath. Know what I mean?"

Maggie looked away from the table in confusion. "Jim Anderson's *wife*..." she said, trying to piece it together.

"Janet."

"Janet confronted Lanie publicly? A week ago?"

"Yup."

"And threatened her?"

"What would *you* call, '*Go near my old man again and I'll slit your throat*'?"

5

Laurent stood in the receiving lobby of the Arles train station. The drive to the station took thirty minutes, yet he remembered not a single minute of the trip—not even the two toll booths he had to pass through from St-Buvard to Arles. He glanced up at the overhead schedule boards. Maggie's brother had called an hour earlier. Grace had spoken with him.

Why do I get the feeling I will not like this man? he thought, frowning, hands on his hips. A slight vibration in his hip pocket alerted him to the call he'd been waiting for all afternoon. He sighed heavily and answered it.

"So," he said, his voice solemn, "have you decided?"

The brief hesitation before his friend Michel spoke told Laurent all he needed to know. In fact, he might as well hang up now. Because not only did Laurent know what Michel had decided, he knew their friendship was over as a result of it.

"Laurent, my friend," Michel said, "you must understand how hard this decision was for me to make."

"I understand of course," Laurent said, turning his attention to the long receiving hall that led to the train platforms. One had just gotten in, although not yet the one from Nice. A woman and her two young children were hurrying past.

"Estelle would kill me to even think of such a thing."

"Did you tell Estelle about my offer?"

Another hesitation. "I did, yes. It affects the whole family, Laurent. I can't make this kind of decision on my own."

"Of course not," Laurent replied drily. "I have another call coming in, Michel. I will talk with you again soon." Laurent disconnected and tucked the phone back into his pocket.

Merde. He wasn't surprised, but he had held out hope that he might be. And now he was coming to the end. Michel, Geoff, Jacques and Robert. There was Jean-Luc, of course. But he wasn't enough. And Jean-Luc had married into money. He could afford to torch his whole vineyard if necessary.

Laurent thought of Maggie's excitement about the upcoming trip back to the States this Thanksgiving. Unless he imagined it, she talked of little else.

No, he was glad for Jean-Luc's new financial comfort but he had no such luxury himself.

He rubbed a hand across his face. He would think of another way. He was sure there was another option. He just hadn't thought of it yet. He shook out a cigarette from his crumpled pack and put it between his lips. Perhaps now was not the best time to quit.

It was good fortune that Grace was still here, he thought. He did not feel very sociable at the moment and the effort to entertain Maggie's relations was not one he felt necessary to expend. If her brother had been interested in knowing him better, he'd had five years to reach out. Coming here now was at best an act of boredom.

And at worst, suspicious.

His eye caught the slender form of a woman walking quickly from the train platforms toward him.

She walks fast, like Maggie, he thought. Very American in that way. He also noted that she was trim, with full breasts and long blonde hair. His face was impassive as he studied her. He saw her hand go up in a wave as she recognized him. Laurent's gaze shifted to the tall man walking behind her. Laurent had seen photographs of Maggie's older brother—and had heard the stories. Ruthless. Cold. Arrogant.

Just like every mark Laurent had ever had on the Côte d'Azur in the old days he thought as he watched Ben Newberry approach. The arrogant ones were always the easiest to rob. They suspected everyone of trying to take advantage of them except the one whose job it was to do precisely that. A small smile curved on Laurent's lips. There had been satisfaction in feeling their trust in him.

It made the inevitable con all the sweeter.

"Yoo hoo! Laurent, right?" the woman called to him from fifty feet away. Laurent would never get used to the American habit of yelling out to people in conversation. It was a personal blessing to him that Maggie had stopped doing it years ago.

He crushed his cigarette under his heel and went to join the couple. Ben Newberry was allowing his wife to carry a heavy shoulder bag as well as drag a good-sized Pullman behind her, while he pulled a small roller bag. If he didn't know anything about this man and hadn't heard a single one of Maggie's stories, he would know the full make of him in just these first five seconds.

It was going to be a long week.

"*Oui*, I am Laurent," he said, reaching out to shake hands with Haley before taking her bags from her. "The trip wasn't too bad, I hope? Sometimes it gets crowded early in the week."

"We really appreciate you coming to pick us up, Laurent," Haley said, looking like she didn't know what to do with her hands now that her burdens were removed.

"*Bien sûr*," he said. He nodded to Ben. "The car is just there." Then he turned his back and led the way.

"Maggie didn't exaggerate how big you are," Ben said. "What are you? Six three?"

"Close enough," Laurent said over his shoulder as he led them to the parking lot. It was after eight in the evening. For Laurent, it was barely dinnertime but he knew most Americans ate early. "Have you eaten?" he asked as the piled their luggage in the back of his Renault.

"No, and we're starving," Haley said. "We snacked on the train."

"*Bon*," Laurent said opening the front seat passenger door for Haley. His quick assessing glance took in her blonde hair, pale complexion and, although she'd made an effort to hide it with makeup, a black eye. "We will dine at Domaine St-Buvard," he said.

Ben took his wife's hand and pulled her away from the car. "Haley will be more comfortable in the back seat," he said. "I usually sit in front because of my longer legs."

Perhaps he wouldn't have done it if he hadn't gotten Michel's phone call just minutes before they arrived. Perhaps if he'd had a better night's sleep—he never slept well when Maggie was not in his bed. But for whatever the reason, he was in no mood to be preempted by a guest who did not know how to behave as a guest.

Laurent put two fingers against Ben's chest and pushed. The man grunted in surprise and took a step back.

"You will adjust, *je suis sûr*," Laurent said, before turning and taking Haley's elbow and guiding her into the front seat.

~

WHAT THE HELL *was her problem?* Randall thought in frustration. She *knew* he wanted to be discreet. It was probably his very desire for secrecy that was the reason Desiree insisted they be seen at every café along the Côte d'Azur.

"We were together and that's all anybody needs to know," he said to Desiree as she watched him over her untouched glass of Pinot. "As long as you don't talk too much, these French cops are about as backwater as you can get."

"Why must you be so offensive?" she said, frowning at him. "You are as bad as the American slut."

"And why must you rise to the bait every time someone says *freedom fries*? If *anybody* should worry about what the cops think, it's you, Desiree. Everyone knows you hated her. And more than a few know you were alone with her that night."

Desiree took a long drag on her cigarette.

She knows I hate how she tastes after she smokes.

She blew a puff of smoke in his direction. "As were you."

"That's not true."

"No, you told the *police* that's not true. I know the real story."

"Look, now more than ever, Desiree, I think it makes sense for us to take a breath and maybe a step back. Everyone will be watching us—"

"You want me to sneak up to your room at night but not sit next to you in the light of day?"

"It's not like that. I'm just saying we should be careful since this murder investigation shines a harsh light on everything it—"

"I am not your whore to be shoved under the rug!" Desiree said, standing up and jabbing her cigarette angrily into the ashtray on the table.

"Will you please stop causing a scene and just sit—"

Desiree snatched up her purse hanging on the back of the chair and flounced out of the café, prompting a line of interested café patrons to turn and look at Randall. He felt sweat coat his brow as he waved to the server to get his attention.

"L'addition, s'il vous plait?"

The waiter appeared to shrug and then turned away, which

could either mean he was getting the bill or wasn't up for it. Randall sagged in his seat, defeated. Desiree knew he counted on her to handle this kind of bullshit. Why did he put up with her? *Bitch!*

He poured the contents of Desiree's glass into his own and turned to stare at the Mediterranean, unseeing. His stomach churned painfully. This whole tour had been a disaster from the start. He hadn't wanted to do it in the first place and now...this. He downed the wine glass and closed his eyes.

Dear Lord, I know I deserve damn little, but if prayer works, and if someone who could take a life for their own benefit deserves any kind of consideration at all in your book, then please God, I'm begging you, let the cops look elsewhere for Lanie's murderer.

∽

THE TWO-HOUR DRIVE BACK to St-Buvard helped calm and focus Maggie's thoughts. When it came time to finally say goodbye to Annie, Maggie hadn't been surprised by how difficult it was. What *had* surprised her was the feeling that she was also saying goodbye to Lanie. While they hadn't been in contact in the last several years, she had been a friend at one time. How many times in the last couple of days as Maggie accompanied Annie to the police station or sat with her holding her hand and talking had she gotten flashes of the Lanie she had known?

So full of life, so determined to have the happy family and the love that had escaped her mother. To end up killed in a bathtub on the French Riviera and only the mother she was estranged from to claim her...

Maggie shivered. She didn't need to compare her own life to Lanie's to feel grateful.

Why had *she* been so lucky when poor Lanie had not?

Maybe it was the friends Lanie had chosen? Even in high school, Maggie remembered Lanie's friends as being largely fringe: tattoos, foul language, some drug use. Maggie's thoughts quickly fast-forwarded to the people who shared the tour with Lanie. Was Dee-Dee telling the truth? If Janet really did threaten to kill Lanie, did the police know?

Her phone rang and she glanced at the GPS screen on the car dashboard to confirm she had at least another hour before she would be pulling into the driveway at St-Buvard.

"Maggie here" she said into her phone.

"Hi, sweetie, tell me you're about to pull into the driveway, I beg you," Grace said.

"Why? Is the visit going badly?"

"We hate your brother. No, I take that back. I haven't shared notes with Laurent on the subject. *I* hate your brother. Is that wrong?"

Maggie laughed. "Don't worry about it, Grace. Ben is an acquired taste. What's he doing?"

"He's just a dick. Nothing is good enough for him. He doesn't even *look* at Jemmy. I guess he thinks he's at a hotel or something. That's how he acts."

"How's Laurent handling him?"

"He's handling him…infrequently."

"Oh, he's at the village café a lot?"

"I don't know where he goes to be honest."

"So you haven't had a chance to talk with him?"

"I'm sorry, darling, no. But you're right. Something's up with him."

"Yeah, this visit with my brother is probably ill-timed. What do you think of Haley?"

"She seems normal but I can't imagine what would prompt her to marry your brother. He treats her like a servant he doesn't like very much."

"Poor Haley."

"Didn't you say Ben met her through you?"

"Yeah, we were friends in high school—with Lanie, actually."

"So the three of you were a girl group?"

"Well, not for long. That was about the time Lanie decided she didn't need the competition any more and gave me the heave-ho. As a result, Haley and I got closer."

"And then you did Haley the mother of all favors and introduced her to your horrible brother."

"In my defense, he wasn't always horrible. I have some very endearing memories of growing up with Ben."

"Really?"

"Alright, not really, but he's a good provider."

"I can't believe you just said that."

"You can't be happy with no money, Grace. Haley spends her days playing tennis and shopping at Lenox Square. Not really a hard gig."

"Trust me, I know that gig. I divorced that gig."

Grace and her then husband, Windsor, had lived in Provence for three years before Laurent and Maggie arrived. Unlike Maggie, Grace always handled the language, the villagers, the food and the clothes as if she had been born to them. In that way, they were a study of complete opposites. Where Maggie was compulsive, scribbling madly outside the lines, Grace was languid and careful, her eye always on the style, the mode, the rules. Somehow, against all logic, they had become the closest of friends.

"So you saw Annie off safely, I presume?" Grace asked.

"I did. She decided to have Lanie cremated."

"A lot easier getting past security than a coffin, I imagine."

"I think she was going to have to wait a week if she wanted to bring the body back."

"Wise move. And she's okay, you think?"

"She's concerned the cops may have pinned Lanie's death on the wrong person."

"Don't they have evidence on the guy?"

"They do, sort of, but Annie is convinced Olivier would never hurt Lanie."

"Well, I'm sure that's what Son of Sam's mom thought too."

"I said I'd look into it."

"Does Laurent know this?"

"I'm almost positive I mentioned it to him."

"I'll take that as a *no*."

"Look, Grace, I'm not doing anything. I told Laurent I'd come home today and *voila*, here I am practically back in my own little kitchen with an apron tied neatly around my waist."

"Laurent doesn't let you cook in his kitchen."

"The point is, I'm home—as promised."

"So you'll investigate it from St-Buvard?"

"That's the plan. I just need to probe enough to feel okay about telling Annie I tried. I have no reason to believe Olivier is innocent. The cops got him. Let the cops do their job."

"That so doesn't sound like you."

Maggie laughed. "Is Jemmy near? I thought I heard laughter in the background."

"He and Zouzou are watching cartoons. Haley's been great with both kids. Why don't she and Ben have any?"

"You're asking me? I have no idea."

"Well, I've roped her into babysitting *twice* and she's only been here not quite eighteen hours."

"What's my brother doing all this time?"

"Texting on his phone. He went with Laurent this morning to do the rounds of the vineyards—"

"You're kidding."

"No, I was surprised Laurent agreed. He's been so grumpy."

"I'm flabbergasted Ben would be interested."

"Well, he was. Very interested. Maybe he and Haley are looking for a summer home? Or investment property in France?"

"He hates France. He hates everywhere."

"Well, he's been dogging Laurent. He's at the café in the village with him right now."

"That does *not* sound like my brother."

"I think you are going to owe Laurent as many big favors as you can count. He is not having a good time, trust me."

"I'll make it up to him somehow."

"If he's like most men I think you can be fairly sure of exactly *how* he'd like you to make it up to him."

Maggie laughed. "As singular as Laurent is in all other ways," she said, "I have to admit he is like most men when it comes to how he prefers to be recompensed."

"You're a lucky woman, Maggie Dernier. I hope you know that."

"I do. Now go kiss my baby boy for me. I'll be home soon."

∼

BEN SAT at the café table listening to Laurent rattle off his French gibberish to each of the buffoons who approached the table. He was amazed to see the man was something of a French godfather to these bumpkins. Dernier sat at his table—the best spot on the south terrace under the largest plane tree—drinking *pastis* and the locals just lined up to pay him homage.

It made him sick.

Thirty minutes earlier, when he had asked Laurent if he could accompany him, the man's forced patience wasn't lost on him. It galled him to smile and act the accommodating fool. In fact, this whole trip was galling but the endgame at Maggie's house was the worst.

It had better be worth it.

"This is your first visit to France," Laurent said.

Yeah, you manipulating frog bastard. Make small talk. I know you don't want me here any more than I want to be here.

"Yes, it is. Haley has wanted to come for ages. And, of course, we've been intending to visit you and Maggie ever since she moved to France."

Laurent grunted and his eyebrows twitched.

Don't these people know how rude it is not to answer someone properly? I've just paid you a compliment, you grape-swilling surrender monkey. The least you can do is be gracious.

Another filthy peasant rambled up to the table. This one had the nerve to pull out a chair and sit. A glance at Laurent's face showed he didn't seem annoyed at the effrontery. He even poured the man a glass of *pastis*.

Disgusting stuff. Tastes like licorice dipped in kerosene.

The French flew between the two men and Ben couldn't help but wonder if it was a cultural thing not to see how rude it was to speak a language in front of someone who didn't understand it. He probably should just give up now if he was looking to find an area where the people over here weren't going to seriously disappoint him.

He saw Laurent gesture in his direction and the village troll he'd been talking with glanced at him. They continued talking, and it was absolutely clear they were now discussing him.

Unbelievable!

"This is my good friend, Jean-Luc Alexandre," Laurent said to Ben. He said it in an offhand way while looking at something over Jean-Luc's shoulder. Ben had never felt more inconsequential in his life.

And he hated Dernier for it.

"*Bonjour, Monsieur,*" the troll said, smiling a gap-toothed grin and reaching out to shake Ben's hand.

Jean-Luc's hand felt oily and Ben resisted the impulse to wipe his palm on his jeans.

"Jean-Luc is a *vigneron* as well," Laurent said. "His property lies next to my own."

Well, *that* was interesting. Ben looked at Jean-Luc with somewhat heightened attention. Maybe winemaking isn't as difficult as they try to make it sound. If *this* creature can do it.

"And does he make his own label, like Domaine St-Buvard?" Ben asked innocently.

He could have sworn that Laurent gave him a closer look for the comment—as if surprised by it. One thing he'd learned very quickly in the twenty-four hours of the man's acquaintance: if Dernier didn't want you to know what he's thinking, you didn't.

"*Non*," Laurent said, watching Ben, "he uses the co-op, as we all do, but his is an amalgamated product."

"Oh, that's interesting that you have a wine co-op here. I've read about them back home. Napa and all that. Winemaking is becoming quite the thing now. More and more co-ops are cropping up to enable backyard vineyards to come to table."

His Internet research on the flight over hadn't been in vain. He'd practically written the script out—just waiting for an opportunity.

He had Laurent's attention now.

Just as he'd planned.

"It is true that America leads the way in the new virtual co-ops," Laurent said, watching Ben closely.

I've got him.

"It's really ingenious," Ben said, edging up his enthusiasm level just a tad. He wanted to appear knowledgeable to keep Dernier engaged, but not so informed as to not be believable. "It's been a boon I understand for those winemakers who don't have the big bucks to produce their product without a co-op."

Jean-Luc finished his drink, said a few words to Laurent and left the table.

Laurent stared at Ben. "You know a little about winemaking," he said.

He forced a confused look on his face. *Had he said too much?*

"I just know what I read in an article I found in the pocket of the seat on the plane coming over," Ben said shrugging.

Laurent nodded slowly, then finished his drink and stood.

"*On y va*," he said abruptly. "Maggie will be home."

Ben didn't even care that he was following the man around like a fawning Yorkie. He'd gotten his attention—without revealing his hand. He felt a flutter of excitement dance in his gut as he followed Dernier out the café toward the parked car.

What happens next...well, the big French bastard won't even know what hit him.

6

Maggie had to admit it was good to be home. Even just a few days away had her relaxed and humming as she drove up the long driveway toward the house.

An old farmhouse, Domaine St-Buvard was built with materials from the rough landscape. Stones of varying sizes were cemented into sloping knee walls, corralling thick hedges of lavender with stalks of whimsical pink penstemon peeking out from the other side. Cherry-colored roof tiles spanned the entire roof and bright blue shutters, handmade in the village and latched with ironware forged in the seventeen hundreds, punctuated the otherwise bleak façade of the *mas* with a gesture of wit and insouciance.

She parked next to Laurent's Renault and wondered what her brother had thought when he'd first seen Domaine St-Buvard.

The front door to the *mas* swung open and Grace stood framed in the doorway.

"Need help with bags?" she called.

Maggie climbed out of the car, pulling her carry-on behind her. "Nope. Where is everyone?"

Grace stepped aside as Maggie entered the front door.

"Laurent is in the kitchen, Haley's playing with the babies in the living room, and here's you and me hugging hello."

Maggie laughed and wrapped a free arm around Grace. "I'm so glad to be home," she said. "I've got to see my little man before I go into withdrawal."

She set her bag down on the pale, yellowing stone tiles of the large foyer just as Zouzou burst into the room and threw her arms around Maggie's knees. Behind Zouzou, Maggie saw Haley, dressed in skintight jeans and a linen tunic with little Jem balanced on her hip.

Maggie kissed Zouzou and picked her up. She was surprised to see how thin Haley was.

"Welcome home, stranger," Haley said as Maggie set Zouzou on her feet. She held Jem out to her.

"Oh, I've missed this!" Maggie said, hugging Jemmy as he squealed with giggles. "What a happy boy you are. Did you miss me at all?"

"He missed you as only a boy can miss his *maman*," Laurent said, coming into the foyer, a smile on his lips.

"Hello, you," Maggie said, going to him as he pulled both her and Jem into his arms. "Got everyone settled in I see."

Laurent kissed her and patted her bottom. "Dinner in an hour," he said before turning back to the kitchen.

"I love your home, Maggie," Haley said as the three women went into the living room.

A tray of iced drinks sat on the coffee table. "Oh, my God, that man is a mind reader," Grace said, seating herself and reaching for one of the glasses.

Maggie settled next to her with Jem on her lap. He clapped his hands together and pulled at her silk scarf, stuffing one end of it into his mouth. Her little poodle mix, Petit Four, jumped up on the couch and settled against her thigh. Maggie touched the dog's topknot curls absently.

Haley patted the couch next to her and Zouzou clambered up.

"I see your uncle Laurent hasn't forgotten you," Haley said, handing the child a section of *socca* from a plate of still-warm chickpea cakes.

"*J'aime ça!*" Zouzou said, stuffing the cracker into her mouth and looking in the direction of the coffee table for more.

"How much work have you done on the place?" Haley asked Maggie.

Maggie sighed and reached for her drink. "Well, I did get Laurent to agree to get the bathrooms updated, thank God. And we repaired the terrace because I kept tripping over the broken pavers, but that's it. I wish we could do more."

"Well, it's simply gorgeous," Haley said.

Maggie knew Haley was being generous. She and Ben lived in one of the wealthiest zip codes in Atlanta. Maggie was sure Haley's idea of French Provincial was nothing like the living room in which she was currently sitting, which was anchored on one wall by a massive floor-to-ceiling fireplace of stacked stone and had a double set of French doors on the opposite wall which led to the terrace.

You're never truly dissatisfied until you look at a thing through someone else's eyes, Maggie thought.

Domaine St-Buvard was comfortable. It was big and rambling, but it was nobody's idea of a French country estate by any means. The kitchen had its original stonewalls, two-foot thick and exposed. The terra-cotta tiles on the kitchen floor dated back to the nineteenth century and the ceiling arced to an apex that held a large, circular skylight. The cabinets were glass-fronted to show colorful local earthenware bowls and plates within.

Off the kitchen a steep staircase led to the wine cellar—and because it was used for wine storage, it was the only room in the house with air-conditioning. Old, stained oaken barrels lined the cellar's limestone walls. A rack holding at least one hundred bottles of wine faced the staircase, minimizing the steps necessary to replenish party supplies.

Maggie flinched when she thought of their basement. Something terrible had happened down there one Thanksgiving five years ago. To this day, if she didn't have to go down there, she didn't.

"I would kill to live your life," Haley said, sipping her cocktail.

"I didn't know you were interested in France," Maggie said, tipping her head to the side to see Haley better. "You should have visited before now."

"I know we should have," Haley said solemnly.

"I wasn't fussing at you. I didn't mean it like that."

Grace stood. "Glad you're back, sweetie," she said to Maggie. "I think I'll help Laurent in the kitchen."

"He lets you do that?" Maggie asked. She kissed Jem's cheek. "Daddy doesn't like us anywhere *near* where the magic happens, does he?"

Grace laughed and left, her drink in hand.

"He doesn't really keep you out of your own kitchen, does he?" Haley said.

"Are you serious?" Maggie grinned. "Trust me, it's *his* kitchen."

"Well, I guess everything is different over here."

∽

AN HOUR LATER, showered and dressed in a simple linen sheath with sandals, Maggie slipped into the kitchen, where Laurent faced a full panoply of pots and pans on the stove.

"*Tiens, chérie,*" he said, gruffly. "Go to the terrace. It is too hot in here for you."

He turned and wiped a sleeve across his cheek, his eyes taking her in, fresh from her shower. He wore his dark brown hair almost to his shoulders and shaggy. His eyes were dark, nearly pupiless. Maggie always found them sexy, but a little disconcerting too.

"But *you're* in here," Maggie said, stung at being ordered out—especially after Haley's comments.

"And I will be in our bedroom later," he said, a smile edging his full lips, "where you may have my undivided attention."

"It's not all about sex, you know," Maggie said as she swiveled on one foot to make a dramatic exit.

"Yes, it is," he called after her.

She strode to the double set of French doors, opened wide to the terrace. It was after nine but still light out. She saw Grace had lit candles and placed them in nearly every room visible from the outside where the table was set for dinner. The heat of the day had given away to a definite chill and while not uncomfortable, the stack of sweaters and light shawls by the door would be welcome later.

Haley stood at the outdoor table, her jeans replaced by a long tunic dress. She'd put her hair up too, Maggie noticed. She turned when Maggie stepped out onto the terrace.

"Grace said you had a babysitter come over to take care of the kids tonight," she said by way of greeting.

"I did. Danielle Alexandre's grandniece is visiting. The kids love her and she loves babysitting."

"I would have been happy to give them their baths tonight."

"Well, you can do it tomorrow night," Grace said as she joined them. "Isn't it heavenly out here? Maggie's got a small plantation of lavender planted just over there. Can you smell it?"

Haley frowned and looked in the direction where Grace pointed.

"The candles are perfect, Grace," Maggie said. "And the table is beautiful. I'm such a slouch."

"You were tired after your long drive from the coast," Grace said. "Setting the table is fun. It's the washing up afterward when you'll be hard pressed to find me."

Maggie laughed. "Laurent does that, too, although he may leave it 'til morning tonight."

"Oh? Reward redemption night, is it?"

"You are so amusing, Grace."

Haley turned away and rubbed her arms as if cold.

"There are wraps by the door," Maggie said to her. "Shall I get you one?"

"I'm fine. Thanks."

"Where's Ben? I haven't even seen him yet."

"Is that a criticism, because I warn you I'm not as desperate to please as some people."

Maggie turned to her brother as he stepped onto the patio. He wore jeans and a polo shirt with loafers. Although she didn't expect a hug, a smile would've been nice.

"Everything okay?" she asked.

"What is *that* supposed to mean?" he said as he found a seat and slumped into it. Laurent came out onto the patio carrying five wine glasses and a bottle of wine.

Grace turned to Haley. "So, Maggie says the two of you were in school together. Is that how you met her brother?"

"That's right. Ben was three years ahead of us."

"So you knew Lanie, too."

"Not really," Ben said. "She was just one of my little sister's amorphous-faced silly little friends. Made no impression."

"Unlike, one would presume, another of her little friends?" Grace smiled at Ben and nodded in the direction of Haley, clearly indicating that now would be a good time to compliment one's wife.

Ben didn't respond.

Haley said, "Did I mention, Maggie, that Ben and I went to my fifteenth reunion at Pace?"

Maggie smiled. "No, you didn't. Was it gruesome?"

"No, not at all. I was surprised I could convince Ben to come with me, but I think he ended up enjoying himself. Didn't you, Ben?"

"Oh, for Christ's sake," Ben said and reached across the table to take one of the wineglasses that Laurent had filled.

"Was Lanie there?" Maggie asked turning back to the conversation. Laurent got up from the table and returned to the kitchen.

Haley frowned. "I didn't see her. Did you, Ben?"

"How would I know? I barely remember what the woman looked like, for crap's sake," he snarled.

"Well, *you* know Lanie," Haley said to Maggie. "If she *were* there, we would've known." She turned to Grace. "Lanie wasn't the shy type even back in high school."

"Those are usually the most fun types," Grace said.

"I'm afraid Lanie didn't have a very fun high school experience," Haley said sadly. "Wouldn't you agree, Maggie?"

Maggie squirmed. The embarrassing fact was that right after she and Lanie parted ways, Maggie had become obsessed with a new student named Jeremy (or was it Joshua?) who had absorbed the whole of her concentration until he graduated—the year before her—and left her briefly heartbroken. She simply hadn't thought much about Lanie that year.

"I guess so," she said. "I know Annie said the two of them were going through a lot because of Annie's divorce." She decided not to mention Annie's drinking.

"Oh, Laurent," Haley said. "What is it that smells so heavenly?"

Laurent emerged from the kitchen and set down a large, heavy casserole on a platter stacked high with thick-sliced homemade toast.

"Oh, it's *brandade*," Grace said. "And Laurent's is killer. Did you double-dose it with garlic?"

Laurent rolled his eyes as if to imply, *what else?* The table laughed.

"Yeah, I hope you're not sensitive to garlic," Maggie said,

picking up one of the pieces of toast. "Laurent brought on early labor for a friend of ours after she ate his *bourride*." Maggie used a spoon to dip into the steaming casserole and settled a large dollop on top of her toast, which she held carefully over her plate.

"What in the world is it?" Haley asked, reaching for a piece of toast. "It smells like...like the best thing I've ever smelled in my life."

"Wait until you taste it," Grace said. "It's salt cod, right, Laurent?"

Haley's hand froze over the dish. "Fish? This is fish?"

"Well," Maggie said, "it's fish pulverized with olive oil and potatoes and artichokes and about a ton of garlic. We normally only have it in winter and, believe me, you can weed half a hectare after lunching on this."

Haley nibbled on her toast and eyed the casserole unhappily.

"What's the matter, dear?" Grace said.

"She doesn't eat fish," Ben said, scooping up a large serving onto his plate. "I don't suppose you have any chicken tenders for her?"

"Ben, stop it," Haley said under her breath, her gaze dropping to her lap.

Maggie knew Laurent's policy on picky eaters and she knew he would be pretty seriously disgusted by Haley's inability to behave as he felt a guest ought to. Even so, she also knew he had strong views on how a host should behave, which is why she wasn't surprised to see him remove Haley's plate and retreat to the kitchen.

"There is leftover pizza from lunch," he said over his shoulder.

"You are an embarrassment to me," Ben said between his teeth.

"Oh, settle down, Ben," Maggie said, smiling encouragingly to Haley. "It's no big deal."

Grace helped herself to the *brandade* and passed the breadbasket to Haley. "Fresh from the *boulangerie* two villages over," she said brightly.

"Thanks," Haley said softly, taking the basket.

Ben ate his *brandade,* ignoring Haley's discomfort.

This was going to be a long visit.

"So, Maggie," Grace said, "how was Annie? Is she going to be okay, do you think?"

Maggie waited until Laurent placed a plate with two pieces of *pissaladière* in front of Haley. She noted that Haley didn't look much happier with the pizza than she had the fish.

"Well, she's pretty devastated, obviously. I don't know what kind of support system she has back home, but she does have a parish and I think she mentioned she's active in it."

"That's good," Grace said.

"She asked me to look into the evidence the police have on Olivier Tatois—"

The fork Laurent dropped was not an accident and Maggie knew it.

"Why in the world do you think Olivier is innocent?" Ben asked her, spooning himself up more *brandade*. "You don't even know him."

"I don't necessarily think he *is* innocent," Maggie responded. "I'm just trying to confirm that the police have the right guy."

"Why don't you think they do?" Ben asked.

"I don't have an opinion one way or the other. As you said, I don't know him. But Lanie's mom asked me to make sure."

"So, as usual, this is Maggie thinking she knows more than the professionals."

"Wow. That's a little more direct than we're used to from you, Ben," Maggie said. "Refreshing."

"I've heard the stories of your so-called sleuthing escapades. I *am* in contact with Mom and Dad, as it happens."

"Good to know. Just not at Christmas or Thanksgiving."

"I have my own family, Maggie," Ben said pointedly.

"Which most people don't use as an excuse not to see their parents," Maggie retorted. "Besides, no offense, but a *couple* is not a family."

Haley sucked in a gasp of breath, her face a mask of hurt.

"*Chérie*, may I see you in the kitchen, please?"

"In a second, Laurent. Think about it, Ben. If you and Haley were to break up right now, it would be no big deal in the larger scheme of things. But that's not the case if there was a kid in the mix."

"Maggie, *now*," Laurent said.

"How dare you, Maggie!" Haley was on her feet, her chair knocked to the floor behind her.

Maggie felt Laurent wrap his hand around her arm and tug her out of her chair.

"We have recently learned the benefits of time-outs," Laurent said over his shoulder as he guided Maggie toward the kitchen, his hand firmly on her back. "And we will return momentarily when we are using our inside voices."

Maggie stomped into the kitchen and then whirled on Laurent. "I need that jerk to realize he's the worst son in the universe."

"As he is not *your* son, perhaps you are not the best judge of that, *chérie*. Besides, your brother wasn't listening to you but you were upsetting your brother's wife very much."

"I'm sorry about that," Maggie said, clenching and unclenching her fists. "He is a pompous, uncaring jackass."

"*Bien sûr*," Laurent said pulling her into his arms and stroking her hair with his large hand down her back. "Breathe, yes? Big breath."

"Don't treat me like Jem," Maggie said crossly.

"Of course not. Jem would be spanked by now," Laurent said, shaking a finger in her face and grinning. "I am treating you like a naughty grown-up girl."

Maggie laughed and eased into his arms. "That guy makes me so mad."

"On this I believe we are all clear," Laurent said, kissing her and rubbing her back. "Can you behave when you return to table? Even knowing there must be an apology first to your brother's wife?"

"Yes, yes, I know," Maggie said, sighing. "I got carried away. I shouldn't have said all that."

"Especially not to one trying so hard to have the *bèbè*."

"Really? You think so?"

Laurent shrugged and Maggie didn't probe further. The things he picked up on with people and their subtle reactions would rival Sherlock Holmes. She'd long ago learned to take his observations as fact and move on. Saved a whole lot of time.

"Now I really feel bad."

"Tcht," Laurent said, making that dismissive sound he did with his tongue. Maggie had heard him use it many times with the dogs. It didn't thrill her that he was using it on her now. "Just apologize and go forward," he said.

"Easier said," Maggie said, straightening her shoulders and taking a deep breath.

When they returned to the table, it became clear that Maggie's apology would have to wait.

"Where did Haley go?"

"Oh, I don't know. Something about needing to cry herself to sleep," Ben said sarcastically. "I'm sure she'll have recovered by tomorrow."

"I'll go up and see her," Maggie said, but Laurent already had a hand on her arm. She glanced at him and he shook his head.

"Yeah," Ben said. "Please let her get over tonight before you launch into her again."

"Piss off, Ben," Maggie said.

"Always with the delicate repartee." Ben stood and tossed his napkin down onto the table. "I was thinking of a smoke on the terrace. Care to join me, Laurent?"

"You go," Laurent said. "I'll come, *bientôt*."

Ben shrugged and gave Maggie a half-smile before exiting the room.

Grace let out a long exaggerated breath. "Well, that was tense," she said. "But fascinating. Whatever possessed you, Maggie to light into Haley?"

"I wasn't!" Maggie said. "I mean, I didn't intend to. I thought I was going after Ben."

"Well, she got good and caught in the crossfire, that's for sure. You do know she's trying desperately to get pregnant, right?"

Maggie glanced at Laurent but he was already clearing the table. "I didn't," she said. "But I do now. Did she tell you?"

"Mmm-mm," Grace said, standing with a dish in her hand. "She's all but given up. So your little *you're not a family unless you have a kid* tirade was pretty ill-timed."

"I feel terrible."

"You let him push your buttons."

"I can't seem to help it."

"That's siblings for you."

Maggie stared through the French doors, where she saw her brother standing on the terrace smoking. "What I want to know," she said thoughtfully, "is what is he doing trying to chum up to Laurent?"

"Now isn't *that* the million-dollar question?"

Maggie joined Grace in the kitchen, where Laurent was running hot water over a sink full of dishes.

"Go," Maggie said to him. "You cooked it. Let us clean it up."

"I don't mind."

"I know you don't, but only you can find out what my jerk brother is up to."

"He *is* up to something," Laurent said grimly as he dried his hands.

Maggie pulled the towel from him. "Go smoke with him and see what he wants. Do your sneaky, *I'm looking at you but you don't know I am,* thing."

He ran a hand down her back and kissed her mouth before exiting the kitchen without a word. Even in this absent-minded gesture, Maggie could sense his mind was elsewhere.

"He already knew your brother was up to something."

"No one will ever surprise Laurent," Maggie said, grinning. "Trust me, I've tried. Wash or dry? Oops. Hold that thought." She pulled her vibrating phone out of her pocket and looked at the screen. "It's Annie," she said.

"Go on," Grace said as she turned the hot water back on in the sink.

"I won't be long." Maggie walked toward the living room, grabbing her wine glass from the table as she went.

"Hey, Annie," she said as she sat down on the couch. "You get home safe and sound?"

"Yes, thank you, Maggie," Annie said, her voice cracked and heavy with exhaustion. "I wanted to thank you again for everything you did for me. I don't know how I would have navigated through the necessary channels without you."

"Well, no need to thank me," Maggie said. "My French may not be good enough to argue philosophy but it's just barely good enough for most everything else."

"I also want to thank you for agreeing to look into Lanie's death more. Olivier has a lawyer, who told me she would be open to sharing information with you. I gave her your contact information and wanted to make sure you had hers, too."

"Okay. Sure. Can I ask you, Annie, *why* you think Olivier might not be guilty? I mean, I know you met him and liked him and all but..."

Maggie heard Annie take in a long ragged breath before answering.

"Well, to be honest," Annie said, "at first I didn't believe it because I felt that I had special information that seemed to... prohibit the possibility of him being guilty. I didn't want to say anything to you before. It just seemed like an invasion of Lanie's life and I have done such a bad job of protecting her when she was alive."

"Special information?" *What the heck was she talking about?*

"The French coroner told me after the autopsy..." Annie broke down in tears and Maggie sat up straight in anticipation. "He...he told me when he gave me Lanie's...remains something utterly heartbreaking."

Maggie remembered that Annie was weepier than usual when she waved her off on the airplane, but she assumed it was because everything was coming to an end. Now her mind raced: *What could be so heartbreaking after losing your only child?*

"Lanie was pregnant."

There you go.

"Wow, Annie. I am so sorry."

Annie sniffled loudly. "So, of course, I knew it couldn't be Olivier. Only a monster would knowingly..." Maggie listened as Annie made an effort to get a grip of her emotions. When she spoke again, her voice was stronger. "Olivier agreed to a DNA test. Understandably, his lawyer believed it would be helpful in establishing that he could not have killed Lanie. That he had no *motive*. His lawyer told me Olivier was eager to take the test, the results of which we got today."

Oh, don't tell me...

"The baby wasn't his."

7

The next morning, Maggie was up early, but still not before Laurent, of course. She found him in the kitchen talking to Jem, who was in his high chair scrutinizing a mashed-up peach.

"I need two coffees," Maggie said, kissing the baby and then moving to the counter where Laurent had just made a full pot.

"You are expecting a stressful morning, *chérie*?" Laurent said, smiling as she drew two mugs from the cabinet.

"They're not both for me. Did you see Haley come through here?"

"She's in the northeast quadrant of the vineyard."

"Wow, really? Why, I wonder?" Maggie poured the coffees. "I don't know how she takes hers."

"The point is the effort, *chérie*."

"Yeah, good. In that case..." Maggie reached for the antique china ewer of cream on the counter and added it to both mugs, along with two spoonfuls of sugar. "Can you get the door?"

Laurent walked her to the French doors and gave her shoulder a light squeeze as she passed through. "*Bonne chance,*" he said, closing the door behind her.

Maggie stood on the terrace for a moment and squinted into the horizon. The northwest quadrant got the sun first and there was a bench out there, so she figured that was probably why Haley went that way. It was also the furthest point from the house.

Maggie steadied the two coffees and walked gingerly over the uneven ground until she reached the first of several long rows of well-tended aisles of grape vines. To her immediate right on the perimeter was a stand of gnarled olive trees providing nothing useful but a thought to their historical role. They'd probably been fruitful during Laurent's uncle's time, but now they weren't even good for shade.

There was an apple orchard on the far side of the vineyard but it too was not harvested. Maggie had stepped on a snake there the summer before and decided on the spot there was no real need to ever go back.

Laurent's vineyard was sectioned into fourths, with the main intersection a wide dirt tractor road. Although she rarely came into the vineyard—*Laurent's kingdom and domain*—Maggie knew she was nearly to the northwest quadrant when she came to the road. Her foot caught a small root and she spilled coffee onto her hand.

"Ouch! Dammit!" She stopped and put both coffees down on the ground to wipe off her hand.

"Maggie? Is that you?"

Maggie looked up to see Haley, hidden until this moment, rise from the bench on the other side of the tractor road. Laurent must have moved the bench. She didn't remember it being so close.

"Yes, it's me," Maggie said. "How did you know? The early-morning cussing?"

Haley laughed and walked across the road to meet her. "Pretty much," she said. Haley was wearing a pair of loose linen slacks and a short-sleeve cotton top. Appearing fresh and unaffected by the hot morning, she looked like she absolutely belonged in the middle of a two-hundred-year-old Provençal vineyard.

Maggie handed her one of the coffees and in the bright morning sun immediately saw the bruise under Haley's eye. Was that new? Or had it been covered with makeup before?

Why is it you always think the worst when you see a woman with a black eye?

"I am so, so, so sorry about last night, Haley," Maggie said. "Laurent tells me all the time that I don't know what I'm saying half the time but last night I really put my foot in it. Please forgive me."

Haley held the coffee and nodded, her smile firmly in place. "It's okay, Maggie. I knew you when, remember? You always spoke your mind. I overreacted."

"No, you didn't at all," Maggie said. "It was all me. I let Ben get me riled up but that's no excuse."

Haley looked away and Maggie saw the bruise was more yellow than purple. So it had happened a few days ago.

Should she say something about it?

"He's going through some changes at work," Haley said. "And Ben doesn't like change."

"He really seems…edgy. More than usual," Maggie said, grateful to change the subject from her to her brother.

"He'll get through it," Haley said, her eyes going to the span of orderly vineyards all around them.

"What made you come out here?" Maggie asked, following her gaze at their surroundings. To Maggie, it all looked like so many desiccated sticks jammed into the ground, albeit with a bunch of plump, fat grapes attached.

"It's so beautiful," Haley said, her voice holding a tone of surprise that Maggie could even ask such a question. "I like to take advantage of different scenery when I'm away from Atlanta. One morning back home—months from now—when I'm looking out my living room window at the traffic on Peachtree Road, I'll remember this moment when the air smelled like roses and everything was absolutely and perfectly quiet."

"Except for my cussing."

Haley laughed. "I might edit that part out of my memories."

"Did Laurent mention the lemon festival in St-Buvard today? Half the village will be there, which isn't saying much, but it'll still be fun. I mean, if you like imagining you're someplace totally out of reality."

Haley laughed again and Maggie felt her heart settle. She'd been forgiven.

"I wouldn't miss it," Haley said with a smile.

∽

St-Buvard was a small village, Maggie thought with satisfaction, but that didn't mean it didn't hold up its end of the food bargain when it came to *terroir* and pride of produce. Although not ranking anywhere near the level of an Aix or Avignon food festival, the St-Buvard *citron* festival was still renowned throughout Provence.

And after a steady string of murders a few years earlier, being known for a lemon festival was a nice change of pace.

Grace, wearing immaculate white linen slacks and matching top, carried a patent leather red clutch bag under her arm. She shaded her eyes as she stood next to Maggie. The festival consisted of nearly fifty stalls, tables and kiosks that had been erected in the small village square. Laurent had a table near the entrance of the square for his label. Maggie saw he'd hired two of the young gypsy boys to hand out samples of the wine.

Next to them, and clearly the apex of the festival, was a long table with rows of shiny, polished lemons stacked in pyramids. In front them were displayed lemon pies, lemon tarts and dozens and dozens of bottles filled with citrus-infused marinades and oils.

Le Canard, the village pub and café, would serve a full menu today starting with its famous *poulet au citron* and finishing with *les tartes au citron*. Even the small Catholic church of St-Buvard, Sainte-Mère-Église, had a small kiosk of lemon cookies perched on the edge of the flagstone courtyard that was the main stage for the festival.

Of course there were always those vendors who came from outside St-Buvard with their lavender sachets and olives, or even their cheap Paris sweatshirts and knockoff sunglasses, but for once the locals didn't seem to mind. Maggie noticed one stall in particular had a wide banner that read: *Le meilleur à Aix. The best of Aix*—selling a lemon-infused *pastis* and doing a brisk business.

"Don't you already have a veritable dump truck full of lemons from your own trees?" Grace asked as she sampled a lemon-spritzed bite of *chèvre* on a small toast round. She nodded at the proprietor, who promptly shoveled half a dozen wheels of the goat cheese into a small paper bag for Grace.

"Today's not about lemons," Maggie said, shifting her overly full food basket to her other arm. "It's about France's general obsession with food."

Grace tucked her cheese into Maggie's basket. "Uh oh," she said. "What's the matter?"

"Nothing," Maggie said sharply. "Except there's no way anyone can take off five pounds of baby weight living in a country where the sole focus is eating."

Grace nodded. "Only five pounds?"

"Shut up."

"Are you going to talk about last night?"

Maggie stopped and frowned. "I didn't realize Laurent and I were that noisy."

"Funny girl. I'm talking about Lanie's surprise pregnancy."

"And the fact the baby *wasn't* Olivier's." Maggie nodded. "Major shock, that's for sure. Poor Annie. She begged me to keep her updated on what's happening with the case."

"How would *you* know what's happening?"

"Exactly." Maggie approached a wizened old lady behind a counter where a large pot of steaming paella sat. "*Bonjour, Madame Bonet*," she said, kissing the woman on both cheeks. Grace shook the woman's hand and she and Maggie were both promptly handed small bowls of the fragrant rice dish, which they took to a small bench under a large sycamore tree.

"Annie thinks because I can sort of speak the language that the police will tell me what's going on."

"You know, darling, Laurent was out on the terrace with Ben by that point, but I'm almost positive I heard you tell Annie you would find out who killed her daughter."

Maggie took a mouthful of paella and closed her eyes. The saffron mingled with the sharp briny flavors of the seafood and melted into a perfect taste sensation.

"Madame Bonet makes the best paella," she said, opening her eyes.

Grace was watching her expectantly. "Well?"

"I don't see how it could hurt me digging around just a little bit to see what I can find out, for Annie's sake."

"And you're sure it doesn't have anything to do with the fact your brother thinks you'd be insane to get involved?"

"Where does he get off having an opinion one way or the other? What's it to him?"

"I agree, darling. *Laurent*, on the other hand, will definitely have an opinion and I think we both know what it will be. Oh, there's Haley," she said, gazing over Maggie's shoulder and into the festival throng. "She's brave, wandering around by herself with not two words of French to rub together. I understand you spoke with her this morning?

"I did. She was very sweet and I didn't deserve it."

"Where's your brother? Did he come with Laurent?"

"This isn't his scene." Maggie waved to Haley and her sister-in-law broke into a wide grin and hurried over. She, too, carried a basket full of individually wrapped parcels of bakery goods, cheeses and lemons.

"Oh, my God, you can smell the lemons from your *house*, Maggie," Haley said. "I'm in heaven."

"Whoa, you have a serious load of pastries there," Maggie said. "And I have a certifiable weakness for macaroons."

"Well, you'll be able to eat your fill tonight," Haley said. "By the way, I saw Laurent on the other side of the square. He looked to be drinking."

"Well, he *is* a winemaker," Maggie said, smiling at the woman behind a table selling sunflowers. "Kind of goes with the business."

"Yes, but he had the baby," Haley said. "*And* Zouzou. In the States, anyone under twenty-one wouldn't even be allowed to sit in a bar."

"Well, the French are more evolved," Grace said.

"God, you cannot be worried about Laurent," Maggie said, laughing. "Those kids couldn't *be* any safer. Why do you think Grace and I are over here sucking up our freedom like convicts on work release?"

Maggie paid for a dozen sunflowers. "Besides," she said, "didn't you hear Laurent complaining this morning about me leaving the clothes basket at the top of the stairs? He's convinced *I'm* the real danger to anyone's idea of safety."

"Well," Haley said, "he has a point. Even without carelessly placed obstacles, the steps at your house are very slick. I've caught myself several times coming down them."

"Those steps are eighty years old," Grace said. "Laurent's uncle built the house in the late thirties."

"Older than that," Maggie said. "His uncle did the renovations on the existing *mas*. Domaine St-Buvard dates back to the eighteen hundreds."

"So no wonder the stairs are slick," Grace said to Haley. "They've been worn down over the generations. Can you imagine?" Grace looked out over the bustling festival. "I love how old France is. It's like living in history."

"Yes," Haley said impatiently, "but my point is that perhaps—especially with children in the house—a little more care might be taken."

Maggie frowned and chose to ignore the criticism. After all, Ben and Haley weren't likely to visit again any time soon. Best to just smile and let it go.

"Good point," Maggie said, looking around the festival. "Oh, there's someone selling *calissons*. In for a penny..."

"I think the rest of that saying is *in for another pound*," Grace said.

"Gosh, you are so amusing, Grace, I can barely stand it," Maggie said, heading for the candy kiosk. "I'm buying them for Jemmy and Zouzou."

~

LAURENT SHIFTED Jem to his other arm and looked around to see if he could spot Maggie. It was a warm day, not unusual for summer, but the huge plane trees that bordered the square provided ample shade for the festival. He spotted her easily and, as usual, a smile curved around his lips when he did.

It was good that just the sight of her always gave him pleasure. She never seemed aware of herself, how she moved, how she looked. He glanced at Grace next to Maggie, and while he admitted Grace was beautiful, he saw a more relaxed, less practiced way of moving in Maggie. It was this unselfconscious presentation to the world that intrigued and delighted Laurent the most.

To stare much longer would inevitably generate the possibility of catching her eye, and just now that was not his intention or desire. He turned and slipped behind the awning of a tall kiosk selling barrels of glistening olives bobbing in oil. He didn't need to look down to know that Zouzou was by his thigh. The child was devoted to him and mindful, even at her young age, of the necessity of not wandering off—at least not from *Oncle* Laurent.

He sat in a wooden chair pushed up to a table well hidden from view and settled Jem on his lap. Zouzou stood next to him: solemn, alert, curious.

"*Bonjour*, Laurent."

He smiled at the woman who seated herself in the chair opposite him, then leaned over and kissed her proffered cheeks in greeting. She was flawless in that way of French women who know their assets and step into them as comfortably as breathing. He had often compared her to his Maggie. Adele Bontemps was completely secure in her effect on men. That was clear from the message in her eyes to the smile on her pink, full lips.

"Are we hiding today?"

"Not at all. Are we drinking?"

Adele smiled and held up a single, slim hand without taking her eyes off Laurent.

A bottle of clear amber *pastis* was set on the table between them, with a crystal ewer of water and two small glasses. Adele poured a healthy shot into each glass and added a small amount of water. Instantly the yellow liquid clouded.

Laurent watched her eyes go to Zouzou as she lifted the glass to her lips.

"Never mind," Laurent said to Adele as he reached for his own glass. "The little ones keep my secrets."

8

"*Non.* I forbid it."

"Okay, stop that, Laurent. You know you can't forbid me."

"I am doing it."

"Well, no, you're not. We live in the twenty-first century."

"You said this woman was no longer a friend of yours. Not for years. Why does this matter to you? Explain this to me."

"Okay. Lanie's mother used me as the paragon of perfect daughterhood with Lanie growing up. Annie was going through a bad time and she—"

"But this is something *she* did. Not you."

"I'm not doing it because of guilt."

"That's not true. That's all this is about. Your guilt."

"She *asked* me, Laurent."

"Hasn't she caused enough problems? First with her own daughter, and now making you feel that her death has anything to do with you?"

"I feel sorry for her, Laurent. And yes, I feel guilty because I left the friendship and I didn't try to find out why she didn't want to be friends anymore. I just gave up on her."

"And you think this giving up led to her death? You think if you had stayed friends she would not have divorced? Or been bitter and angry? You think you have that much power, *chérie*? *Vraiment*?"

"I played a part in it. Lanie needed my friendship—"

"You said she turned away from you."

"Yes, so what? She needed me!"

"You are seeing this relationship through different glasses now, no? It is like an adult child of divorcing parents rewriting his memories of his childhood."

"Maybe it's seeing the truth for the first time."

"I think it is foolish and self-indulgent to go."

"But?"

"But I suppose I can see no real harm in it—as long as you do not climb out on any tree limbs. Eh? Promise me that? No skulking in caves or slipping into abandoned mines?"

Maggie burst out laughing. "You've been reading Jemmy's *Hardy Boys*."

"It is much the same with you, no? Promise me you will not be stupid. You are somebody's mother now. Jemmy needs you in one piece. As do I."

"I promise. Two days. I'll ask some questions—all of which will no doubt confirm that Olivier is the murderer—then reassure Annie and come home to my little family."

Laurent grunted but pulled her into his arms for a long kiss.

∼

GRACE TURNED off the car but didn't immediately get out. She listened to the sounds of the engine click and shudder as it settled into silence. She was pretty sure she was the only one who ever stopped at this dirt turnaround, half of a mile before the sign for the village of St-Buvard was visible. She didn't remember when she'd gotten in the habit of stopping here. When she used to smoke, that's for sure, she thought wryly as she noted the impulse to dig through her purse for a cigarette. She'd quit two years ago.

Annoying, she thought with a smile. It was always so much more pleasant with a cigarette.

Grace loved *St-Buvard*. That was almost the worst thing about leaving France a year ago, leaving this little world behind. Perched on the side of a hill with the remains of a Roman aqueduct at its base, *St-Buvard* was tinier than most little French villages. With one *charcuterie*, one *bureau de tabac*, and one café, *St-Buvard* was indeed *petit*. That was precisely why Grace and Windsor had settled there over eight years ago in a small, renovated *château* ten kilometers outside the village.

Had it really been so long ago? So much had changed. So much was gone.

She glanced at the cell phone sitting in its recharger dock in the console. She reached out and tapped it with a finger and then decided against calling.

What would I say? *Hi there. I'm sitting out in front of the village remembering how it used to be. Is your girlfriend there? Can you talk?*

Grace curled her outstretched fingers into a fist and placed it in her lap. She glanced at her watch. Maggie was probably en route about now, but there was a section of country from Aix to St-Tropez where cell reception was nonexistent. Perhaps Maggie was nearly to the coast? She picked up her phone.

I am the last person to need advice on affairs of the heart. And God knows, Maggie is the last person I'd be mad enough to look to for answers in that category.

Wasn't it just amazing dumb luck that Maggie had found Laurent? And then kept him?

Grace dropped the phone back in its dock. *Now that's a thought. What if it really is a skill you're just born with?*

Because while it was absolutely true Maggie had the fashion sense of a demented Minnie Pearl, and equally true she tended to blunder her way though her marriage like a bull on steroids, it was also true that her friend had a man who was deeply in love with her.

Grace turned the car on. She had plenty of time—thank you, Haley. She had a good three hours before she was to meet Gabriel at *Le Deux Garçons* in Aix. Her stomach clenched briefly when she thought of him.

Stop that, she admonished herself. *You're just nervous.*

She would arrive in town with plenty of time to park and see if there were any new boutiques on the *Cours Mirabeau*. It was positively startling to her that it had been so long since she'd been to Aix.

She drove down the narrow tree-lined road away from St-Buvard, feeling the cool breeze of her car's air conditioning gently rearrange her long curls as they framed her face. Bless Haley for watching Zouzou today, she thought again with a smile, and felt her mood lift.

Her eyes strayed to her purse. Perhaps she would stop at a *tabac* in Aix. Surely one cigarette wouldn't hurt.

∼

Maggie tapped the pedometer but the numbers didn't budge. There was no way she hadn't walked more steps than it was reading.

Stupid thing. Probably measuring in kilometers or something useless like that. She sighed and clipped the pedometer back onto the waistband of her white linen shorts. Grace had begged her not to wear the shorts—said they'd make her look big-bottomed and she'd never be able to keep them from wrinkling desperately —but they were cool and comfortable.

She really wished she'd listened to Grace.

Laurent had driven her to the Aix train station early that morning, where she caught the train to Fréjus on the coast. Her brief conversation on the phone with Bob Randall assured her she'd have "loads of fun" and would finish the tour in a little more than two days.

That was just about the limit of Laurent's patience. To be honest, Maggie wasn't sure what she would do on the tour or even what questions to ask. She had no overriding reason to believe Olivier was innocent. Really, she was just collecting information, talking to the people who had known Lanie, and then checking it off her list so she could call Annie back and tell her she'd done her best.

What did it mean that Olivier was not the father of Lanie's unborn child? Could it have been as easy as the fact that Lanie had an affair? Well, she certainly had never reported a rape, so it was a pretty safe bet if it wasn't Olivier's that Lanie had stepped out on him.

Unfortunately, the baby not being Olivier's now gave him a motive. *Poor Olivier*, Maggie thought, shaking her head as she watched the flat expanse of French countryside fly by her window. *Way to have that one turn around and bite you on the butt.* She hoped his attorney would at least argue that if Olivier had known the baby *wasn't* his would he logically have begged for a DNA test? Clearly, he assumed the baby was his.

But if you took Olivier out of the picture for just a moment the news meant that the father of Lanie's baby—whoever that was—might have a class-A motive for killing her. Especially if, say, a knocked-up tour guide on your popular television travel show displayed a propensity to reveal her sources?

Talk about public broadcasting, Maggie thought grimly.

The parting at the train station with Laurent had not been exactly icy, but neither had it been very mushy either. Maggie knew he wasn't thrilled with her leaving—especially not with a house full of guests—but she also picked up on a certain amount of relief to have her gone for a bit. In many ways, that scared her more than anything else.

What in the hell is going on, Laurent? She prayed that Grace would have better luck in the next two days.

When her train arrived in Fréjus, Maggie saw Desiree standing on the platform waiting for her.

Guess she got the short straw.

It was just barely midday and Maggie found herself wondering where lunch fit into the itinerary. She cursed Laurent for keeping her too well fed. She was always hungry now, and the time when she could walk away from a *tarte de pomme* or even a simple *cassoulet* was long ago. At this rate she would never lose the baby weight.

"*Bonjour*, Desiree," she said brightly as she descended from the train onto the platform.

The woman nodded curtly at her and forced a return greeting out between clenched teeth. It was probably her association with Lanie, but it was very clear Desiree didn't like her. In fact, hadn't liked her from the get-go.

"We are to meet the others at lunch," Desiree said, turning away as Maggie ran to keep up. Desiree was wearing four-inch heels on her sandals, but her long legs were athletic and she had to stop more than once to wait for Maggie to catch up to her. That was all the more embarrassing because Maggie knew Desiree was older than she was.

It didn't matter. She consoled herself that she was logging in the steps on the pedometer, which might allow her to indulge in a little dessert at lunch. With a sinking heart, she saw as they left the train station, that Desiree was not leading Maggie to a parked car. Clearly the woman had walked to the station.

The more steps I rack up, Maggie told herself reasonably, *the more I can relax at lunch.* She thought that she would look at her two days away from Laurent and his kitchen as an opportunity to fast—or at least cut down to three meals a day—but she felt her resolve waiver the closer she got to the restaurant section of Fréjus.

The aroma of cooking seafood, saffron and garlic seemed to fill the air as she and Desiree turned down one narrow cobblestone street. Directly ahead, Maggie saw the road dead-end into a large outdoor restaurant. The umbrellas over the tables were a deep green and gave the impression of a lush garden among all the stone and brickwork. Dee-Dee stood up from one of the large tables and waved to them.

Everyone was there. Jim and Janet Anderson looked up from their wine and dishes of olives and smiled blandly at her and then went back to their conversation. Bob Randall stood up from the table and spread his arms out to Maggie although he had not even looked in her direction when they met in Nice.

"Madame Dernier," he boomed out. "Come sit next to me. I can't tell you how grateful I am that you agreed to serve as our guinea pig for this tour!"

Maggie noticed that Desiree simply sat down and lit up a cigarette. Her job was done.

"We have a huge order of fried calamari coming," Dee-Dee said, pouring Maggie a glass of rosé wine.

So much for the diet, Maggie thought with resignation as she reached for the wineglass.

Lunch was prolonged and wonderful. After the first hour, Maggie stopped keeping mental notes to share with Laurent and just sat back and enjoyed the *foie gras au torchon*, the heavenly *moules Provençale* steamed in white wine, olives and garlic and, oh, the amazing rack of lamb with the juniper demi-glace. Maybe she would tell Laurent about that one. She tucked her pedometer into her purse. It felt like it was pinching her waist every time she turned in her seat.

Just from a cursory examination of the small tour group, she could see that Jim and Janet were a closed society unto themselves, caring only for each other's conversation or company. Dee-Dee had said they were wealthy, so it was possible they used that as a reason not to socialize too closely with the others.

On the other hand, the others were all deeply crazy in one form or another.

Randall was the sun around which everyone revolved, that much was clear. Maggie could still feel the charm radiating off him. It wasn't just that the sought-after prize came at his discretion, and that it included working closely with him. It was also because the man had an aura of charisma that seemed to draw everyone into his sphere—even waiters and shopkeepers, Maggie noticed.

Full and thickheaded from the afternoon wine followed by multiple cups of espresso, Maggie wondered how any of them were going to perform in any kind of coherent manner for the afternoon tours.

"We took the day off because of you," Dee-Dee said.

"Oh, I didn't realize that," Maggie said, her eyes watching as Desiree drunkenly tugged at Randall under the table.

"Well, *some* of us will be working, of course," Dee-Dee said tartly. "*Some* of us are always working."

"*Tais-toi*," Desiree snarled.

"Now, girls," Randall said, his arm going around the back of Desiree's chair. "We've had a lovely lunch, haven't we? Let's don't ruin it. Are you tired, darling?" he said to Desiree, his eyes glossy with drunken lust.

Looking at Dee-Dee and not Randall, Desiree smiled slyly and nodded. Maggie thought it was the first smile she'd seen the woman give. It wasn't pretty.

Randall and Desiree stood up and staggered away from the table without a backward glance.

"Disgusting," Dee-Dee said, watching them retreat down the long street and disappear.

Maggie turned to her. "I thought you said they weren't an item. I thought you said it was all in Desiree's head."

A loud bark of a laugh made Maggie turn in surprise to the

Andersons at the end of the table. They were both watching Maggie.

"Is that what Dee-Dee told you?" Jim said. "Well, that is truly pathetic. Even for our little Dee-Dums." He laughed again.

Dee-Dee jumped to her feet, lost her balance and fell back into her chair, knocking her wineglass over onto the table. She was successful on the next try, grabbing her purse and making the best possible show of swanning out of the outdoor restaurant. Maggie watched her go and then looked back at the couple.

"So Dee-Dee's got a torch for Randall?" The couple exchanged a look, trying to decide if it would be appropriate to condescend to converse with her.

Finally, Janet leaned across the table. "It's a fascinating study in human behavior. Dee-Dee wants Bob but Bob wants…wait for it…Lanie."

Maggie frowned. "But isn't he sleeping with Desiree?"

"Didn't I say it was fascinating?"

"Don't forget the best part," Jim said as he placed a hand on his wife's arm. "The best part is that Desiree *knows* that Bob really wanted Lanie."

"But Lanie said no?"

"Supposedly," Janet said, her eyes glittering with cryptic meaning. Maggie reminded herself that according to Dee-Dee, Lanie *had* said yes to Jim. And while that might give him bragging rights since it sounded like she wasn't totally undiscerning, it also gave his wife, Janet, motive.

Maggie looked back down the narrow road where Desiree and Randall had vanished.

"So Desiree is sleeping with Randall, but everyone knows he preferred to be with Lanie—who he couldn't have."

"Exactly."

"Wow," Maggie said. "Desiree must have hated Lanie."

"You could say that," Janet said, leaning back into her chair and reaching for her wineglass.

Grace walked across the lawn, a basket of just-cut zinnias in her hand. The sun hadn't set yet and the warmth of the day seeped into her thin linen tunic.

Zouzou burst out from the underbrush and tackled Grace around her legs, making her falter but not fall.

"Zouzou, you little monster!" Grace laughed, wrapping her arms around her daughter and trying to tug her into her arms. "If this is an ambush, I'll have you know I can retaliate with rapid-fire tickling." Zouzou shrieked and twisted out of Grace's grasp. She ran back around a large lavender bush that anchored the north corner of the flagstone terrace.

Haley appeared from inside the house and set down a tray of drinks glasses on the large outdoor dining table. She had little Jem snugly tucked into a carrier she wore in front. He was awake and, unlike how Maggie usually wore the carrier, was facing outward. Actually, Haley's way made more sense, Grace realized.

The baby was kicking his feet and looking at the world around him, his fists reaching out to grab at the trees, the tablecloth or the ears of Laurent's big hunting dogs, Arlo and Marthe. Little Petit Four, Maggie's scraggly poodle terrier mix, wisely spent most of her time under tables and away from Zouzou's insistent demonstrations of love.

"Drinkies, Grace," Haley called to her. "Laurent thought this would lure you in."

"The man knows me too well," Grace said, dropping the flower basket on a chair and surveying the tray of drinks. She picked up a cold crystal glass with crushed ice and cut limes in it. One sip told her it was vodka, but infused with something she couldn't put her finger on. *Basil?*

She settled in a chair and put the drink down before reaching out for Jem. "Shall I take him? He looks heavy."

"He's absolutely no trouble at all," Haley said, unbuckling

him and slipping him out of the harness. "But it is a little warm." She handed him to Grace and sat back in her chair and smiled. "You should have another," Haley said. "You look beautiful with a baby in your arms."

"I look even better when it's somebody else's baby," Grace said. "Did you have a good day? Did Zouzou behave herself?"

"She was an angel. I could eat her with a spoon. Did you get a lot of work done?"

Grace took a long sip of her drink, turning her face away. "Not near enough," she said. "I don't really know what I'm doing."

"I'll bet you're doing better than you think."

"Thanks. I suppose time will tell."

Later—much later—Grace would remember the next several seconds as happening in slow motion. She would realize that time had slowed down and along with it the ability to move or react or think until all she could do was sit frozen in her chair, a baby on her lap, and listen to the terrified screams of her child as they reverberating across the lawn and into the atmosphere.

9

After her lengthy and heavy lunch, Maggie's first day on the tour ended with a nap that didn't finish until the next morning. Furious that she'd wasted the evening when she knew Laurent was counting the hours until she returned, she vowed to redouble her interviewing efforts of the group to make up for lost time.

That morning, she met the rest of the group in the lobby of their hotel off the N7 Highway.

I guess the magic begins after breakfast, she couldn't help think. Her hotel room had been charmless and basic, and while a continental breakfast was on offer in the small breakfast room, one glance confirmed it was a stale selection of reheated frozen croissants, canned juice and bad coffee.

Randall was talking through Desiree to a young man draped in various video cameras. Obviously he was trying to get some local talent to pinch-hit for the still missing Olivier. She smiled as she joined the Andersons and Dee-Dee as they stood waiting for Randall to finish.

Janet wasn't as friendly as she had been the night before, but she'd already tipped her hand to Maggie that she was an easy talker once she started drinking. Maggie would remember that.

"Everyone sleep well, I hope?" Maggie asked cheerfully. If their faces were any evidence at all, it looked as if the Andersons hadn't stopped imbibing after lunch the day before. Jim looked ill and every minute of his sixty-one years. Janet wore sunglasses even in the hotel lobby and clutched her arms in a protective gesture that warned all to stay away.

Dee-Dee was drinking a diet soda from a can and didn't respond.

"May I ask what's on the agenda today?"

Dee-Dee sighed, as if it were a terrible imposition to respond. "We'll do a tour of the Roman antiquities," she said. "That was supposed to be Lanie's part and Bob hasn't decided who'll do it now."

Maggie wondered how deluded you'd have to be to believe you were having a relationship with someone who was having a relationship with someone else. She wasn't sure she'd ever even heard of it before. She smiled at Dee-Dee but the woman refused to look at her.

She's probably embarrassed, being called out in the open like that yesterday.

A loud handclap made Maggie and Dee-Dee turn their heads to see Randall shaking hands with the boy and turning toward them. Desiree continued to speak to the new cameraman.

"We are in business, people!" Randall said, rubbing his hands together as he approached the group. "Young Sage here won't be with us past St. Raphael, but we'll use him up before then. Are you ready to see Fréjus?"

Maggie smiled politely and noticed the Andersons weren't bothering with that kind of courtesy.

"Who's leading today?" Dee-Dee asked.

"Well," Randall said, "as young Sage is new to our little group and speaks no English, I thought it might be less wear and tear on all of us if—"

"Never mind," Dee-Dee said with disgust. "You answered my question."

As they all walked to the SUV to begin the day's tour, Maggie's phone began to vibrate. A glance at the screen made her answer it immediately.

"Hey, Annie," she said. "Is everything okay? I'm just about to join the others for the tour."

"Yes, darling, I won't keep you. But I wanted to let you know that I found out from that nice police detective that the main reason they're holding Olivier is because of the keycard they found in his wallet."

Maggie slowed her pace. "What about it?"

"That's just it," Annie said with a sigh. "Detective Massar sent me an email and that's all I could unscramble from it. May I forward it to you?"

"Sure."

"Maggie, are you coming?" Randall called from the parking lot.

"Be right there!" Maggie called back. "I have to go, Annie."

"Of course, darling. Just let me know what he said when you have a moment, okay?"

"Will do." As Maggie hung up, she saw the email struggling to come through on her phone. She would read it in the SUV.

The tour began with a drive down the center of Fréjus. Maggie shared a seat in the SUV with Jim and Janet and looked out the window at the tidy, tree-lined residential sections of town. Souvenir shops, dress shops and bookstores seemed to line the people-clogged streets. Maggie was amazed to see so many tourists and assumed they must be French.

Most people back home would never have heard of Fréjus. And the fact that it wasn't near the beach also seemed to make it a surprising popular stop for visitors.

They sailed past the shops and a beautiful arch of stone that Maggie could see served as some ancient entranceway. Beyond it and the tips of the trees, she spied the spire of the town's ancient cathedral set off a small, graceful square and wondered why they weren't being told anything about it.

Randall drove with Desiree in the passenger's seat while the new videographer, Sage, and Dee-Dee sat in the cramped rear seat. Sage wasn't homely, Maggie thought, but he was awfully young. She wondered if Dee-Dee was thinking about making a move. A few covert looks in her direction seemed to confirm that Dee-Dee was trying to decide the same thing.

"We're not doing the town, itself?" Maggie asked.

Randall turned to look at her and instantly she wished someone else would answer. The roads were narrow and the stonewalls unforgiving. And, she thought, he drove too fast.

"Not this trip," he said. "Just a taste of the highlights. What do they call it when it's food, *chérie*?" He turned to Desiree and it was all Maggie could do not to cringe when he used the endearment. He mangled it so bad it sounded like he was calling her the name of the fruit.

"*Amuse-bouche*," Desiree said promptly, not taking her eyes off the road.

Maggie made a point to remind herself that just because she was starting to seriously dislike someone was no reason to consider them guilty of a crime.

Although I have been pretty accurate in the past. And, she admitted, wrong as many times, too.

"I just need to remind everyone that even *I* have not yet heard Desiree's presentation," Randall said over his shoulder. "Mademoiselle Badeaux—ever the dedicated professional—only rehearses in the privacy of her hotel room so as to keep the excitement level cranked to its very highest level. I'm sure we'll all appreciate that."

Desiree turned and smirked at Dee-Dee sitting behind her in the backseat.

Thirty minutes later, Randall pulled the SUV over to the side of the road and everyone piled out. Maggie noticed they were just beyond a large roundabout that headed toward the main highway. The massively high pillars loomed overhead like crumbling but majestic giants. Roman aqueducts. They were impressive, and she couldn't help but try to imagine the men who had built them and the villagers in the Middle Ages who had toiled, lived and died in their shadows.

"Wow," Maggie said, her voice tinged with awe. She stood off to the side of the road—a road with few cars on it in spite of its direct access to the N7—while Randall and Desiree and Sage took their places. Sage set up his tripod in front of the aqueducts, no more than twenty yards beyond them, and Randall stood in front of the camera waiting patiently.

The young man adjusted the lavaliere mic on Randall's lapel and then stepped back behind the camera before pointing to Randall.

"Greetings from Fréjus," Randall said into the camera, his smile genuine with delight. "If you are English-speaking and visiting this relentlessly beautiful town on the Côte d'Azur, I will know you heard my voice. Why is that? Because Fréjus is a hidden jewel in the crown of southern France."

Then Randall snapped his fingers at Sage. "And we'll do a cutaway there," he said. "Go ahead and get some B-roll, okay? Desiree? Tell him to shoot the aqueducts and maybe some of the skyline. I can't remember your script. Do you mention Fréjus is mostly inland?"

"I do not," Desiree said, straightening the peplum of her cotton blouse. Maggie saw she had freshened her lips and foundation while Randall was performing.

"Okay, don't worry about it then. Rolling?" he asked Sage.

Maggie saw Sage shrug, but as he continued to look in the viewfinder she thought it was a safe bet he was still filming.

Desiree plastered on a wide smile that startled Maggie in its patent falseness and stepped into the foreground of the shot as Randall stepped out.

"*Bonjour* from Fréjus," she said and swung her arm out to take in the view behind her. "A medieval city created by the Romans in 49 BC, this amazing structure you see behind me, this aqueduct, was built in the middle of the first century BC and functioned for a thousand years. Can you imagine? Forty-two kilometers long, providing the village and the surrounding area with its water."

Desiree turned as if to give the structure an admiring glance.

"We French have at least a few things to thank the Italians for, no?" she said smiling.

"No, cut!" Randall said, waving his hands at Sage. "Desiree, no. Why did you say that? Now we'll have to do it again."

Desiree blushed furiously.

"I thought it would feel more...organic to refer to the fact that as a Frenchwoman presenting this amazing town to our listening—"

"Your *Frenchness* is not the point, Desiree," Randall said. "It is not *near* the point. Stick to the damn script. Can you just do that? Honestly, people..." Randall ran a hand through his thinning hair and turned to Jim and Janet, who were standing impatiently in the summer heat.

"Did that last bit feel right to you? I mean as tourists? Mrs. Dernier? Please be honest. Desiree is a professional. You won't hurt her feelings."

Maggie's mouth fell open and for a moment she forgot she was posing as a tour member. She felt Desiree's gaze drill into her. "Uh, it felt okay to me," she said, shrugging.

"You see, Desiree?" Randall said. "Do it again." He turned to Sage and made a rotating motion with his finger. "*Encore*? *Encore* that scene? Tell him, Desiree."

"He understands," Desiree muttered, taking her place in front of the camera again, her smile not yet in place and the blush still evident on her neck.

"Should I mention the dog crap visible on her shoe?" Dee-Dee said loudly. "Or will you crop that in post?"

Desiree looked down at her feet. There was no dog mess anywhere near her. But when she glared back at the camera, her eyes darting to Dee-Dee as she spoke, it was clear she was done for the day. Fuming, she turned and stormed back to the SUV, which she climbed into, her arms folded in an angry, protective clench.

"All right, everyone," Randall said wearily. "Take five."

Maggie watched him get into the car and put a hand on Desiree's shoulder. She shrugged it off but her body didn't move away from him.

Dee-Dee went over to Sage as he broke down his camera tripod, her voice high-pitched and silly as she attempted to engage a non-English speaker in conversation. The Andersons stood silently, staring up at the looming aqueducts, neither speaking. *Probably neither seeing, either,.*

Reminding herself of Annie's email message, Maggie pulled out her phone and opened the forwarded email. She scanned its contents quickly. Annie had been right. Massar said the main piece of evidence against Olivier was the fact he had in his wallet the keycard used at the time of the murder.

Pretty damning, Maggie thought, wondering for the hundredth time why Annie thought Lanie's boyfriend was innocent.

∼

"You have no idea how dysfunctional everyone on this trip is," Maggie said on the phone that night. "Everyone either hates everyone else or is sleeping with everyone else. Sometimes both at the same time."

Grace laughed. "Sounds like great fodder for your next novel."

"I'm done with writing novels."

"Too bad. Laurent said it kept you busy."

"I'll just bet he did! Honestly, he doesn't even try to hide how patronizing he is."

"You should get on her your knees and thank God for Laurent," Grace said, still laughing.

"How's Haley? I didn't get a chance to talk to her before I left."

"Your sister-in-law is my personal hero about now," Grace said. "You're not going to believe this, but Zouzou fell down the well."

"Are you serious? I *told* Laurent that thing was dangerous!"

"Well, he's a believer now. When it happened, Maggie, I just froze. I don't know why but the horror of hearing that scream coming from my baby...I just sat there. And Haley was up and racing to the well before I even got to my feet."

"Was Zouzou hurt? How did she get her out?"

"One little scratch. Haley just threw the board that was on top of it out of the way and jumped down. She didn't even look around for another way. Of course, Laurent was there by then and he pulled them both up. If I live to be a hundred, I will owe that woman."

"Well, she always was very athletic. So besides rescuing children from wells, what does she do all day?"

"She reads a lot and takes long walks through the vineyard. She watches Laurent cook and she babysits."

"And Ben?"

"On his laptop in the bedroom or on the phone."

"I wonder what his deal is. Haley told me in Nice that he was under a lot of pressure about something. What about you? How's the business? Have you heard from Windsor?"

Grace sighed. "No to Windsor, but I've been meaning to talk to you about something. Frankly, I am not sure of how to handle it. As far as business, I have a meeting next week with the owner of a children's boutique and for once it's not someone acting like she's doing me a big favor. I really like her clothes, too."

"That's great. Where is she? Paris?"

"Yes, but she has a store in Aix."

"Too bad. It's nice to have an excuse to spend the weekend in Paris."

Grace laughed. "That's what I thought. And then I reminded myself I'm supposed to be thinking like a businesswoman."

"I hate when that happens."

"But when you have a few minutes—not now, I understand you're in a rush—but when you do, I have something I could use your help with."

"Sure. How about when I get back?"

"I may need you before then. Oh, I think I hear Laurent home downstairs. He's been in such a bad mood lately."

"Tell me about it."

"Oh, stop. Laurent worships you."

"Except when he's yelling at me."

"Darling, I *live* here, remember? Laurent never yells at you."

"That may be true, but he has a raised eyebrow that can scorch."

"But as far as whatever's going on with him, I really think you need to grab this particular *toro* by the horns."

"Laurent doesn't respond well to the direct approach."

"He responds very well to *your* approach, dear. You need to talk to him."

"It's a thought."

"Darling, I'll put this in plain language for you: *Come home, your husband needs you.*"

Maggie laughed.

"I'm serious, Maggie."

"Grace, trust me, he wouldn't welcome me trying to butt into his business."

"It's your business too. The vineyard is what supports your house, your groceries, your lifestyle. You can't let him manage it alone."

"He prefers to."

"Zouzou prefers to eat ice cream at every meal," Grace said. "Doesn't mean she should."

"Laurent needing me...huh, that's a new one. What next? The Earth orbiting around the sun?"

"I believe the Earth *does* orbit around the sun, dearest."

"You know what I mean."

"Alright, before I hand you over to your hunky hubby, whom I hear climbing the stairs, tell me in one sentence or less what you've found out in your elongated stakeout thus far."

"I've found out that Desiree—one of the tour guides who was competing with Lanie for the TV job—is sleeping with the boss *and* she hated Lanie."

"Well, that's motive. Anything else?"

"Since I don't have access to the police records on the case, I don't know if she has an alibi for the time of death or anything. I'll have to find that out on my own."

"I don't suppose just asking her...?"

"She's not very nice. I try not to ask her for the salt when she's sitting right in front of it."

"Too bad."

"Then there's Olivier. He had motive for killing Lanie because of the baby not being his and we all know he had opportunity."

"Not exactly what Annie was hoping to hear."

"Well, I'm hoping what she really wants to hear is the truth."

"Anybody else look suspicious to you?"

"Not really. They're all pretty horrible, but it takes a special kind of horrible to kill someone in cold blood."

"This is true. Oh darling, Laurent is here and he has a sleepy baby in his arms whom I know you are going to want to Face-Time with. Promise you're not taking chances and that you'll come home on schedule. I have a special reason for asking you that."

"I will, Grace. Thanks."

∼

AFTER DINNER on the walk back to the hotel it began to rain.

"So, this must be a nice break for you. Are you friends with Randall?" a slurred voice asked close to Maggie's ear. Maggie turned to see Janet by her elbow. The woman had been solidly drunk all during dinner. Maggie had no idea how she was able to stay upright for the two-block walk back to the hotel.

"I wasn't needed at home and just thought I'd finish up with y'all."

"You're from the South? How come your brother doesn't have an accent like you do?"

"I have no idea." Maggie noticed that Janet didn't really seem to be waiting for a reply but was looking around, distractedly, as drunks do.

"You know about my husband I suppose," Janet said, moving alongside Maggie and gripping her arm for support.

Maggie turned her head to see Jim trudging along behind them. Although not quite as inebriated as his wife, he walked with his head down, as if carefully, single-mindedly watching every footstep that would lead him to his bed.

"I'm not sure what you—"

"About him sleeping with that slut. I'm sure you know. Everyone knows."

I know you're the first person I've heard call her that, Maggie thought, her stomach tensing, *and I know the word "slut" was written on her dead face.*

"She came on to *him*. Did you know that?"

"I did not."

"Well, she did. You know why?"

Maggie didn't answer. Janet was leaning heavily on her now, which slowed their progress. A few feet ahead of them, an equally drunk Dee-Dee was trying to walk without falling. Randall and Desiree had left the table an hour ago.

"Because she thought we were rich, that's why."

"You're not rich?" *This was news.*

"Ha! You thought so, too. Everyone thinks so. You know why?"

This guessing game was getting tiresome. But the last thing she wanted to do was shut off the flow of information.

"No, why?"

"Because Bob told everyone we were. Truth is we're only here because Bob's mother is Jim's sister. She made him take us."

"Shut up, you stupid bitch," Jim snarled.

Maggie jumped at the intensity and the closeness of his interjection. He had obviously been listening to every word.

"And when Lanie the slut found *that* out," Janet continued, unperturbed, "she told the world what up to then only *I* knew—"

"If you say one more word, you disgusting bitch," Jim said, grabbing his wife's arm and jerking her away from Maggie, "I will divorce you the minute we return to the States."

Janet cackled and her laughter brought her to her knees. "Promise?" she said from her position on the sidewalk. Maggie held back to allow Jim plenty of time to jerk Janet to her feet and guide her in the direction of the hotel.

She couldn't help but wonder what Janet had been about to say before she collapsed.

What had Lanie told the whole world that up to then only Janet knew?

∽

THE NEXT MORNING, Maggie found herself crammed up against

the window in the middle seat of the tour SUV as the group left Fréjus and headed toward Marseille. She was scheduled to leave the group to head back to St-Buvard tomorrow morning so she knew she needed to make today count.

Squished inside a seven-person vehicle with all the suspects ought to do it.

The drive down the coast to St-Tropez was nothing short of breathtaking. Minus the notorious hairpin turns found around Menton and Villefranche-sur-Mer, the coastal drive ambled alongside carefully placed stone knee walls, the heart-stopping beauty of the Mediterranean laid out before them like an undulating carpet of azure blue. White sailboats dotted the bays and inlets, making Maggie think the whole world must be on vacation.

Who owns these boats? Are they here all year long? Is life just one long party to some people?

Sage had reluctantly agreed to continue on with the group but even Maggie had picked up on an attitude that hadn't been there before. Surely, Randall was paying him? She glanced in the back seat where Sage sat hunched over his camera equipment, his gaze seaward but not seeing. Dee-Dee was staring out the other side of the car where the view was a long series of bushes and cement bulwarks edging the southern side of the E80.

"Ben said your husband owns a vineyard in the Languedoc area?" Jim said abruptly to Maggie.

She hesitated before answering. Jim Anderson hadn't said a word to her before now. Was this because of his wife's drunken revelation to Maggie last night?

"Well, yes," she said. "But it's Provence. Not Languedoc."

"And your husband runs it and produces wine, does he?"

Why don't I like you? Maggie thought as she tried to smile in response.

"He does. His label is *Domaine St-Buvard*. Mostly reds but he's starting to experiment with rosés now."

"Your brother was asking me if I knew anything about vineyards."

Janet snorted and Maggie looked at her but Janet kept her focus out the window. It occurred to Maggie that last night was the second time Janet had tried to cast suspicion on someone in the tour group—first Randall and then her own husband. Might that be a logical ploy if you were trying to divert suspicion away from yourself? She hadn't forgotten that Dee-Dee believed Janet had plenty of animosity against Lanie.

"I told him," Jim said, "I own several, but was never really interested in the day-to-day."

Maggie shot a covert glance at Janet but the older woman didn't turn around. Clearly Jim was fully committed to maintaining the fiction that he and Janet had money.

It was strange that Ben would talk about Maggie and Laurent —even if all he did was mention their vineyard. After so many years of disinterest on his part in anything that had to do with them, it was startling and vaguely unbelievable to imagine him talking to a stranger about her. She looked at the sea and hoped they were going to stop soon for lunch. Breakfast had been nonexistent, as usual.

"I got the impression he was about to invest in one here in France," Jim said. "I told him that was a frankly idiotic idea. Well, if one hoped to make money, that is."

Maggie stared at him. *Ben was thinking of investing in a vineyard?* She looked away and tried to remember how her brother acted at dinner at Domaine St-Buvard. *Was he thinking of investing in Laurent's vineyard? Does that even make sense?*

"He hits her, you know," Janet said, still staring out at the unbroken canvas of interminable blue water.

Maggie snapped her attention back to the interior of the car. "What?"

"Now, we don't know that for sure," Randall said from the front seat. "Let's don't pass on rumors."

"I *heard* them," Dee-Dee said from the back, her voice high and whiny. "I heard the slaps, and I heard the cries."

Maggie felt her face flush with heat. Her mind whirled as she tried to take in what they were saying. She clawed for the window opener.

Even without breakfast, she could feel an oily nausea creep up her throat.

10

Grace watched Laurent pull out of the driveway. The man had been downright evasive this morning—even for Laurent. As taciturn and phlegmatic as he normally was, the difference was just noticeable enough to cause alarm.

Maggie was right. There *was* something going on. A queasy, hard ball formed in the pit of her stomach. *Am I right, too, though that it couldn't possibly be another woman?*

*Just because Windsor dropped the ball...*Grace quickly did a mental shout of *Stop!* when the thought formed in her mind. It was one of the tricks she discovered in a magazine while waiting to get her hair done in Aix. *If you have an unwelcome thought pop into your head, just scream Stop! in your thoughts and it kills the thought.* Too often, if one thinks of something unpleasant, Grace reasoned, it feels as if you're meant to hold it up to the light, dissect it, probe it...and that never ends well.

After all, what was the point? Windsor found someone else and remembering or thinking or analyzing the whys of how that happened wasn't going to improve her day.

Her mind flashed a memory of the smile from her lunch

companion the day before in Aix and she was surprised that her first instinct was to use her thought-stopping trick on that too. No, she didn't want to overthink that lunch and she had enough on her plate to allow herself to get distracted by such things. It was enough that she'd shown up since there was a moment there when she wasn't at all sure she would.

Grace approached the bicycle propped up against the house and frowned. She hadn't ridden one since she was a teenager. She looked in the direction Laurent had gone. She certainly wasn't walking the two miles to the village and back. She pulled the bike away from the house and pointed it in the direction of the main road. Besides, a woman on a bicycle? Laurent would never in a million years think it was her.

Within five minutes, Grace was coasting down the incline of the road outside Domaine St-Buvard toward the village. There was very little traffic. She knew she'd have to navigate the single hairpin turn at the little cement bridge just before the village, but she'd already tested the brakes—several times—and was sure she could manage it. The surprise was how much fun it was—sailing, coasting, drifting down the road, her hair flying out behind her, her cotton skirt flapping against her legs.

The giant plane trees lined the road, their overhead boughs thick with cool green leaves, shading her as they had shaded the marching Roman soldiers, and of course the advancing German army in the last war.

Is there a single place in the States that can transport you back into time like this? she thought, her heart already lifted and buoyant. *A single place that can make you feel both light and free and yet entrenched in history?*

The bridge was visible from the last graceful turn she negotiated and Grace backpedaled to slow her speed. She saw a car coming toward her so she coasted to a stop on the side of the road. When it passed, she rode slowly around the sharp turn, and the entrance to the village opened up immediately on the other side.

From here she could see Le Canard, the café facing the ancient stone square, which was punctuated by a fountain that didn't work and a trio of mammoth plane trees cemented right into the square itself. Across from Le Canard, she saw Laurent's car.

So he did come to the village. Grace glanced at the terrace of umbrella tables in front of Le Canard as she rode past. She had no reason to think he would look at a woman on a bike. They were not uncommon in and around St-Buvard, although the riders were usually in their seventies. Grace rode to the front of the *tabac* that anchored the opposite side of the square and parked her bike. She felt flushed from her accomplishment.

Who needs a car? Who needs a taxi? She smiled at the proprietor of the *tabac,* who watched her enter with stark surprise and then moved to look behind her as if he expected to see a saddled elephant tied up out front. Grace slipped into the side room of the *tabac* and took a seat at the window. There was no coffee or *cocas* on offer here—not with Le Canard a mere thirty steps away —but the French liked to rest and reflect, Grace thought. There would always be a spot to sit and think even if one's hand wasn't filled with a drink.

She squinted at the busy café across the street. Laurent was unmistakable anywhere he went. Too large to be hidden, true, but also because he carried himself with the affect of someone who didn't care who saw him.

I wonder how that worked during his years as a conman, Grace found herself musing.

She quickly picked him out of the group of patrons seated at one of the six outdoor tables of Le Canard. She frowned. She hadn't expected him to be alone. Laurent was very popular in the village, spending half his time exchanging kisses and handshakes with literally every person he met. So she wasn't surprised to see he was with someone.

She just hadn't expected that someone to be so beautiful.

Grace had never seen her before. She was clearly French, although Grace couldn't put into words how she knew that exactly. Perhaps it was her easy elegance and nonchalant way she wore her beauty, perhaps it was the comfort with which she spoke to Laurent and the waiter when he appeared with their drinks.

This can't be what I'm seeing. Grace was stunned when the woman leaned over and placed her hand on Laurent's arm—in a way that indicated it wasn't the first time she'd done it. *There's no way this is what I'm seeing.*

Laurent was partially hidden from view by a table of boisterous village men but Grace had a clear line view of the woman. Grace knew a little something about the body language of women on the prowl.

This cat was hunting.

Maggie, where the hell are you? You need to be home dealing with this, not prancing around the Côte d'Azur looking for closure for someone else's problems!

She felt a light tap on her shoulder, and when she turned she saw the *tabac* proprietor's wife standing there with a stern look on her face.

"Are you here to buy something, Madame?" she asked acerbically.

So much for the French attitude of reflection and rest, Grace thought as she got up from the seat with as much dignity as she could muster. She'd forgotten to bring any money.

"*Non, merci,*" she said haughtily and exited. She released the kickstand on the bike and pointed it back out of the village, glancing briefly at Le Canard before she climbed on.

The woman was gone but her purse still remained at the table so she would be back. Laurent was studying a paper in his hands, oblivious to his surroundings. Grace saw a thin curl of smoke rising from the ashtray in front of him.

She rode past the café, her head turned away, and already felt a light perspiration forming on her upper lip. It had been an easy downhill coast most of the way to the village. Clearly, the return trip was going to be a different ride.

∼

THE SEA SPARKLED like glittering glass, Maggie thought. No wonder the world's rich and celebrated chose Saint-Tropez as their personal paradise. Even today with the glamour of its fabled past well behind it and the encroachment of an unbroken string of t-shirt kiosks lining its main drag, nothing could detract from the natural beauty of the water—so blue it looked like a shimmering cerulean mirror.

And as exquisite as the picture before her was, her stomach still roiled painfully when she called to mind Haley's bruised face.

He was hitting her. Her brother.

And everybody on this tour knew it.

Who are you, Ben? What happened to you?

When her phone rang, Maggie jumped as if she'd been goosed. A quick glance at the screen showed it was Annie. Maggie hesitated, tempted to let the call go to voicemail. She had nothing to tell Annie and she didn't feel up to lifting someone else's spirits.

"Hey, Annie," she said brightly into the phone. She saw Desiree appear at the entrance of the restaurant where they'd just had lunch and motion for Maggie to come. It must be time to leave for Cassis. "What is it, eight o'clock your time?"

"Hello, dear," Annie said. "Yes, just a bit after. Where are you today?"

"Saint-Tropez."

"Oh, that's nice. I was wondering if you have any news about...anything?"

Maggie sighed. This whole trip was a waste of time. Except for discovering that her brother was a wife beater, she hadn't learned a single new bit of information. "There really isn't much, Annie," she said. "Except a confirmation that just about everyone here on the tour was seriously jealous of Lanie."

"You mean, professionally?"

"Uh, yes."

"I suppose that's not surprising."

"You know, I have to say, it's starting to look like Olivier isn't such a bad choice as a suspect after all."

"But then why would he agree to take the DNA test?"

"Just because he was convinced the baby was his doesn't mean he didn't...you know."

There was a brief pause. "I really appreciate you doing this, Maggie and I know you could be home with your baby, so if you want to call it quits I completely understand."

"It's just that there doesn't seem to be anything to find out," Maggie said. Desiree was gesturing more vividly now, her whole face was flushed with her obvious annoyance at Maggie not coming immediately when called.

"No, I understand. Did you get a chance to talk to the maid at the hotel?" Annie asked.

Now Desiree was stomping over to Maggie.

"The maid?"

"I can't believe I forgot to tell you," Annie said. "One of the maids approached me as I was leaving and was trying to tell me something. I guess I was distracted by everything that day."

"Sure, you would be."

"Do you think you might call and find out what it was all about?"

"Is there a reason why you think you're so important you can keep all of us waiting like your pathetic servants or slaves back where you come from?"

Maggie looked into Desiree's twisted face. "Are you serious?" she asked the Frenchwoman coolly.

"Maggie?" Annie said on the phone.

Without taking her eyes off Desiree, Maggie said to Annie. "I'll check with the hotel in Nice and find out what the maid wanted, Annie, and then call and let you know, okay?"

"Thank you, dear. And God bless you."

After she hung up, Maggie put her phone in her bag and stood. "My goodness, Desiree. It would be a shame to pee yourself in one of the most glamorous places on earth."

~

AN HOUR LATER, Maggie was sitting in a boat in the *Massif des Calanques*, an inlet running along a twelve-mile stretch of beach that ran all the way to Marseille. She had spent the car ride to Cassis staring daggers at Desiree and concomitantly trying to mull over what possible news a maid could have wanted to pass on to Annie. Twenty minutes into the ride, she called the hotel but was told it was hotel policy not to reveal the names of their employees on the telephone.

"Beautiful Cassis," Desiree intoned from where she stood at the helm of the small boat. "Home to the *Calanques*, steep-sided valleys enclosed by majestic limestone cliffs that are actually Mediterranean fjords."

Maggie sat opposite Jim and Janet Anderson in the small six-person boat. Dee-Dee and Desiree stood at the head of it taking turns steering and presenting their recited tours.

When Desiree finished the first part of her spiel, she sat down and reached for a water bottle. She looked at Maggie. "Because our program does not target armchair travelers," she said, "Bob insists we hike or kayak to many of the Côte d'Azur's special destinations spots. He is very attentive to the true French experience."

"I notice he isn't hiking with us today."

"He has done this tour many times. The first time I saw him was on his show. He was standing at the tip of the *Calanque d'En-Vau*, stripped to the waist, explaining how the sea level would rise—"

"Where was the mic clipped?" Maggie asked.

"*Comment?*" Desiree turned to her in exasperation.

"Well, you said he was stripped to the waist. I was just wondering—"

"There was a boom mic."

"Oh, sure. I can see that. On a ledge of a fjord. Wow. No wonder he's the best. That's some good television."

"I don't need to be fluent in your language, Madame, to comprehend your sarcasm."

"Oh, I think you are totally fluent in my language, Desiree."

Desiree bristled and turned to face the Andersons, who were gripping the side of the small boat with matching grimaces on their faces. Janet wore a broad-brimmed straw hat in clear hopes of avoiding the sun. Jim just winced into the light with a let's-get-this-over look on his face.

"For many travelers to this area," Desiree said, standing again and addressing the little group, "the most *calanque merveilleux* is the *Calanque d'En-Vau,* which is an easy two-hour hike that—"

"Is she supposed to use French words?" Dee-Dee said loudly. She held her phone to her mouth as if it were a walkie-talkie. "Bob? Desiree is using a mixture of American and French words."

"Tell Desiree to stick to the script," Randall said over the phone's speaker. Maggie could hear the noise in the background of wherever he was. Sounded like a bar.

Desiree gave Dee-Dee a sour look and then readdressed the Andersons and Maggie as the facsimile of her someday TV audience.

"The most extraordinary *calanque*," she said, "is often considered to be the *Calanque d'En-Vau,* which is an easy two-hour hike that plummets to a thrilling and quite steep descent to the beach below."

"Like hell I'm going on that mother," Jim said flatly.

Desiree sat down in the boat with a thud. "I cannot believe I must do this without a cameraman," she said. "I could kill that stupid Olivier for his selfishness!"

Before Maggie had a chance to react, she heard a violent splash and a startled squawk. She twisted in her seat to see Dee-Dee standing at her seat in the boat, pounding her fists against her thighs in fury and frustration.

"Damn duck!" she screamed. "He bit me! Did you see that? Goddamn him!"

What Maggie saw when she turned to the vortex of churning water off the side of the boat was a flurry of feathers and bursts of foam. She held her breath, hoping she wouldn't see blood, too. Bobbing on top of the maelstrom of agitated, escaping duck, was a sparkly periwinkle blue cell phone case that quickly submerged and sank from sight. Maggie looked at Dee-Dee, who was now shaking her fist at the wounded animal—her omnipresent blue cell phone nowhere in evidence.

These people are insane.

∼

GRACE LAID out the tablecloth on the grass and set down the picnic basket. Her morning bike ride had pretty thoroughly depleted any desire to do much of anything for the rest of the day. After a long, cool shower and a vow never to get on a bicycle again, Haley's suggestion of a picnic seemed to perfectly fit Grace's energy level.

She shielded her eyes against the sun, though the spot they'd chosen was mostly shaded. A large Cypress tree spread its limbs overhead allowing the stark sun to peer through in speckles and flashes. The distraction did little to keep her from focusing on the fact Laurent might very well be having an affair.

"Just put him down on the cloth," she said to Haley, who knelt next to her with the baby in her arms. "He can't walk yet, thank God, so that's one less thing to worry about."

Haley gave the infant a quick hug and set him down on his tummy. Instantly, he grabbed at the cloth and army-crawled to the edge where the grass was.

"Not that you can totally ignore him," Grace said, laughing as Haley pulled him away from the grass.

"Mama!" Zouzou said, running over to the women and tumbling down onto the cloth. "*J'ai faim!* Really, really *faim!*"

"I think it's precious that your little one speaks French," Haley said.

"Well, it's really sort of Franglais. I have the only four-year old who is fractured in two languages. Her English is as misguided as her French."

"I think it's charming."

"I hope her teachers share your opinion when she starts school next month."

"Is there a school in St-Buvard?"

Grace opened the wicker basket and pulled out a banana. Zouzou grabbed it and bounded away.

"Don't go beyond the boundaries," Grace called to her.

"Boundaries?"

"*Oncle* Laurent walked the perimeter of where she's allowed to go, which is basically not out of my sight. Zouzou likes rules. Laurent always knows how to handle her."

"Is he good with children?"

"Laurent?" Grace looked at Haley with surprise. "Laurent is good with everyone." As soon as she said the words, she flinched. *Too good, maybe?*

Haley pulled Jemmy back onto the cloth and then turned him over on his back and tickled him until he giggled.

"But to answer your question," Grace said, "yes, there is a kind of school in the village. I'm not sure Maggie and Laurent won't allow Jemmy to go there at least for a few years. It's Catholic, of course. And it's close by."

"But not for your little girl?"

Grace pulled out a plate of deviled eggs and pulled the clear wrap from the top. Laurent had made the eggs earlier that morning using *aioli* instead of mayonnaise. Grace considered it a major strength of character that she hadn't eaten them all before the picnic.

"I don't intend to live with Maggie and Laurent forever," she said. "In fact, I was looking at apartments in Aix last week. There's a wonderful *école maternelle* there."

"The tour group spent an afternoon in Aix last week," Haley said, her voice serious now. "On our way to Nice. It was beautiful."

"Yes, it is. And so are these *gougères*. Where Laurent gets the time to get his vineyard ready for harvest *and* make *gougères* I have no idea. The man's a marvel."

"Is that why Maggie found an excuse to leave yesterday? Because she's married to such a wonderful man?"

Grace turned to look at her. "Maggie and Laurent are very happy." *Am I trying to convince myself?*

"If you say so."

Grace looked out at the horizon of the vineyard until she spotted Zouzou's form skipping through the vines. She had awakened this morning to the sounds of sobbing that, irrationally, she thought must be Zouzou's until she burst into the little girl's bedroom to find the child sleeping. It was when Grace returned to her own bedroom that she heard the harsh male whispering coming from Haley and Ben's bedroom and realized the crying sounds had come from there.

"Maggie is on the coast," Grace said carefully, setting out a large bowl of olives, "because she made a promise to a friend and, take it from me, I know what those promises mean to her."

"But Maggie barely knows Annie," Haley said, frowning. "Is it possible she's finding motherhood harder than she thought it would be?" Haley ran a gentle hand over Jemmy's head as he swiveled it around to regard her.

"I heard you crying this morning," Grace said quietly, her eyes still watching her daughter in the field.

Haley sucked in a quick breath. "It's not what you think."

Grace looked at her. "I'm not an idiot, Haley. Ben's hurting you." She held up a hand as if to stop any protest on Haley's part. "Even if he's not physically hitting you, although I wouldn't put it past him. If Laurent hears him do it, Ben will walk with a limp for the rest of his life, brother-in-law or not."

Haley pulled Jemmy up onto her lap and hugged him close. Grace saw she was fighting tears.

"I always thought if we could just have children, everything would be fine. Ben would calm down and not be so angry all the time. But I just can't make it happen." A single tear trickled down her cheek and she rubbed it away.

"I'm so sorry, Haley," Grace said, reaching out to take Haley's hand in hers. "And I know you don't want to hear this, but trying to fix an unhappy marriage by adding kids to the mix is always *and without exception* a bad idea."

"I know," Haley said, kissing Jem. "But at least I'd have the kids, you know? It wouldn't matter then what Ben did."

"I'm almost positive it doesn't work like that," Grace said sadly.

∼

MAGGIE SAT in her hotel room. The window faced the sea, and while the interior was rudimentary and bare with linens that had certainly seen the last world war, the view was incomparable. She watched it now, the intense blue of the Mediterranean, speckled with the copious white sails of the rich and idle.

The others in the tour had already walked to the little seaside restaurant they'd scouted out earlier in the day and Maggie was edgy from the combination of anticipating what she knew was going to be a difficult phone call and a nearly constant state of hunger.

"Hi, sweetie," she said as soon as Laurent picked up. "Everything okay there?"

"What have you been drinking?"

"That is so rude, Laurent. Why would you say that?"

"Because you sound like you're cranked up on a six-pack of Red Bull and it is seven o'clock at night."

"I *am* a little tense, Laurent, if you want to know. I'm sure you think this is a vacation for me but it's a gigantic pain and most of these people are horrible. It is *not* a pleasant experience at any level."

"So I am assured you will be home tomorrow as you promised."

He was not going to make this easy for her.

"Look," she said, "it turns out I have to take the train to Nice in the morning. I forgot something and want to check to see if it's at the hotel."

"They have phones in that part of Nice."

"I *did* call and the concierge said he couldn't give me that information over the phone."

"If you are stalling, Maggie..."

Surprised, Maggie sucked in a quick breath. Laurent never called her by her first name; he always called her *chérie*.

"I said I'd be home by lunch time and I will."

"By way of Nice."

"Yes, but so what? That doesn't affect my deadline."

A moment of tension passed between them. She had tried to

circumvent him about the reason she was going to Nice and he'd called her on it. Usually she suspected he *knew* when she was playing fast and easy with the truth—but he'd never *said* anything before.

Everything was different these days.

Besides, she *had* forgotten something in Nice and it *was* at the hotel. And she *had* called and been told a telephone interview wouldn't be possible. She was sure, however, that these sorts of details would not assuage Laurent.

"Is everything okay there?" she asked suddenly.

"*Non*," he said. "You are not here."

"I mean besides that. Is everything okay with the harvest?"

"Of course."

"It's just that you're acting strangely lately."

"*Impossible.*"

Maggie had to suppress a grin. "Well, not *very* impossible if *I've* noticed it."

"Everything is fine. Just come home and be a hostess to your guests."

"Laurent, please let me finish what I started out to do."

"Lunchtime."

"Yes, dearest. And I must say, after all this fuss I'll expect nothing short of a six-course meal to explain your absolutely panic to have me back home. Is my brother being a pain?"

"*Oui*, but he's not bothering anyone but his wife."

"Poor Haley. Have you talked to her at all?"

Laurent snorted and again Maggie was surprised she knew what the sound meant without words. Translation: *Why would I talk to your brother's wife?*

"She and Grace went into the village," he said. "For tonight's bread."

Due to an unfortunate series of murders early in their tenure at St-Buvard, the village *boulangerie* had been shuttered, although it was unthinkable for any self-respecting French village not to have a bakery and a daily supply of fresh bread. Since that time, most of the people living in St-Buvard had depended on the bi-weekly arrival of the traveling bread truck. Laurent usually just drove to Aix.

"I'm glad Grace is there," Maggie said.

"Especially since you are not."

"Okay, Laurent, I get it. You're annoyed. I owe you."

"You do. But I will settle for seeing you at the Arles train station at precisely thirteen hundred hours."

Damn. Was he looking at a train schedule? She wouldn't put it past him.

"I'll be there," she said sweetly.

∾

THE WALK from the restaurant back to her hotel was only ten-minutes, but it was all uphill. As usual, Maggie had eaten more than she'd planned to and now she was uncomfortable and seriously annoyed with herself.

Like everywhere in France during the summer, it was still light out at ten o'clock at night. Maggie heard the voices of the others in the tour group as they headed in the opposite direction of the hotel—toward town—for drinks. *How they could eat and drink as much as they did was the big mystery,* Maggie thought as she picked her way across the cobblestone street.

"Hello there, Maggie, hold up!"

She turned to see Bob Randall trotting over to her. Behind him, Desiree waited on the curb. Even from the twenty yards that separated them, Maggie could feel the woman's irritation barreling down the road toward her.

"Hey, Bob," Maggie said when he reached her. "You not going with the others?"

He looked a little winded from trying to catch up, but she knew the florid face and panting could just as easily be the result of the two bottles of wine he appeared to consume single-handedly at dinner. She noticed purple splotches down the front of his shirt.

"Oh, I am. I just wanted to make sure you got back to the hotel safe and sound. You sure I can't convince you to stay out a little longer?"

Maggie smiled and turned to resume her walk. "Positive. I'm beat."

"You're leaving us in the morning?"

"I am. I'm going briefly back to Nice and then from there, home."

"I hate that you're going to miss the rest of the tour."

Maggie stole a glance at him. He hadn't spent much time talking with her since she'd joined the group two days ago so this attention was a surprise. "I enjoyed it," she said. "Although you'll have your hands full deciding between Desiree and Dee-Dee."

"Oh, I've already decided."

Maggie stopped walking. "Really?"

"It was always going to be Desiree," Randall said, shrugging. "Well, after Lanie dropped out of the running."

You mean dropped dead, Maggie couldn't help but think.

"Then why do all this?"

"My production company insisted. We want it to look all above board." He waved his hand in the air. "No, it *is* all above board. We just want to dot all the i's is all. We have to go through the process."

"So Dee-Dee is giving her presentations but she doesn't stand a chance?"

Randall peered at Maggie and grinned. "You were on the boat when the crazy bitch killed a duck, right?"

Maggie suppressed a laugh. "Yes. Although I understand the duck lived."

"She's totally mental," Randall said. "Can you imagine her being co-host? We'd be sued in every city we shot in."

"I can see your point."

"I wasn't going to say anything," Randall said, his voice dropping a level as he looked over his shoulder to where Desiree was still standing on the curb. "But we had an issue with her at the start of the tour."

"An issue how?"

"Seems she came on to Lanie's boyfriend while we were in Orange, and not only did he turn her down, but he told Lanie about it."

Maggie gave him her full attention.

"Lanie basically laughed it off," Randall said, "but unfortunately she did it in a very public way."

"She humiliated Dee-Dee."

"Yeah. Well..." He leaned in closely, as if his next words were extremely important and covert. "You saw how Dee-Dee went off on a poor duck, right?"

"What are you saying? You think *Dee-Dee* might have wanted to kill Lanie?"

Randall held up his hands as if to defend himself. "I'm just saying she's crazy and Lanie did a number on her. Someone else might want to connect the dots on that one."

Especially someone trying to deflect suspicion from himself?

"Anyway, I just wanted to mention it because I saw the two of you chatting in the car earlier and I wanted to put a bug in your ear."

"Sure. Thanks. I appreciate it."

"Listen, if you can walk yourself the rest of the way from here, I'd better get back. Desiree is definitely hot-blooded, and while sometimes that can be a good thing—if you know what I mean?" He grinned lasciviously at Maggie. She worked to keep her lamb vindaloo from coming up.

"No problem," Maggie said. "You probably won't see me in the morning. I'm catching the seven o'clock train."

"Well, good travels," he said as he turned to head back up the street. "And thank you for filling in. The company will send you an online eval to fill out."

He jogged back up the street to where Desiree stood on the corner, smoking and waiting. As Maggie turned to head back to the hotel, she tried to imagine what Randall was up to throwing Dee-Dee under the bus like that. And why to Maggie? Because she was Lanie's friend? Was he covering for Desiree?

As Maggie reached the hotel, her phone vibrated and she checked the screen. It was Grace. For the first time in her friendship with her, Maggie pushed *Decline*.

She knew something was going on with Grace. She had been hinting at needing to talk about it but tonight was not the night. Maggie didn't have the emotional or physical energy to hear it, let alone help with it.

She would call first thing in the morning after she'd gotten a decent night's sleep. She quickly texted Laurent to tell him goodnight and to kiss their baby for her, then found her way to her hotel room on the ground floor.

Was there something in the wine? She couldn't remember ever feeling this exhausted. She set the alarm on her phone, stripped her clothes off and left them on the floor then slipped between the sheets of the bed, groaning when she did. She was asleep in seconds.

Some time in the middle of the night she awoke, her senses tingling with the scent of a man's aftershave mixed with sweat thick in her nostrils.

Someone was in the room with her.

11

Maggie flung the bedcovers back to scramble out of bed when she realized she wasn't wearing a nightgown. She grabbed the sheet and lurched to her feet.

She saw a dark form hunched by her bed, as if ready to climb into it.

"Who are you?" she cried out, hating the tremor she heard in her voice. "I'm American so I'm armed." She backed away from the bed toward the door.

The form stood up slowly from the shadows and she saw him raise his arms in her direction. "Don't shoot," he said. "It's only me."

Maggie turned to the lamp on the dresser and snapped on the light.

Bob Randall stood before her totally nude. He was grinning.

"What the hell are you doing in my room?" Maggie sputtered. She spotted Randall's jeans and t-shirt in a crumpled heap on the floor next to her own clothes.

"I would have thought that was obvious," he said, reaching for the duvet on the bed and winding the fabric around his waist.

"How did you get in here?" Maggie's heart was still racing from being awoken so abruptly. She clutched the sheet across her breasts, twisting it in her hands.

"Well, this is my rodeo, isn't it, darlin'? I have access to all the rooms. Sorry about this. Guess I misread our little conversation earlier."

"Are you demented? You thought I wanted you to show up in my room in the middle of the night? Is that what you figured Lanie wanted? Did you show up in *her* room uninvited too?"

"Whoa, whoa! I did not visit Lanie in her room in the middle of the night, or any other time." The smile fell from Randall's face. He went to his pile of clothes and snatched up his pants.

Maggie backed up to the door, ready to bolt if she had to. He dropped the duvet and pulled on his jeans.

"Maybe you had the same crap sense of communication then that you do now," Maggie said. "Only instead of leaving peacefully you got mad and hit Lanie across the head with a wine bottle."

Randall stopped dressing. "That's how she died? She was hit with a wine bottle?"

"Like you don't know."

"Did the police find the bottle?"

"We're not having this conversation. Get out of my room this minute before I call the cops."

"Trust me, the French police don't care about two consenting adults in a hotel room."

"I'm not *consenting*, you moron. That's kind of the whole point."

"Well, how was I to know that? I thought I got the green light from you."

"By what possible stretch of the imagination did you think that?"

"You said you enjoyed your trip with us and then you licked your lips and looked right into my eyes."

"You are seriously deranged. Get the hell out. *Now*."

"And for your information I have an alibi for the night Lanie died. I was with Desiree and she'll confirm that."

Maggie jerked open the door and stepped aside as he passed her. He walked into the hallway.

"I hope this little miscommunication doesn't ruin what I thought was a very—"

Maggie slammed the door and latched it. She stood with her back to the door listening to her heart pound in her ears.

After a moment, she walked to the dresser and turned on her cell phone. Three a.m. Too early to get up for the day, too late to even think about trying to go back to sleep. She dragged a desk chair over to the door and wedged it under the doorknob and then went to take a shower and begin her day.

∽

BEN STOOD in the hallway of the old house and listened. He knew Laurent was usually up before anyone else. He glanced at his wristwatch. Four in the morning. He glanced at Haley's sleeping form in the bed. He was fully dressed. He went to the door and moved quietly down the slick, wide stairs to the living room. The two big dogs lifted their heads when he passed through the room. They knew him and so didn't bark. But they watched him as he opened the exterior French doors.

He slipped out onto the terrace just as his cell phone began to vibrate. He closed the door behind him, glancing up at Laurent's bedroom window above the doors. It was dark.

"Newberry," he said into the phone as he moved silently to the edge of the terrace. He didn't expect his voice to carry into the house but it sounded loud in his ears in the otherwise still night.

"Have you talked to him?"

"He speaks French, you know," Ben said acidly. "Which I don't speak, if I have to remind you."

"Strange you didn't mention that fact when you insisted you were the man for the job," his caller said, a tone of menace lacing every word.

"I am still the man for the job," Ben said. "It's just taking time to win his trust."

"What do you know at this point?"

Ben was ready to give his report but was surprised to realize he was experiencing a twinge of discomfort. Except for that first day, Laurent had been okay with him. Almost friendly. He shook off the feeling. He was doing this for everybody's sake.

"I know he's just about given up recruiting any takers to restarting the co-op. Except for one old geezer, they're all either selling out or signing with us."

"So what's his next move?"

"He…I…you have no idea how secretive he is. I found out through my *wife,* who found out through my sister's best friend, that *she* doesn't even know where his money comes from."

"We *know* he's secretive, Ben. We knew this wasn't going to be easy. Can you *not* get him to change his mind?"

"Of course I can. I just need you to appreciate the difficulties."

"We don't give a damn about the difficulties. If you want your little problem back here to be resolved you need to get him to fall in step with his neighbors and get him to sign the papers."

"I just need a little more time."

"No can do. It's all going down the middle of next week. If you can't talk him out of this little act of rebellion of his, you're going to need to bring pressure on your sister and get *her* to sign the contract. Jesus. Can you handle it or not?"

"I can. Yes."

The line disconnected and Ben realized he'd been holding himself rigid for the duration of it. He let out a long breath.

Remember why you're doing this. He turned back to the house. This is the hard part. He wiped a line of sweat off his forehead although the chill of the early morning had produced goose bumps on his arms and legs.

When Ordeur contacted him two months ago it had seemed like an answer from God. Ben had literally been moments away from picking up the phone to call the old man when all his problems were swept aside.

True, at first they made it sound like they needed his services as a corporate attorney, and he'd been flattered—and stupid—enough to believe it. When the meeting came down three weeks ago where they told him they were aware he'd laundered money for a client through his trust account for a fifteen percent fee he was frankly surprised he hadn't seen it coming.

The way they presented his current "opportunity with the company" was: *take a tour of Provence with your wife to visit your sister, and while you're there convince her husband to sign the contract with Ordeur or expect a visit from a DEA confidential informant upon your return.*

Ben looked forlornly at the dark hulk of the house. *If you dance with the Devil*, he thought, *expect to get your ass singed.*

He and Haley were scheduled to fly back to Atlanta on Monday. That gave him two days to finish the job here before his deadline of next week.

Just the thought of what would happen if he failed prompted a shiver that sped up his spine and ended in a painful twinge in his neck.

Laurent didn't trust him and he wasn't ever going to. Ben saw how the man watched him and it didn't bode well for any heart-to-hearts. Besides, Ben's people skills were never his strong suit. No, it was pretty clear he needed to go straight to Plan B.

He slipped back into the house and stood quietly in the living room. One of the dogs growled. "Shut up," he whispered. "It's just me."

What's with these people and their obsession with pets? He sidled past the two large dogs. Maggie's poodle must be upstairs in

Maggie and Laurent's bedroom. He walked to the hallway and stood quietly again, waiting for the dogs to settle, waiting for complete silence to return to the house once more.

Laurent's den was off the kitchen. The door was closed but Ben had watched the big Frenchman come and go and knew it was never locked. He walked silently to the room and pushed the door open. Quickly, he turned on the flashlight on his cell phone and closed the door behind him. He could feel his heart racing as he approached the broad oaken desk.

Dernier didn't have a computer that Ben could see, or a landline. That meant the contract the conglomerate sent him was likely filed the old fashioned way. He scanned Laurent's desk. There were receipts for handmade barrels and casks and for a shipment of bottles. Since Dernier didn't crush his own grapes, Ben didn't expect to see evidence of any kind of equipment purchase. All of that would come to a screeching halt when the co-op closed for good.

It was obvious Dernier didn't have a choice. Not if he wanted to continue to make wine. *Why was he being so stubborn about it?*

He flipped through a magazine where Dernier had earmarked an article on something called *cork taint*. Whatever the hell that was.

He stood back and surveyed the man's desk. He obviously didn't spend much time in here. Just three days as a guest in his house told Ben that. Laurent walked his vineyard and he pressed the flesh in town—when he wasn't in the kitchen cooking.

Where the hell could it be?

A thought came to him and he circled the desk looking for a trash basket. He crouched next to it and shined his light into it.

The crumpled contract from Ordeur rested on top.

"I see it is time for our little talk."

Laurent's voice was so close to where Ben was kneeling that he jumped and fell backward at the sound. He scrambled to his feet and shone the flashlight in Laurent's direction, but before

Ben could think of the lie to explain what he was doing he realized he still held the contract in his hand.

∼

AN HOUR after she'd showered, packed and dressed, Maggie was dragging her wheeled bag down a narrow tree-lined pathway with orchards on one side and a vineyard on the other. The train station was just under two miles from the hotel. She hated the sound her luggage made on the uneven pavers of the path, as if to announce to the world that a lone female was attempting to cross the city in the dark.

Praying that most felons or hoodlums wouldn't be up this early, Maggie lifted the bag off the ground and used the shoulder strap to deaden the noise.

Even without coffee, her mind was buzzing with the events of the last several hours. She was still reeling with the horror of waking up and realizing that someone was in her room with her.

Should she report Randall? Was it too late to do that? And then the bigger question: should she tell Laurent? He had enough on his plate right now just getting the grapes in from the field without driving to Marseille to kill a national television personality.

Thinking of Laurent made her think of sweet little Jemmy and she felt a sudden hard twinge in her stomach when she brought the baby's face to mind.

Am I a bad mother? I miss him desperately. I would love nothing more than to hold him right now.

Maggie pushed open the ancient wooden door of the tiny Cassis train station and stood in the lighted foyer for a moment. A sudden sickening feeling sidled into her stomach. To her left was the ticket seller's booth, yet unmanned this morning. To her right was a small café kiosk being set up. She headed for the café and arranged her bags around a chair.

"*Un café crème, s'il vous plaît,*" she said to the owner, who nodded and disappeared.

The horrible fact was she was in no hurry to go home. Laurent wasn't wrong about that. But it wasn't because she was running away from Jem!

The owner brought her coffee and a croissant on a pretty china plate. Maggie was surprised—and delighted. She looked up at him before he left. He just shrugged.

Who knows why the French do what they do? Maggie thought, picking up the warm croissant and realizing she was very hungry. Maybe they're so in tune with food they can just *see* when someone needs to eat without being told.

She was alone in the little train station but could see the encroaching light of the new day peeking into the large palladium window over the front door.

Did Laurent think she was trying to escape her motherly duties? Did Grace? She glanced at her cell phone. Five o'clock was too early to call Grace back. She'd do it on the train.

Maggie closed her eyes and took a long sip of the hot, milky coffee and when she did she got a vivid image forming behind her eyes—a memory of when she and Ben were children. He was the eldest and only boy of the three children and he had always taken his role as brotherly protector seriously.

In her mind, Maggie saw Ben sitting between her and her sister, Elise, at the top of the stairs on Christmas morning waiting for their parents to get up. He held both their hands and helped pass the interminable minutes until they could go downstairs by telling them stories of Santa and his elves.

Maggie had forgotten that moment, when she had felt so connected to him by their mutual excitement of the magic of the day and by his palpable love for his sisters.

When had that changed? When had *Ben* changed?

Two bowls of *café crème* later, Maggie bought her ticket for the three-hour trip to Nice and boarded the train. There was nobody in her train compartment so she spread out her bags, sent a quick text to Laurent, and closed her eyes.

She awoke to an insistent rapping on her compartment window and realized she had slept the entire trip. Flustered, she gathered up her belongings and hurried out into the brilliantly bright light of Nice at midmorning. She'd meant to call Grace and sort out what she was going to ask the concierge. She'd intended to process how Randall could suggest it was Dee-Dee who killed Lanie.

Weird, unbalanced Dee-Dee. Was she capable of murder? The image of Dee-Dee throwing her cell phone at the poor duck came immediately to mind.

Maggie walked briskly down the busy sidewalk of tourists and shoppers, wondering if she would have enough time to do everything she needed to do before racing back to the train station as she'd promised Laurent.

Why is he making everything so hard? Why can't I just do what I need to do?

It occurred to her that Laurent never raced around like a maniac to make sure she wasn't left alone at the house or to ensure some casually made promise was kept. She slowed her steps. *Why am I stressing? I'm going to do what I need to do. If he loves me, he'll respect that.*

The Soho Hotel loomed at the end of the block, the stark blue horizon of the Mediterranean serving as a dramatic backdrop behind its marble white façade. She marched into the hotel. The concierge stood at the front desk, empty of waiting guests, watching her come.

Maggie parked her wheeled bag in front of her.

"*Bonjour*," she said. "I called earlier about needing to talk to one of your maids."

The man stared at her and didn't speak.

Maggie took in a covert breath to steady her patience. She knew she shouldn't have just blurted that out. The French like more finesse and preamble. Laurent always said she shot herself in the foot when she charged in without taking the time to set the stage.

Laurent always set the stage.

She switched to French and dropped the ingratiating smile, but kept her voice steady and pleasant. "It is very quiet for a Friday, no?" she said.

The man's eyebrows edged upward. "*Oui*," he said. "We are expecting an influx of Germans at any moment."

She knew he wouldn't be amused at any joke referencing the German occupation of Paris in 1940, but it took all her self-control to refrain from attempting one.

"Well, everyone loves the Côte d'Azur," she said, reigning hard at her impulse to just get to the point.

"*Bien sûr*. Does Madame know which maid she needs to speak with?"

Bingo!

"She will have been the maid who cleaned my room during my last stay," Maggie said. "Room 205."

He nodded and picked up the phone, spoke briefly, and then turned back to Maggie. The sheerest of smiles hinted around his mouth.

"*Bientôt*," he said, directing her with a glance that indicated Maggie should wait in the lobby.

She thanked him profusely and patted herself on the back for behaving contrary to her natural inclinations. *Maybe I am learning a few things.*

She didn't have to wait long. A few minutes after she sat down, a young, dark-haired woman slipped silently into the lobby, her eyes probing Maggie's questioningly.

Maggie stood. "I'm here on behalf of the American lady whose daughter was killed in the hotel two weeks ago," she said in French.

The woman nodded but looked around the lobby as if uncomfortable to stand there.

"Shall we go somewhere else?"

"Outside?" the woman said, pointing to a hallway leading away from the front door and the frenetic *Promenade des Anglais* outside it.

Maggie picked up her bags and followed the maid down a long, dark hallway, which opened up to an alleyway. In the alley was a large dumpster and a wooden picnic table shoved up against a tall, stone wall. Wild bougainvillea poured off the wall in casual, vibrant drapes of bright purple.

"My name is Ooli," the woman said as she sat at the picnic table and drew out a pack of cigarettes from her uniform pocket. "Cigarette?"

Rule number two, Maggie reminded herself as she nodded and accepted the cigarette. *Don't do anything to make your only source of information pull back.*

Ooli lit Maggie's cigarette and then her own. "I told Madame that I had information about the death."

Maggie nodded. "Madame Morrison doesn't speak French. She didn't understand."

"I thought perhaps that was so. I don't want to talk to police, you understand?"

Maggie nodded again.

"First," Ooli said, holding up a finger but looking around her as if expecting someone to be listening to them, "I saw who visited the dead woman's room that night."

Maggie's excitement surged. *Had she seen the murderer?*

"Second, I saw who visited her room other nights."

Maggie frowned. "Other nights?"

Ooli nodded and sucked in a long inhalation of smoke, her dark eyes watching Maggie carefully. A moment passed between them and Maggie reached into her bag and took out a pad of paper and a pen. She drew five boxes on the paper and wrote the room numbers for Dee-Dee, Randall, Desiree and Olivier inside each. She marked a heavy line around the box that was Lanie's room. She showed it to Ooli.

"You know these rooms?" Maggie asked.

Ooli smiled nodded.

"Please, show me," Maggie said.

Ooli picked up the pen and drew a line from the box marked 208 straight to Lanie's room box. She looked at Maggie and smiled.

Room 208 was Desiree's room. Maggie found herself getting excited. She reached for the pen but Ooli withheld it. When Maggie looked at her in confusion, the maid drew a sixth box, wrote the number 210 inside it, and drew a line from it to Lanie's box. She put the pen down and pushed the paper back to Maggie.

Maggie looked at the paper and felt her fingers grow cold.

Room 210 was Ben's room.

12

"You can't just throw us out! What will you tell my sister?"

"Your sister seems less able to endure you than even I," Laurent said dryly as he stood across the desk from Ben. "I'll call you a cab."

"Haley will be mortified to be thrown out like this."

"I am not throwing *her* out."

"But that's not how it works, is it, sport? You can't give *me* the heave-ho and expect my wife not to leave with me."

Laurent shrugged. "So you both leave. *Voila.*"

"I'm telling you that you will do irreparable damage to your relationship with your American in-laws if you do this. I don't know how people are over here, but family means a lot to Americans. Especially Maggie. You heard her little dog and pony show at dinner last night."

"I don't think she means you when she talks of family."

"Well, you'd be wrong. You don't have to like me, Laurent, but I'm family."

"Why are you here?"

"I got turned around in the house when I got up to—"

"Why are you in Provence? Why are you at Domaine St-Buvard?" Laurent gestured to the Ordeur contract now lying on the desk between them.

Ben ran a hand through his hair. Laurent saw the man weighing his options—and the degrees of the lies he would tell.

"I...I work for Ordeur," he said finally. "I work for the American company that's signed up all the growers from your co-op."

Laurent's face never changed, not even to reflect his surprise that Newberry had chosen to tell the truth. "Why are you here?" he repeated.

"I'm here to ask you to reconsider signing the long-term contract with us."

"Reconsider."

Laurent looked at the contract on the desk before them. Ben Newberry hadn't been about to ask Laurent to *reconsider* signing it. He'd been about to sign it himself.

Laurent picked up the contract and ripped it in two. He let the pieces float to the floor. "I would have challenged the signature in court," he said with a shrug. "You must be an inferior kind of counsel back in Atlanta."

"Look," Ben said, gritting his teeth and snatching up the scraps of paper, "you've got to sign this or sell your holdings to Ordeur. They'll give you a great price. You'll never have to work again."

Laurent held up a hand to indicate he'd heard enough.

"If you don't sign it," Ben continued, his eyes beginning to dart around the room in desperation, "I'll go to prison. Is that what you want? I may not be Maggie's favorite person but ask her if she wants her only brother to go to jail."

"One hour." Laurent turned and left the room.

"What the hell?!" Ben blurted in frustration to Laurent's retreating back.

∽

GRACE HELD Zouzou's hand and squatted next to what could only be described as a stuffed monkey wearing a lampshade. While this wasn't the first flea market she'd ever been to, it had been many, many years since the last. This particular market in Arles was only held once a month, so it held the promise of many undiscovered finds. Or so that's what Haley had told Grace this morning when she begged that they might take the children and go.

"Grace, did you find something?" Haley called.

Grace stood and saw Haley several yards away with Jemmy in his stroller. Haley was looking at a large white pitcher. Even from here, Grace could see the chips in the rim of it. She could also see the delight on Haley's face.

"You'll never get that in your suitcase," Grace said as she and Zouzou walked over to join her.

Furniture was stacked on top of itself—bistro chairs, painted end tables, full dining room sets that looked like they belonged in a Victorian mansion. Since this was Provence, there was an abundance of fabric, tablecloths and pottery, blunt and dark yellow with contrasting stripes of deep blue in platters, vases and saltcellars.

To Grace it looked more like an enlarged yard sale than a proper monthly event. It certainly had nothing on the markets in Paris, of course, or even the monthly one in Aix that stretched the full length of the Cours Mirabeau on both sides of the street, around the dolphin fountain and back up again. But Haley had made the argument that it was nearby and because it was so deep in the country they were more likely to find real treasures.

Well, *Haley* was likely to. Grace wasn't interested in previously owned goods no matter how well maintained they might be.

"I can ship it back," Haley said, but she put it back down on an antique marble table. "Can you believe all this stuff?"

"Truly, I cannot," Grace said dryly. She stood next to a rack of vintage Arlesian clothing: blouses, colorful shawls, and wide, flouncing skirts no one in their right mind would be caught dead or dying in.

"I adore the cicadas," Haley said, picking up a fragile looking ceramic one and turning it over in her hand. "They're so unusual and so representative of the region."

"Yes, and they look like big colorful roaches," Grace said. "Oh, please, let's do hang some in the kitchen where people eat."

"You're funny, Grace," Haley said, digging in her purse for her wallet. "You really have never been here before? How is that possible?"

"Well, it never occurred to me, frankly. And of course Maggie wouldn't have the patience for it."

"Why doesn't that surprise me?" They both laughed.

After Haley paid for the cicada, she spotted a child's peasant skirt in layers of red, yellow and blue chintz.

"Oh, Zouzou would look precious in that!" she said, picking up the skirt. "Would you like it, darling?"

Zouzou jumped up and down and clapped her hands. Grace knew the child didn't care, but she did love getting presents.

"May I buy it for her, Grace? I can't wait to see her in it."

"Sure. Thank you, darling. That's very thoughtful." Grace looked out over the crowd of shoppers at the market. They looked to be mostly tourists—the professional antique dealers had likely gotten first pick before the market opened. A blond head in the crowd caught her eye for a moment and she held her breath until he turned and she saw it wasn't Gabriel. He'd called twice since their lunch in Aix. Once, she had let the call go to voice mail and the other, just this morning...

"Penny for them, Grace?" Haley said as she helped Zouzou slip her new skirt over her shorts. "Oh, my, you are so beautiful, Zouzou!" she said to the little girl. "Isn't she, Grace?"

Grace looked at her daughter, already pirouetting in the new skirt to show it off.

"Yes, just lovely," Grace said, smiling absently.

"You okay, Grace?" Haley smiled, but her eyes were soft with concern and Grace tried to remember the last time she'd had a conversation with someone who cared that much about how she was feeling. Seeing it now almost made her want to cry.

"Yes, fine," she said, watching Zouzou bend over Jemmy's stroller to give him a kiss. "Did I mention to you that I went on my first date since the divorce?"

Haley's mouth fell open and she grabbed Grace by the arm and shook it. "No, you did not. We are going to find a café right this minute so you can tell me everything."

A warm flush of relief seeped into Grace at Haley's words. "There's really nothing much to tell," she said.

"The hell there isn't. Come on, kids, Mommy and Aunt Haley need an espresso with some major pastries on the side. When did this happen? Where did you meet him?"

Grace took Zouzou by the hand and led the way out of the crowd. She found herself feeling excited about the prospect of talking about Gabriel. Maybe it would help her sort out her feelings about him. As she stood at the curb facing the intersection, she felt a surprise twinge of guilt.

This is normally the kind of thing Maggie and I would do.

But Maggie hadn't called or answered her phone for the last two nights. Which, considering Grace wasn't totally sure what to do with the information about Laurent and his mystery woman, wasn't as upsetting as it might be.

As she stood on the curb with Haley and the children waiting to cross the street to a bustling outdoor cafe, Grace felt a burst of intimacy and affection and, without thinking, turned to Haley.

"Can I tell you a secret?" she said.

∽

TWO MORE MAIDS joined Maggie and Ooli where they sat at the outdoor table. Even for late summer, Maggie felt a breeze coming off the Mediterranean. One of the maids set a large platter of chicken wings down on the table. Maggie watched the women eat and gossip and laugh and felt like she was watching the scene from another planet or dimension.

Ben visited Lanie's room.

Ben was sleeping with Lanie.

Ben lied.

She sat with her hands in her lap, unwilling to move one step in front of the other when a sudden cold knot twisted in her stomach.

Lanie's baby...

"Madame?"

Maggie turned to see Ooli standing in front of her.

"You come with me, yes?"

Maggie grabbed the handle of her luggage. "Come with you?" she asked, shaking her head to clear it.

"I have not yet told you the most important part."

There's more? Maggie felt a tightening in her chest as she followed Ooli down the long alleyway to the street behind the hotel. "Where are we going?" she asked.

Ooli dropped back a step and took Maggie's arm so the two were walking abreast on the sidewalk. "I was just about to destroy it," she said conspiratorially. "One more day and, pftutt, it would be gone."

"*What* would be gone?"

At least they were walking in the right direction. The train station was only six blocks away. She'd be home in time for dinner. Laurent would be so pleased.

"The evidence," Ooli whispered in Maggie's ear.

Had she found the wine bottle?

Maggie started to ask another question but Ooli put her finger to her mouth to indicate she would say no more and they walked in silence for another block until they came to what appeared to be a cyber café. Ooli pulled Maggie inside and settled them both at a table with a computer terminal. When the waiter approached, she ordered two espressos.

She turned to Maggie and put her hand on Maggie's as it rested on the table.

"You will need to pay me for this," she said softly.

"Oh!" For a moment Maggie thought she was talking about the coffees, but as she reached for her billfold, she hesitated. She had one hundred euros in her wallet along with her train ticket to Arles. "May I see what it is you have to show me first?"

The waiter set two tiny cups of coffee in front of them and hurried off. Ooli didn't seem to take offense at the suggestion. She pulled her cell phone out of her uniform pocket and studied it for a moment.

"Do you have headphones?" Ooli asked.

Maggie shook her head. *What in the world was she up to?*

Ooli held the phone to Maggie's ear and pressed a button.

Maggie heard static and someone screaming. She pulled away and then took the phone to position it better. The recording was brief and, at first, unintelligible. Maggie frowned in confusion and handed the phone back to Ooli.

"I was washing the baseboards in the hallway," Ooli said. "I saw the woman from Room 209 enter the dead woman's room, and when the screaming began I turned on my phone to record it."

Room 209 was Desiree's room.

Maggie stared at her and then reached for the phone again. This time, as she listened, her eyes widened. She could easily identify Lanie's voice, if not her words. At one point, she heard her scream, "Desiree! You must be joking!"

She turned and looked at Ooli who smiled.

"Worth fifty euros, *oui*, Madame?"

Maggie nodded as Ooli pulled a patch cord from a wooden bowl on the table and connected her phone to the computer. Then she dug out a small plastic jump drive from the same bowl and inserted it into the back of the computer. After she transferred the audio file to the jump drive, she erased the master recording from her phone and sagged with relief.

Desiree was on tape having a screaming fight with Lanie the night she was murdered. There could be no doubt as to whom Lanie was fighting with. *She called Desiree by name.*

"Madame?"

Maggie shook herself out of her thoughts.

"I need to return to work, yes? You will pay our bill?" Ooli handed Maggie the jump drive and kept her hand out. Maggie dug out a fifty-euro bill and gave it to her.

"Thank you, Ooli," she said.

Should she go straight to the police station? She had Massar's number. Maybe she should call first?

Ooli stood and touched Maggie on the shoulder. "Please tell the lady I am sorry about her daughter." She turned and left the café.

Maggie sat alone, her eyes on the little plastic jump drive next to her coffee cup until the waiter approached with the bill. Five minutes later, cell phone in hand in case Laurent responded with an irate phone call to the *I may be a few minutes late* text she just sent, Maggie hurried down the sidewalk toward the police station.

This had to be case-breaking information! Ooli intimated that the police hadn't interviewed the maids—although it was true they had all worked to be as invisible as possible.

As Maggie jogged down the sidewalk, careful not to bump souvenir displays or café tables with her clumsy wheeled carrier, she glanced at her phone screen. He still hadn't responded. That wasn't entirely surprising. Laurent rarely carried his phone and he spent much of the day outdoors. It was possible he hadn't received her text.

It was also possible he was already in Arles, doing some market shopping and getting ready to meet her train.

As she looked away from where she was walking to glance again at the screen, she felt a sudden bone-wracking jolt to her shoulder as a strong, unseen arm slammed into her. Maggie staggered, windmilling her arms to stay upright, and pitched into a vertical postcard carousel. As she tumbled to the ground, she felt the strap of her handbag wrench off her shoulder. Metal prongs from the postcard holders scraped her cheek as she plunged into the display. She twisted around on her hands and knees amid the ruined jungle of metal and fluttering cards to see the back of a running form dart into the crowd.

Her suitcase and her cell phone lay on the sidewalk at her feet.

But her handbag—with the jump drive—was gone.

13

Maggie sat on a bench facing the *Promenade des Anglais*. She held her cell phone in both hands and kept her suitcase wedged between her feet, although rationally she knew there was little chance anyone would try to steal either of them. As she stared out at the relentless blue sea, dotted with bobbing yachts and powerboats, she tried to ignore the chill that crept up her bare arms.

Someone had followed her. Someone had been watching her.

She took in a long breath to steady her nerves. It couldn't be a coincidence that her purse with the jump drive was stolen, could it? Had she simply been mugged?

She wanted to believe that. She wanted to believe it was just bad luck that fate had chosen this day of all days to add her to the list of the clueless tourists getting ripped off on the Côte d'Azur.

But she didn't believe that.

That jump drive pointed the finger at Desiree as Lanie's killer. Pure and simple. Before Maggie met Ooli, there wasn't even circumstantial evidence to point in anyone's direction. The frustration pinged off her when she thought how close she'd come to being able to tell Annie of her progress.

A trio of young girls walked by on the boardwalk. They must be French, she thought. They were all beautiful, their clothes simple, elegant, and brief. One of the girls walked brazenly topless next to her friends, her hips swaying in a low-slung sarong, her young breasts tan and taut.

When Maggie's phone vibrated in her hands, she was so startled out of her reverie that she nearly dropped it. She looked at the screen to see she'd gotten a text. It was from Dee-Dee.

<You'll never guess. Olivier is back!>

Maggie stared at the text, uncomprehending. Olivier had rejoined the tour? She quickly tapped in a response.

<How did that happen?>

She stared at her screen, willing Dee-Dee to answer her.

<He said L's mom paid his bail. Think they were screwing?>

Dear God, what is wrong with that woman? Maggie thought in annoyance.

<Are you in Marseille yet?> Maggie typed.

<Yeah. Waiting for Des to get back.>

Maggie felt a tingling in her fingers as her excitement began to ratchet up.

<Back from where?>

<Who knows? Who cares?>

I care. Especially if Desiree's little excursion included following me to Nice.

The sound of a horn made Maggie look up. Laurent pulled to the curb in front of her and the car behind him wasn't impressed. Maggie hopped up and pulled open the back seat door and pushed her small suitcase in the back before joining him in the front. "It's two hours from St-Buvard," she said, leaning over and giving him a quick kiss before he turned the car into traffic.

"*Oui?*"

"Well, I only called you ninety minutes ago."

"I got held up."

"You sure you don't have a stockpile of speeding tickets somewhere I don't know about?"

Laurent gave her a glance and accelerated into traffic down the main avenue toward the A8.

"I brought one of your other handbags," he said. "It's in back."

"Oh, thanks, Laurent," she said, looking in the back for it.

"How did you lose your purse?" he asked.

"I left it under my chair when I stopped for coffee." She pulled a small handbag from the back onto her lap. It occurred to her she only had her cell phone to put in it.

"You weren't required to pay for your coffee before you left?"

"I paid when they served me. So, what's happening at home? How's the baby?"

"Fine."

"And Ben and Haley?"

"They may be leaving soon."

"Did something happen?"

"Country life is not to your brother's liking."

Maggie studied Laurent's profile, implacable as usual. If she wanted to know why Ben and Haley were leaving early she'd probably be better served by asking them.

"How's Grace?"

Laurent looked at her. "You are not in constant touch with Grace as usual?"

"We...I've been so busy. I've missed some of her calls."

He nodded and focused back on the road.

"It's a beautiful day," Maggie said. "I wonder when the last time was that you took a little holiday from your work at the vineyard?"

Laurent grinned. "You are getting much better at this, *chérie*. I'm proud of you."

Maggie laughed. "I just thought it wouldn't take that much more time if we went home by way of Marseille."

"It is not on the way."

"No, but it *could* be, without a whole lot of extra time."

"You want me to drive you to Marseille."

"It's a beautiful day and you haven't been to the beach in forever."

"Marseille is not what I would call a beach."

"I need to talk to a couple people on the tour," Maggie said, dropping the animation from her voice. "I just need one hour more. Something's come up."

"*Quoi?*"

"Well, Olivier was released on bail—Annie paid for it, it seems—and...and I heard something really suspicious about Desiree that I'd like to check on. It wouldn't take long at all, Laurent. Please?"

"*Bon*," he said, shrugging.

Maggie's mouth fell open. "Really? You don't mind?"

He smiled. "I am with you," he said, "and the day is indeed beautiful. Your brother's wife is babysitting *les enfants*. We will finish your little mystery together and then go home. Together."

A surge of happiness fluttered in Maggie's chest as she faced the road and ran through the questions she would ask Olivier... and then Desiree. She would need to call Annie, too, and inquire why in God's mysterious world she had paid Olivier's bail.

"And it gives us time to talk," Laurent said.

Maggie looked at him and frowned. "Talk?"

"*Oui*. You can tell me how you got the cut on your forehead."

∼

HALEY DECIDED the French countryside was at least as pretty as the North Georgia mountains. That was a surprise. Or was it just here on Maggie and Laurent's farm where the sky and the land seemed to meld in such a comforting hue of harmony? She stretched out her legs and repositioned little Jem on her lap. He was sleepy now after a morning of rambunctious crawling all over his father's vegetable garden. Haley believed strongly that a little dirt didn't hurt anyone.

He nestled in her arms and she felt the tremor of his happy sigh as he succumbed to sleep. Over his head, she watched three bees dodge and weave an aerial pattern over the tops of Maggie's zinnias. The air was scented with lemons and rosemary. *No wonder the French like their food,* she thought with a wry smile on her lips. Their whole world surrounds them with it.

She was surprised at how much she was enjoying France. She'd deliberately never traveled outside the U.S., and if it hadn't been for Ben's insistence early last spring that they visit Maggie this summer she wouldn't be here now. The thought of Maggie made her frown.

It didn't bother her that Maggie—and now Laurent too—had left the premises for whatever errand was so much more important than a house full of overseas guests. Although, granted, Haley would likely milk it for what it was worth when she described the visit to Ben's mother.

Imagine, Elspeth. Her only brother comes to visit for the first time ever and Maggie just up and leaves?

On the other hand, there was no sense in upsetting Elspeth. The woman would no doubt find a way to explain away Maggie's poor behavior—as she always did—and Haley didn't want to look like a complainer in her mother-in-law's eyes.

So far the biggest surprise of the trip had been Grace. Haley could not remember anyone as warm and instantly accepting as her new friend. Grace trusted Haley with the care of her precious child. *And* her secrets. Haley smiled at the memory of her coffee with Grace in Arles after the flea market.

Grace admitting that she was afraid to fall in love again after Windsor didn't seem to Haley to be much of a secret. Why not tell the world? Who cares? But maybe Grace came from a world where people do care about such things. Maybe she had learned to protect herself—and her heart—by recognizing that some things are better kept to oneself.

Haley looked down at the baby and ran her fingers through his fine hair. *How on Earth could Maggie leave this little angel? He's so tiny, so dependent, so vulnerable.*

It wasn't fair. Haley would give her soul to have a little one such as this—would never even run to the grocery store without him, let alone gallivant up and down the French coast for three days. She snuggled Jemmy tighter in her arms and felt the sun's rays warm the top of her head.

My time will come, she reminded herself as she reached out to the patio table to make sure the baby monitor was still on. Zouzou was a good little napper, but that didn't mean Haley wanted her waking up by herself in her room, regardless of what Grace said. Haley would give her ten more minutes and then go up to her.

One of these days, I'll have a house full of children of my own and wonder what I ever did with myself when I was childless.

Even the word, said silently in her head, caused a faint chill to run down her arms. *Childless.* She glanced involuntarily at the bedroom window where she and Ben slept. The chill deepened and she had to stop herself from rubbing her arms. It wasn't cold, she admonished herself. It was a beautiful sunny day deep in the south of France.

But Haley's eyes didn't leave the bedroom window, and while she was able to prevent herself from disturbing the baby by rubbing the goose bumps on her arms, she wasn't quite able to stop the feeling of acrimony when she thought of her husband.

~

LAURENT AND MAGGIE stopped for a late lunch of mussels and *pommes frites* with a very good bottle of Rosé and then drove the coastal road south to Marseille. Maggie had assuaged Laurent's concern about her cut ("I tripped over my suitcase and fell into an outdoor postcard carousel") and congratulated herself for not misrepresenting the truth too badly. She rationalized that she knew she couldn't avoid his worrying about her safety, but the least she could do was not make it any harder on him.

She sent a group text to Randall and Dee-Dee explaining that she and Laurent would be briefly rejoining the tour. Randal responded by sending directions to a restaurant in Marseille.

Once in the town center, Laurent turned onto the Boulevard la Canebière. The street was teeming with tourists, who reflected a strong Arab presence. Maggie knew Marseille had a huge Moroccan population and they seemed out in force today. She looked at the navigation tool on her smartphone.

"Turn left on the Rue Longue des Capucins," she said. "The restaurant should be on our right."

Laurent slowed for the turn. His phone rang in the console, but when she went to reach for it he snapped it up.

"Whoa, Tiger," Maggie said. "Your girlfriend should know better than to call you in the daytime."

"I always enjoy your humor," Laurent said, looking at the screen of his phone.

"Everything okay?"

He tucked the phone away in the pocket of the driver's side door, his face unreadable. "*Bien sûr*," he said. "Just something about the vineyard."

"Isn't it always? Oh, there it is on the right. That's Randall standing out on the sidewalk."

Laurent pulled up to the curb and stopped. Maggie turned to him in surprise.

"You're not going to park?" she said.

Randall came over to the car and Maggie rolled down the window, still waiting to hear Laurent's answer.

"Glad you could make it," Randall said, his face flushed and his eyes darting from Maggie to Laurent.

He probably thinks I brought my husband here to beat the crap out of him, Maggie thought with satisfaction. *Let him stew a bit.*

"*Bonjour*," Laurent said to him through the window before turning to Maggie. "I must get back to St-Buvard."

"But we just got here!"

"Enjoy your day. When you're finished, take the train to Arles. I will pick you up at the station this evening."

"Are you serious? What's going on? What was that call about?"

"It was nothing, *chérie*. Go on now."

Randall piped up. "We can give her a ride to the train station. No problem."

"*Bon*," Laurent said, leaning across Maggie to open her door. "Call me when you are there. If I can't meet you—"

"What do you mean *if you can't meet me*?"

"I have a sudden engagement that may go into the evening."

"Laurent, you are so lucky I'm not the jealous type because you are being seriously mysterious and I don't mean that in a good way."

"If Maggie is free tonight," Randall said, looking over his shoulder where Desiree appeared in the doorway of the restaurant, "and she could possibly stay on one more night, we're doing the final show from Arles tomorrow. And then we can take her straight to her front door in St-Buvard."

Maggie stared at Randall in surprise but Laurent didn't hesitate.

"*Bon*," he said, unhooking Maggie's seatbelt. "Her bag is in the backseat."

Maggie watched in astonishment as her husband worked in tandem with Randall to hustle her out of the car and onto the street. Laurent gave her a quick kiss before she climbed out of the car and then drove away.

She stood on the sidewalk watching his taillights disappear in the crowded street.

"Wow. He's a big guy," Randall said as he picked up Maggie's bag.

She turned to him. "I still might call the cops," she said. "Just watch yourself."

"I always do, my dear," he said, sweeping an arm out to indicate she should precede him into the restaurant. Desiree stood to the side to let her pass, and when Maggie looked into her face she saw that Desiree was smiling.

It was not a nice smile.

No words needed to be exchanged. It was as clear to Maggie that Desiree had followed her to Nice and stolen her purse as if the Frenchwoman had stood up and admitted it to her face.

Desiree killed Lanie and now had possession of the only piece of evidence that proved it.

Maggie's stomach roiled as she passed the Frenchwoman, but she straightened her shoulders and marched into the darkened interior. It was an African restaurant and smelled of incense mixed with the fragrance of curry, onions and many unidentifiable spices.

Maggie allowed her eyes to adjust to the dark until she saw a large round table with the others gathered around it. Three bottles of wine pinned the center, with multiple glasses in front of Jim and Janet. Jim sat with his head propped up on an unsteady elbow and Maggie saw Janet's eyes glittering with excitement from six feet away.

"You came back!" Janet said, clearly drunk. "You'll want to meet our guest of honor. Or is that the reason you came back? It would be for me."

Maggie saw the young man sitting to Janet's right—the infamous Olivier, she thought as she took a seat next to him. Desiree and Randall rejoined the table.

Maggie wasn't surprised that her reentry to the group had been treated with little fanfare. In fact, she preferred it that way. Except for smug glances in her direction, Desiree largely ignored her, spending the rest of the afternoon nearly sitting on top of Randall at the table. From what Maggie could see, the Frenchwoman ate very little.

Maybe that's how French women really stay slim, Maggie thought, pulling at her now snug waistband. *They just don't eat. Big secret.*

"*Bonjour*, Madame," Olivier said to Maggie. His easy smile made his handsome face even more appealing. He was dark-haired with cerulean blue eyes and full lips. Maggie couldn't help but think, *Well done, Lanie.*

"*Bonjour*," Maggie said. "You're Olivier, I guess."

"*Oui*." As if the introduction clearly came with reason to sober his happy expression, he promptly frowned.

"I'm so sorry about Lanie," Maggie said, wondering if anyone else had thought to offer him condolences. *Innocent until proven guilty*, she reminded herself.

"*Merci*, Madame," he said solemnly.

"Call me Maggie."

"Maggie," Dee-Dee said, slurring the word just a bit. "I got a new cell phone." She held up a phone with a pink fuzzy cover on it.

"I know. We've been texting back and forth, remember?"

"Oh, right. Also? I'm doing the final presentation tomorrow. Olivier will be able to tape it too. I'm so excited."

"Oh, that's cool," Maggie said, her glance taking in Desiree, who seemed to be working hard at ignoring the conversation by burying her face in her wineglass. "Where?"

"The Arles Amphitheater," Dee-Dee said. "I've got a kick-ass presentation, too. Everyone's going to love it."

Desiree snorted but said nothing.

A waiter approached the table with a wide tray of steaming plates and began distributing dishes around the table. Plates of *bourek* and *pastilla* wraps made the rounds, with everyone heaping their plates with the fragrant potato wraps. Although she and Laurent had eaten not two hours earlier, Maggie felt her mouth water at the overpowering scent of spicy chicken, almonds, and onions. She put two wraps on her plate and prayed they weren't more than five hundred calories a serving.

She turned to Olivier, who poured a glass of wine and placed it in front of her.

"Thank you," she said. "So did you know they'd put you straight to work when you rejoined the tour?"

Olivier shrugged. "Bob said I always had a job. I need the money."

"Did I hear right," Maggie asked him, "that it was Annie who helped you?"

"She is like a mother to me. A wonderful woman." His eyes lit up as he spoke and Maggie was struck by how young he really was and what a terrible ordeal the last few days must have been for him.

"Do you have family in France?" she asked. "I think Annie said you were from Algiers?"

"No, no family here," he said sadly. "And now I am grateful for that so they do not see me imprisoned like a dog."

"When do you have to go back to Nice?"

"My lawyer said he would call me."

Maggie was aware that the table had gotten noisier. Only Desiree spoke French well enough to understand her conversation with Olivier, and she was far enough across the table that Maggie didn't worry about her overhearing. Even so, she moved her chair closer to him and lowered her voice.

"I need to ask you, Olivier, if you have any idea of who might have hurt Lanie that night."

Olivier put down the wrap he'd been about to take a bite out of and faced Maggie earnestly. "I know exactly who killed my precious love," he said, tears jumping to his eyes and emotion turning his hoarse whisper ragged. He fought for control and drank down the contents of his wineglass before putting his face close to Maggie's ear. "She calls herself French, but her real name is *murderer*."

When Maggie pulled back to look into his eyes, she saw him glance at the head of the table...where Desiree sat licking grease from her fingers.

∼

IT HAD to be the noisiest hotel Maggie had ever attempted to sleep in. She sat up in her bed and worked to push her earplugs in tighter. She wasn't sure what kind of rooms the rest of the people on the tour had ended up with, but hers had definitely been an afterthought. Her bed—a twin with a wilted comforter that made her wonder if the linens had been changed in the last month—was shoved up against the window facing the street.

She touched the wall and wasn't surprised to feel it vibrate with the sound of the live music coming from the bar across the street. A scream, muffled only by the closed window and the shouts from the other street revelers, made Maggie hold her breath until it ended in hysterical laughing. She glanced at her phone on the nightstand. The screen read three o'clock. That meant nine o'clock Annie's time, she thought.

Did she have any real news to tell her? She swung her legs out of bed and went to the room refrigerator for a cola. She opened it. Empty. Sighing, she groped in the semi-darkness for her robe and found her slippers.

Maggie could tell Annie that she finally met Olivier and she saw why Annie thought he was innocent. He seemed like a really nice guy. She opened her hotel room door and peered down the hall. *Doesn't seem like much of a report, though.*

She turned back to the room and picked up a handful of euros and her room key and dropped them in her robe pocket and then slipped out the door into the hallway. She remembered seeing a vending machine down past the elevators. She had no idea if the other members of the tour group were even on her floor but, if so, she strongly preferred not to accidentally run into any of them.

The vending machine stuck out into the hallway like an obscene road bump. Maggie shook her head, wondering how anybody managed to get past it with suitcases in tow. The minute she reached it, she heard a footstep on the far side of it.

Crap. Anybody out and wandering the halls of this dump at three in the morning is probably not somebody I want to bump into. She tucked herself into the shadow of the vending machine to wait for whomever it was to pass.

It had always been Maggie's belief that whispering was more noticeable than just speaking in a low voice. She had that theory confirmed the longer she stood there.

"Rot in hell, bitch," a familiar voice mumbled loudly. "Glad you're dead. I'll show *you* blackmail."

Maggie's scalp crawled. It was Jim. Drunk and clearly half out of his mind, but definitely him.

Was he talking about Lanie? Maggie heard a door creak open on the other side of the machine and held her breath to be able to hear better.

"Get in here, you old fool. What are you doing out there confessing to the world?"

Janet's voice.

"Your fault," Jim said loudly, not bothering to whisper any longer. "I told her. I said some things follow naturally, as dawn follows night. I told her that. Bitches die bashed to death in their own bathwater."

"Shut up! You'll wake the whole hotel," Janet hissed, her whispered voice louder and more distinct than Jim's.

"As natural as the consequence of being an evil bitch," Jim said, the tail end of his words muffled as he entered the room before the door slammed shut. Maggie eased out the breath she was holding.

Was Lanie blackmailing Jim?

She left the shadows and tiptoed back to her room, her thirst forgotten. She settled back on her bed still wearing her robe, her mind spinning and the sounds of the street party still throbbing through her wall. She wouldn't call Annie tonight after all. Not yet.

Not until she found out why Lanie was blackmailing Jim.

And if it had been enough for him to want her dead.

∽

GOD KNOWS he didn't want to have to do this. Ben went to his wife's leather valise and felt in the inside the zippered panel. If that arrogant Frenchman had left him any alternative at all, he wouldn't have to. The pocket held only one long envelope with several sheets of paper inside. At first he hadn't seen the point of all the research—none of it cheap and all of it time-consuming—but he was glad now that he had it. He pulled the envelope out and took a step toward the window and looked out.

Haley was sitting under a beech tree with both children. *They should pay her by the hour.* He took a quick step backward in case she looked up. Satisfied that she was otherwise engaged at least for the present, he went to the dresser in the bedroom and found a letter opener in the top drawer.

He slit the envelope open and withdrew the folded sheets of paper inside. One was a photograph. He didn't bother looking at it. He knew what it showed. Another was an old copy, taken from microfiche, and he treated it gently. As far as he knew these were all originals. Under the circumstances, copies would be useless. They wouldn't stand up in court and they wouldn't hold up to scrutiny that they hadn't been altered. These few pages, even old and damaged, were worth everything to him. Replacing them would be next to impossible. It had taken nearly a year of single-minded, obsessive daily research to obtain these.

He refolded the sheets and tucked them back away then slid the envelope into his front coat pocket.

Why did he feel guilty about this? What possible reason could he have for not reveling in his triumph?

He heard the sound of his nephew squeal with laughter and his heart squeezed at the sound. The boy looked like his father, but there was something in the eyes...something that told Ben the child was a Newberry where it counted.

He touched the envelope through the silk of his jacket lining and looked out the window to the long undulating horizon of hectare after hectare of lush vineyard. *These documents will destroy everything I see now. The vineyard, the house, the marriage.*

Maggie's happiness.

He allowed a tremor of guilt to ripple through his stomach, then shook it off.

In the end, she'll thank me. It doesn't matter that this is now the only way for me to avoid prison. Think of that! That frog bastard would rather see me rot in jail than sign a simple piece of paper that would hardly change his life at all, except to make him richer.

No, Dernier deserved this. It was the bed he'd made and now he could lie in it. As for Maggie, it was her own self-absorption and willfulness that put her in the bed next to him.

Ben hesitated as he turned to exit the room, his hand resting on the bedpost. Would Maggie and his father ever forgive him? *It's true the old man was fond of Dernier, but after all...*

Ben tightened his grip on the bedpost and stuck his jaw out.

... I am blood.

14

Maggie stared at Janet and Jim as they sat in the breakfast room of the hotel. Jim looked ill and Maggie was frankly surprised to see him up and about this early. He'd sounded practically deranged last night. Janet was buttering her croissant and looking around the cramped dining room as if comparing it to the Waldorf. Her mouth was twisted into a grimace of distaste.

Must suck to have to pretend to be rich, Maggie thought, sipping her café crème. She knew she probably should've had an espresso instead. Would've saved about a thousand calories, but since she was putting butter *and* jam on her croissants this morning she thought it best to accept her current *what-the-hell* dietary attitude and just have the drink she really wanted.

Olivier sat by the window with Dee-Dee, which Maggie thought was nice of him. After the duck-maiming incident in Cassis it appeared that even the other crazies in the group were giving Dee-Dee a wide berth. She'd brought the definition of whack-job to a whole new level. Even so, Maggie hated seeing how haunted and wistful the woman always looked.

Desiree, on the other hand, needed none of Maggie's sympathy. She sat with Randall, sipping the espresso that Maggie knew she should have gotten, wearing six-inch heels and a skirt so tight there was no way the Frenchwoman could take a full breath.

The fact was—Jim's drunken and incoherent confession aside—Maggie knew Desiree was still her best shot as a suspect after Olivier. Why else would she follow Maggie to Nice and steal the one piece of evidence that existed against her? Why else except to cover her guilt?

When Randall got up and left the dining room, Maggie walked over to Desiree's table.

"*Bonne matin*," Maggie said. "Did you have a nice visit in Nice yesterday?"

Desiree stirred a sugar cube into her coffee cup and didn't look up. "You are mistaken, Madame," she said coldly. "I was in Grasse yesterday."

"Sure you were. You know, it occurred to me that you knew I was going to be in Nice because you overheard me talking to Mrs. Morrison on the phone about the maid giving her information."

"Perhaps you have started drinking early? You are babbling."

"I know you stole my purse, Desiree. And I know why you stole it."

"False accusations are taken seriously in France, Madame."

"You mean like me accusing you of killing Lanie?"

Desiree finally looked at Maggie. And smiled. "Exactly so. If you wish to formally accuse me, I will need to contact the authorities in my defense. But I don't think you want to do that."

"You really hated her, didn't you?"

"*Oui*. But that doesn't make me her murderer."

Maggie couldn't argue with that—especially since there seemed to be so many people who disliked Lanie—but she forced her face to remain impassive.

"Is this why you have returned to the tour?" Desiree asked. "To lay blame for the slut's death?"

There's that word again.

"Mind telling me where you were the night Lanie died?"

"I was with Bob Randall at the time of Lanie's...passing."

"You mean the night she was murdered."

"*Quoique.*" Whatever. "I'll talk to Bob about terminating your time with us on the tour. I'm sure he will be horrified to discover your true purpose. Especially from a public relations standpoint, *n'est-ce pas?*" Desiree stood abruptly and dropped her napkin on the table. "Meanwhile, please remember what I told you about making accusations—even ridiculous ones—while you are in France."

Maggie took a quick step backward to avoid being physically shoved out of Desiree's way during the Frenchwoman's dramatic exit. Maggie stood there for a moment, watching Desiree leave.

It occurred to Maggie that while she did just learn that Randall and Desiree were each other's alibis for Lanie's murder, she wasn't at all sure she'd made any real progress from her brief interview with Desiree—except, unfortunately, to warn her main suspect that she was on to her.

∽

Laurent watched Adele as she poured the drinks. He saw that she had left the bedroom door open, the bed clearly visible and inviting from the salon.

There was nothing he didn't see. And, of course, Adele of all people would know that.

"I wasn't sure you would come," she purred, turning to him and holding out a glass of *pastis*. His eyes were on hers as he took the drink, but he knew her breasts were falling out of her silk blouse.

"How could I not? Your invitation was irresistible." He sipped his drink and smiled at her from where he sat in the main salon. He'd taken a seat on the couch. Probably only a small tactical error, he realized, unless it became necessary to reject her, in which case it was a mistake from which he and his vineyard might not recover.

Adele sat next to him, picked up the remote control and pointed it at the far wall, which opened to reveal a television screen.

"You will see, *chérie*," she said, "that I have been very busy since we last worked together." She turned to him and smiled coquettishly. "I have been learning new tricks, yes?"

"As we all must," he said. *This balancing act was not difficult. It is not unlike so many I have done in the past with hundreds of thousands of euros in the balance.*

And yet the stakes have never been higher.

Adele put the remote control down and snuggled back into the couch, her skirt riding up on her thighs, her thigh touching his.

A photograph of a wine crushing operation appeared on the screen.

"I bought it last spring," Adele said softly. "Five brands, including Domaine St-Buvard, owned individually yet sharing joint leasing of all equipment."

Laurent felt his pulse quicken and swallowed down the rest of his drink.

"Access to every level of equipment that, separately, the owners could never afford, includes representation in a tasting room..."

The photograph on the screen changed to show a small but tastefully appointed room lined with hanging wineglasses and stacks of bottles ringing the burnished wood walls.

"...as well as connections to local restaurants and retailers that would be unreachable independently."

It will be the saving of Domaine St-Buvard. Laurent watched the slides, one after another, showing the operation that was the answer to his prayers. *If I can pull it off without needing to bed Adele.*

"Each winery is individually licensed," she continued, "operating under an alternating proprietorship that allows them to label their wines as *produced and bottled by*." Adele looked up at Laurent and he tore his eyes from the screen to see her full lips, glistening with the *pastis*, her eyes riveted to his, her message as clear as skywriting: *It's all yours... for a price.*

"Each independent winery works under an alternative proprietorship," he repeated.

"Yes, of course. It's what differentiates you from custom crush. You keep control this way without having to buy all the equipment."

"You were always so canny, Adele," he said to her, turning toward her on the couch. Her eyes went from his eyes to his mouth, and she smiled at his praise. "And the other four brands?" he said.

Adele placed her drink on the counter. She took his hand and held it against her breast, but before Laurent could react she touched the wedding ring on his hand.

"Is this a deal breaker?" she asked softly.

He held her eyes for several long seconds and then gently removed his hand from her breast. "You tell me," he replied.

She watched him for a moment and then turned and picked up the remote control from the table.

"The four other brands, besides your neighbor Jean-Luc Alexandre, are located in the Luberon, and one in Spain," she said. "I have arranged for them to come to St-Buvard to meet with us." She glanced at Laurent, her expression veiled. "To meet with you, your American wife, and myself. We will sign the papers then."

Laurent picked up Adele's hand and kissed it. "*Merci*, Adele," he said, standing. "I will not forget this."

For the first time in four months—virtually since the moment he knew Ordeur was splintering the co-op—Laurent felt a weight lift from his shoulders and his heart. And he felt like laughing.

∽

The Arles Amphitheater was always an impressive structure Maggie thought as she walked up the smooth flat stone steps that led into the main arched entranceway. She'd brought both her parents here when she and Laurent first moved to Provence.

There was something about walking the same stone hallways that people had done two thousand years ago that gave her chills just to think of it. The imposing, ghostly structure had a way of connecting her with the people of 90 AD Arles. After all, could they really be so different?

Olivier carried an unwieldy tripod on his shoulder—the video camera securely attached to it—and entered the arena ahead of her. Jim and Janet Anderson walked slowly, almost reluctantly, behind Maggie. The few glances she'd spared in their direction showed them both looking elderly, even ill. Janet stumbled at one point on the stairs and Jim did not reach out to help steady her.

What had she really heard last night? Maggie wondered. Was Jim being blackmailed by Lanie? And if so, where did that fit in?

"Ça va, Maggie?" Olivier called to her. He was about to disappear into the dark shadows of the amphitheater. Even the brief walk from where the car was parked to the structure's entrance had been hot enough to make a line of sweat visible on his t-shirt. He was, nonetheless, smiling.

"Yep," she said, waving him on. Desiree and Randall were still back at the car for some reason, but it didn't matter. This was Dee-Dee's part of the tour and she would make sure everyone was seated and watching before she started. When Maggie reached the top step, before entering she turned to glance over her shoulder. With the arena built right in the center of town, all she could really see was the first line of restaurants and shops that faced the amphitheater. She turned and went inside.

The coolness of the interior gave her relief from the walk and the heat of the morning. She saw Olivier disappearing through one of the stone archways that led to the seats and the viewing area. She remembered when her father first saw the arena below, ringed by the seating galleries. It literally took his breath away. Maggie smiled at the memory. She hadn't seen her folks since last Christmas. Jem was a newborn then. She couldn't wait for them to see him now. Thanksgiving and Atlanta seemed like a long way away.

Following Olivier through the archway, Maggie gave herself a moment to take in the impressive sight of the four tiers of seats ready for an audience to enjoy barbarous entertainment. She couldn't look at the arena without thinking that it wasn't always used just for bullfights and gladiators.

There had been the odd hungry lion and Christian, too.

"*Bon*, Maggie," Olivier said. "I am setting up here so you and the others should sit over there." He waved to a tier of stone seats off to Maggie's left and up two rows. She saw Dee-Dee, notecards in hand, rehearsing silently, standing in front of where Olivier was putting his tripod. He had positioned her with the dramatic oval of the arena behind her.

Maggie climbed up the rows, sat on one of the stone seats and arranged her purse at her feet. Jim and Janet came through the archway and squinted into the sun until they saw her. Without smiling or waving, they put their heads back down and made their way to where she was sitting. Maggie didn't expect any conversation this morning, and she didn't get any. She watched Janet, wondering if she was at all concerned at the possibility that she'd been overheard last night, but clearly whatever nightmare hangover she was dealing with blotted out all other concerns.

The weather in Arles was good today, if a bit warm. There were no clouds and, fortunately for the tour, no other tourists. Even though it was well past seven in the morning, Randall had guessed correctly that it would be too early for most tourists to venture out. When he and Desiree finally entered the amphitheater, they glanced at Maggie and the Andersons then moved to a row on the same side but out of earshot.

Maggie thought Desiree was working particularly hard to avoid eye contact with her. She felt her foot vibrate where her purse lay against it. She reached in the bag to look at the cell phone she'd tucked in there. It was Annie. Maggie pressed *Decline*. She'd have to call her back.

"Can you imagine?" Dee-Dee said as she walked to the railing that overlooked the sandy arena. She turned and looked into the lens of Olivier's camera and smiled. "Sitting here more than two thousand years ago waiting for the show to begin?"

Maggie got goose bumps when Dee-Dee spoke. *She's good*, she thought with surprise, rubbing her arms.

"Although it was built in 90 AD, the Arles Amphitheater was the reality TV of Roman times—from chariot races and bullfighting, to bloody hand-to-hand battles. Think of it." Dee-Dee leaned toward the camera with an earnest look in her eye, as if she were connecting with each member of the audience.

"Gladiators fought wild animals here to the delight of twenty thousand screaming fans. She turned and pointed to the dark archway that led to the bottom arena. "That was where the Christian martyrs were led in...and there was no other way out."

That's just what I always used to think, Maggie thought, feeling the mystery and the eeriness of the place settle into her bones.

"Some people say the Arles Amphitheater is confirmation of the emphasis the Romans put on sports and that's probably true," Dee-Dee continued. "But I think it's much more. Measuring four hundred and forty-six feet in length and three hundred and fifty-eight feet wide with one hundred and twenty arches, the amphitheater is two-tiered to allow a system of galleries for optimum viewing of whatever was going on in the arena—gladiators, wild animals, or bullfights."

Dee-Dee walked back to the railing and swept an arm in the direction of the arena. The feeling that she was building up to something was palpable. Maggie held her breath, surprising herself by how Dee-Dee's words were creating a feeling of expectation in her. She leaned in closer.

"The floor of the arena was sand, in order to absorb the blood better. Necessary all those years ago, as well as today when bullfights are held here each year." Dee-Dee nodded wisely into the camera, a ghost of a smile on her lips. "And not unlike the entertainment of two thousand years ago, the fights are dramatic, thrilling and bloody. Simply put, no matter what happens down there..." She nodded in the direction of the sandy oval below. "...*somebody* is not walking away afterward."

She turned to Olivier behind the camera with one hand on her hip. "Then I thought I'd segue into a bit I'm working on about how Van Gogh settled here in the eighteen hundreds but always felt like he left a piece of himself behind. You know, the ear thing. What do you think?"

Behind Maggie was the single and steady clapping of one person in the stands. When she turned, she saw it was Randall and that he was standing.

Huh, she thought. *A standing ovation for the one who doesn't stand a chance of getting the slot?* She saw that Desiree, on the other hand, was staring at Dee-Dee in open-mouthed astonishment.

∼

"You were truly awesome, my dear," Janet said, patting Dee-Dee's hand an hour later at one of the outdoor restaurants at the foot of the steps leading down from the amphitheater. "Inspiring. Wasn't she, Jim?"

"Really good," Jim said, handing his menu to the waiter. "Just bring a bottle of your best Rosé," he said.

"I'll have the artichoke risotto with the grilled cod," Janet said to the waiter.

"You're just ordering that to make me ill," Jim said in a low voice. "I swear I'll change seats."

Dee-Dee turned to Maggie. She was so proud of herself she glowed.

"What did you think, Maggie?" Dee-Dee asked. "Would you say it was the best presentation of the tour so far?"

"Well, it was really, really good," Maggie said. *Would Randall change his mind about Dee-Dee after her performance today?*

"*Good?*" Olivier said with surprise as he leaned across Maggie to reach the olive bowl. "It was by far the best presentation yet."

"Really?" Dee-Dee said, grinning at him. "Do you really think so?"

"*Absolument.*"

Weird, Maggie thought. *Surely, Olivier would think Lanie's was the best?* She shook off the thought. *Probably just being nice.*

"Thank you, darling Olivier," Dee-Dee said, grabbing him and kissing him loudly on the cheek. "Did you hear Bob after I finished? I mean, did you *hear* him?" She giggled as she remembered it.

"He was very impressed," Maggie said.

"I'll say he was," Dee-Dee said. "He told me he didn't know I had it in me. He said he was spellbound. He actually said I had *je ne sais quoi*! In front of Desiree, he said that!"

"Pretty historic," Maggie said. The look on Desiree's face when he said it was pretty historic too, she thought. In fact, until the moment when Desiree donned a strident shade of scarlet while Randall was over-praising Dee-Dee, Maggie would have said she was a pretty woman. At the time she looked like a strangling pufferfish.

"Well, it was worth the hours of research and practice in front of the mirror that I put in," Dee-Dee said. "That's all I can say."

"Where are Bob and Desiree?" Maggie asked, looking around the terrace.

"Desiree said she was ill," Olivier said with a grin, "which does not surprise anyone. And Bob said he had to write a check to the hotel or something. He will join us for cheese and coffee."

"I think Bob is giving me a ride home," Maggie said. "What's everyone else doing?"

"We are all taking you to St-Buvard," Olivier said with a grin. "I have heard so much of your husband from Bob, I must see this for myself."

"Well, don't believe everything Bob tells you," Maggie said.

"I never would," Olivier said, winking at her. "And now, we must have a bottle of Champagne, no? Are we all agreed?"

Olivier turned to Dee-Dee, but she was intently studying her smartphone.

"Dee-Dee?" he said. "To celebrate your amazing day?"

She looked up, her face flushed and her eyes darting to the entrance of the restaurant.

"Are you all right, *chérie*?" Olivier asked her.

"I am," she said, shoving her phone in her purse and grabbing her cardigan from the back of the chair. "But I just remembered something I need to do."

"Surely, you are not leaving," Olivier said, as she rose from the table.

Maggie frowned. Did it make sense that Dee-Dee would leave her own party? At her moment of glory?

"I have to. You go on and have fun," Dee-Dee said, leaving the table. "I'll see you…you know…later."

Maggie and Olivier watched Dee-Dee leave the restaurant and then turned to look at each other.

"But she has food coming," Olivier said, his mouth open in surprise as he turned in obvious disbelief to watch Dee-Dee's retreating back.

∽

BEN RUMMAGED in the drawer of the kitchen looking for something to stir his drink with. Ever since Laurent caught him going through his office, Ben felt uncomfortable even doing perfectly innocent activities. He found an iced tea spoon and picked up his vodka tonic and moved into the dining room. It was damn rude that now *both* Maggie and Laurent were out doing more important things than attending to their guests, but he had to admit it was easier on the nerves with Laurent away.

Would he really throw him out? He sipped his drink and walked to the set of French doors that looked out onto the garden and the vineyards in the distance. Fortunately, Laurent had been called away before he could enforce his threat.

Something caught Ben's eye outside and he took a step closer. He was sure that Haley and Grace had taken the kids out for the day. A muffled squeal pierced through the doors and he saw Maggie's little boy crawl into view on the terrace stones. *So. The women must be here after all*, he thought.

The child was good-looking. Brown hair, dark brown eyes. He supposed he looked like Dernier somewhat but he also had strong Newberry lines—the nose, the shape of the head, the quick, alert glances. Ben drank down the entire glass of vodka as he watched the baby. A woman's voice, light and musical, caught the child's attention and Ben watched Jem turn his head and grin at the unseen source.

Would the child have looked like him? Ben realized it was the first time he'd thought of it since he'd arrived at Maggie's. On the train trip from Nice, it seemed he could think of nothing else. *That stupid, stupid bitch Lanie. She deserved what she got—with bells on.* But when it was all said and done—regardless of how tidily things ended up—the fact was she had taken something of his when she went. He gripped his glass before remembering it was empty.

When you start doing insane, self-destructive things, he wondered bitterly, *do they just keep getting easier to do?*

Haley stepped into view and scooped up the baby in her

arms, prompting more delighted squealing from the child. Ben knew it was irrational, but the picture of her cuddling Maggie's child hit him as wrong and somehow unfair.

He must have made a movement because Haley turned toward him and shaded her eyes to see inside the French doors. The happy look melted from her face the minute she saw it was him. He opened the door.

"Where's Grace?" he asked.

Haley turned to call to the little girl, whom up until then Ben hadn't noticed. She was a pretty little thing but shy. She always hid whenever he came into the room. "Come, Zouzou," Haley said. She held out her hand and the child clasped it, never taking her eyes off Ben.

"She had to go into town," Haley said.

"Of course she did. And so here's Nanny Haley just ready to be of service. You're not their servant, Haley. You're letting them take advantage of you."

"I don't mind."

"Oh, good. Will you be cleaning the house later, too?"

Jem turned his head to look at him, and Ben was struck by how intelligent the little fellow looked. Almost as if he could understand their conversation.

"Don't be sarcastic in front of the children," Haley said. "It's upsetting to them."

"You mean it's upsetting to you. They have no idea what I'm saying. Do you, sweetheart?" he said to Zouzou. The child instantly puckered up and began to cry.

"What the hell is the matter with her?" he said, startled.

"*You* are the matter with her," Haley said, her face flushed with anger. "Go back in the house." She hesitated. "Please."

The feeling of the papers he'd extracted from her suitcase felt like they were burning in his inside jacket pocket.

What would Haley think when he used the documents

against Laurent? She pulled the children away from the house, as if protecting them from him.

Well, she'll just have to get over it, he thought with annoyance as he watched her lead them toward the small lawn that lay just before the vineyards. Everything he was doing, he was doing for the two of them.

As he watched her walk away, her back to him, he felt his fingers grow cold and his heart harden.

She'd either see that, or she wouldn't.

∼

THE JOY *of it all was beyond imagining.* Dee-Dee glanced at her reflection in a shop window as she scurried past. She couldn't help but smile at what she saw: a beautiful girl, her hair twisted into a careless but elegant chignon, walking straight, boobs leading the way. She hurried her pace.

Could this day be any better?

She glanced at her smartphone. She'd plugged in the directions as she walked. *He had texted to meet him at one o'clock.* That meant she had less then five minutes to walk to where the phone was telling her was a fifteen-minute route by foot. She held onto the shoulder strap of her purse and began to jog down the pedestrian cobblestone street, praying her heels wouldn't catch on the uneven pavers.

Her phone chimed and she looked down to see what the incoming text read.

<Are you coming? We haven't much time. Cut across rue de clair, near the cemetery. It's a shortcut.>

Dee-Dee squinted up at the street sign in front of her. *Rue du Refuge.* The map on her phone didn't show the road he mentioned. She peered down the alley at the intersection. It was lined with Arlesienne townhouses, old but brightly painted. One had a shutter hanging by its hinge. The phone map was telling her to go down this alley. Would she come across *Rue de Clair* if she did?

She texted him back <Be there soon> and plunged down the narrow residential street.

Where was he leading her? A park? A café? A hotel room?

The townhouse facades were made of uneven stonework topped with rust-orange tile roofs. Several had window boxes with blood-red geraniums bulging out of their containers. The narrow street was uphill and steep. It was barely wide enough for a car to get through, which didn't matter, she reminded herself. This was a strictly pedestrian only section of Arles.

Dee-Dee's legs began to ache and she felt perspiration trickle down her back and underarms and she cursed the fact she would show up bedraggled and damp when she finally arrived at the rendezvous.

Why all the secrecy? Why can't he just invite me to his room? A bottle of Champagne chilled...

The thought of the possibly waiting bottle of cold Champagne buoyed her enough to trudge on. Today was her finest hour. *The look on Desiree's face! The pure joy on Bob's.* Dee-Dee nearly ran up the hill, her face flushed with effort and pleasure. At the top, she looked around and felt her mood falter. The street ended in a dead-end, with a large and very ancient house directly in front of her.

Screw these cryptic text messages, she thought in frustration. Just as she pulled her phone out to call him, she noticed the sign. It was small and tacked unceremoniously on a gate just to the left of the big house. Dee-Dee approached it. The sign was handwritten and read, *Rue de Clair*. A thrill of satisfaction ran through her.

She moved across the cracked stone walkway that led to the front door of the house in order to get to the gate. It was wooden and looked medieval. She was relieved to see there wasn't a lock on it, and when she grabbed the handle it easily creaked opened.

She looked over her shoulder at the street behind her and then entered the garden.

Am I to use this garden as a cut-through, she thought with confusion, *or is Bob waiting for me here with a picnic lunch and a bottle of rosé?* Damn his need to surprise her, she thought with grim bemusement as she closed the gate behind her. Four steps into the interior she realized the area was less a garden than it was a small pasture. Wild roses grew entwined with rusted barbwire along the perimeter of the fenced yard. There was a small shade tree of some kind in the middle of the yard, the whole of which appeared slightly smaller than an American football field. And nowhere did she see Bob lounging on a blanket with a picnic basket. What she did see, directly opposite from where she stood, was another gate. She sighed. *So it is a cut-through, not a destination.* She adjusted her purse strap on her shoulder and moved toward the gate, glancing up at the back windows of the house to see if anyone was at home. A burgeoning and sudden aroma of manure wafted to her the minute she started to cross the field. She looked at the ground to make sure she wasn't about to step in anything and felt her irritation return.

This is ridiculous! Does he really think I'd enjoy this asinine game? She saw her shoes—sixty dollars from Macy's!—were already muddy and she cursed the fact she was indeed going to show up for the assignation reeking of cow shit, if not wearing it.

The movement caught her eye before she was midway to the far gate. Dee-Dee's first thought was that she had interrupted a gardener at work and would now need to come up with some explanation—in very bad French—as to why she was trespassing. That thought died in her mind the minute she turned her head.

The animal stared at her, its eyes glittering and focused on her even from twenty yards away. The smell riffled off it in undulating putrid waves and made Dee-Dee's stomach lurch with nausea. Easily seven feet in height and weighing over a ton, the bull's coat was rough and black, its tiny pig-eyes watching her with unmistakable malevolence. Black spots formed and popped in her vision as Dee-Dee stumbled and then stared in stunned disbelief as the beast lowered its head of dagger-like horns.

A scream fought to escape her throat, but only a whimper slipped out as she wet the ground in a gush and watched in disbelieving horror as the monster charged.

15

Well, this is certainly an odd ending to the whole trial-by-tour-guide thing, Maggie thought as she paid the taxi driver outside the *Centre Hospitalier d'Arles*. She looked at her phone and hurried into the main entrance of the emergency room. She'd put two calls in to Laurent saying she might be late but had gotten no response.

Two hours after Dee-Dee mysteriously slipped away from lunch, she, Olivier, and the Andersons returned to the hotel to pack their bags. An hour after that, as she stood with Desiree and Randall outside the hotel loading up the car for the final presentation, Maggie received an urgent phone call from Olivier asking her to say nothing to the others and meet him at the emergency room in Arles.

Dee-Dee had been attacked.

Brimming with questions and astonishment that Dee-Dee had been hurt, as well as the fact that Olivier wanted it kept quiet, Maggie hurried through the double doors of the hospital emergency ward. The interior of the emergency room looked much like any she'd ever been in back home. The smell of idoform mixed with ammonia was nearly overpowering. The entrance emptied onto a large waiting room ringed by several triage desks. Maggie walked up to the nearest one, but before she could get the woman's attention behind the counter she saw Olivier waving to her from across the room.

"Maggie! Over here!"

She walked quickly to Olivier, who stood outside a treatment room separated from the waiting room by a long vinyl curtain.

"What happened?" she asked, looking past him to get a glimpse through the gap where the curtain ends didn't quite meet. She saw a figure lying on a bed.

"Dee-Dee was gored by a bull," Olivier said. Maggie thought he looked breathless, as if he'd just rushed in from somewhere, but assumed the adrenaline of the situation was reason enough for his condition.

"She left lunch to go to a bullfight?"

"*Non*. She got a text from Randall telling her to meet him. She took a shortcut through a pasture with a very angry bull in it. She called me as soon as they finished stitching her up."

"That's terrible. How badly is she hurt?"

"She was *gored*, Maggie!"

"Will she recover?"

Olivier frowned at her in impatience. "Don't you see what this means?"

Maggie took a step toward the curtain.

"It means Randall tried to kill her," he said loudly.

Maggie stopped, one hand on the curtain and frowned. "How do you figure that? Sounds like a freak accident. Have you called Randall yet?"

"No, he damn well hasn't!"

Maggie turned to see Bob Randall knocking chairs over in his urgency to reach them from across the waiting room. Thankfully, there were few people in the room. "Dee-Dee just called to tell me what happened," he said as he reached them, his teeth bared and fists clenched.

Maggie turned back to Olivier. "Can we see her? Is she in there?"

"She does not want to see him," Olivier said, blocking Randall from entering the curtained room.

"Yes, I do!" Dee-Dee shouted from behind the curtain. "Send him in."

Reluctantly, Olivier stepped aside and turned and pulled back the curtain. Dee-Dee lay propped up on the treatment table, her left leg bandaged and elevated, spatters of blood streaking the eyelet chemise Maggie remembered her wearing at lunch. Her face was white under the jagged streaks of mascara and eyeliner that smudged her cheeks.

"Dear God, Dee-Dee," Randall cried, going to her. "What the hell happened?"

"You bastard! You tried to kill me!"

Randall looked at her with his mouth open. "What in the hell are you talking about? I would never—"

"I have the texts to prove it! You lured me to that pasture hoping the bull would make your job easier."

Randall gaped at her and then turned to look at Olivier and Maggie before turning back to Dee-Dee. "I have no idea what you're talking about."

Olivier picked up the cell phone next to Dee-Dee's bed. "Dee-Dee received a series of texts from you instructing her to meet you by way of the bull's pasture."

"But that's impossible." Randall reached for the phone but Olivier pulled it back.

"Sorry," Olivier said. "The police said not to touch the phone until they arrived."

"The police?" Randall sputtered.

"Yes, the police, you bastard," Dee-Dee said. "I called them as soon as the doctor finished stitching up my leg. I'll see your whole program in flames. You'll be lucky to do the local weather at your affiliate PBS station when I'm done suing you."

"Why in the world would I try to…it doesn't make sense!"

Randall's face registered a realization that apparently made the accusation make sense. "I didn't send those texts," he said weakly.

"You think someone *else* used your phone to send them?" Maggie asked him.

Randall rubbed his hand across his face and didn't answer.

"And here I had done such a magnificent job at the Amphitheater," Dee-Dee said, her voice dissolving into tears. "I gave my best presentation *ever*."

Olivier patted her shoulder and spoke softly to her. "Perhaps that is *why* you were sent the texts. Because you were so good."

"Let's don't jump to any conclusions," Randall said. "If the police really are coming—"

"Oh, count on it. They are!"

"Well, let's have them sort it out then." He pulled his phone out of his pocket and began scrolling through his texts.

"The texts are there, aren't they?" Dee-Dee said, sniffing. She reached up and put a hand over Olivier's where it rested on her shoulder.

Randall let out a sigh. "I just don't understand this."

Maggie turned to Olivier. "You think Desiree sent the texts from Randall's phone?"

"Who else?" Olivier said. "Randall doesn't have any reason to hurt Dee-Dee. All he had to do was just not choose her."

"Exactly!" Randall said and then to Dee-Dee, "Not that I was going to *not* choose you, darling. Your presentation at the Amphitheater was inspired. In fact, if not for…" He waved a hand to encompass Dee-Dee's bandaged leg, prompting a howl of anguish from Dee-Dee that made both Randall and Maggie take a startled step backward.

"So she wins! The bitch wins!" Dee-Dee cried.

"*Non*, Dee-Dee," Olivier said, patting her again and looking fiercely at Randall. "The police will have something to say about that."

~

AN HOUR LATER, Maggie and Olivier sat in the waiting room while Dee-Dee's drugs kicked in and the police questioned Randall in a separate room. Maggie tried to think if the attack on Dee-Dee could have anything to do with Lanie's murder. So far it just looked like professional jealousy...taken to a psychotic extent.

"If Desiree did this," she asked, "will the police be able to tell?"

Olivier shrugged. "Probably not unless she confesses."

"That's not likely, is it?"

Olivier ran a hand over his face. It occurred to Maggie that between helping Janet home from dinner when she'd overindulged and assuaging Dee-Dee's nearly constant hysteria, Olivier had stepped in to being the caretaker of the group. Had he always had that role, even when Lanie was alive?

"Perhaps when she sees her lover shackled and dragged off to prison," he said, "she will step forward."

"Sounds a little too human for Desiree. On the other hand, if Randall *is* indicted for this, can Desiree hope to win the co-anchor spot? She'll have blown the whole point of the attack."

"I don't think she thought this out very well," Olivier said.

"Plus, if Randall's found guilty, can you imagine the social media bloodbath? It'll be the death of his show, just like Dee-Dee said. *'Popular travel guru found guilty of attack with a deadly bull.'*"

Olivier stood up. "I need coffee. Can I bring you one?"

Maggie shook her head and pulled out her phone. "No, thanks," she said as he turned and left the waiting room. She couldn't believe she still hadn't heard back from Laurent. He wasn't normally good at communicating by text message, but he usually got back to her in *some* way.

Did his mysterious phone call yesterday have something to do with the problem with the vineyard?

In the back of her mind Maggie heard the musical ding of the elevator's arrival on her floor, but it wasn't until the shadow fell across her knees that she thought to look up.

"I cannot believe you have the nerve to show your face here," Maggie said to Desiree as the Frenchwoman stood wringing her hands in front of her.

"Where's Bob?" Desiree asked. "He's not answering his phone."

"Maybe he's busy having it dusted for fingerprints."

"Where is he?"

"Aren't you interested in how *Dee-Dee* is doing?"

"I know she's fine," Desiree said with an impatient snarl. "I called the hospital."

"How thoughtful." Maggie peered around the back of her. "Where's the stuffed animals and bouquet of flowers? Where's the card? *Sorry I tried to kill you. No hard feelings.*"

Desiree's face blanched and she started to turn away but Maggie jumped up and grabbed her arm.

"Did your little stunt not turn out the way you thought, Desiree? The cops are booking Randall right now for criminal assault."

"You lie!"

"Why don't you ask Bob? If he's still talking to you, that is."

Desiree wrenched out of Maggie's grasp. "It was an accident!"

"What was? Her surviving the attack?"

"I need to talk to Bob." Desiree brought her hands to her face and, very uncharacteristically, began to chew on a nail. "I didn't think she would be hurt. I just meant to scare her. You must believe me."

"Actually, it's really more the *police* you need to convince. But you're good at that, aren't you?"

A look of confusion on Desiree's face turned to a reddening

glare. "Why do you persist in believing I killed Lanie? I told you, I was with Bob that night."

"I wouldn't put too much stock in that alibi after today."

"Besides, everyone on the tour knows who killed Lanie."

"May I join the party of people who know?"

Desiree sat down next to Maggie and gripped her fingers tightly together in her lap. "The day Lanie died she stood up at lunch and announced to everyone that Jim Anderson was not what he seemed."

Was this the big secret Janet alluded to?

"Go on."

"It appears that Monsieur Anderson is not wealthy, as he pretends to be."

"And you're saying he was so mad that Lanie publicly revealed this that he killed her?"

"*Non*, it was when she announced to all that he was sexually *incapable* that he became enraged."

Maggie frowned.

"Monsieur Anderson was *enraged*," Desiree said. "Ask anyone who was there."

"This happened the day she died?"

"*Oui.*"

Maggie looked up and saw the elevator doors open to reveal Olivier stepping free of them. He saw Desiree sitting with Maggie and quickly joined them.

"What are you doing here?" he said to Desiree. The Frenchwoman stood and straightened her blouse free of wrinkles, attempting to retain some dignity.

"Be so kind as to tell Bob that I will be with the others." She straightened her shoulders and walked woodenly to the elevator, where she got on and disappeared.

"She has some nerve," Olivier said, shaking his head.

"I'm not sure I don't believe her," Maggie said.

He looked at her in surprise. "You think she wasn't responsible for the assault on Dee-Dee?"

"No, I'm fairly sure she was. But she actually sounded kind of sorry."

Olivier snorted. "She is full of guile."

"Were you...can I ask if you were at lunch with the tour group the day Lanie died?"

Olivier rolled his eyes. "Desiree told you that Lanie embarrassed Monsieur Anderson at lunch."

"She did. But I find it hard to believe it was enough to make anyone want to commit murder."

Olivier hesitated and seemed to debate responding.

"Am I missing something?"

"I don't want you to think badly of Lanie."

"Look, Olivier, was she blackmailing Jim Anderson?"

"Lanie could be...impetuous," Olivier said. "She had a big heart but often she spoke before thinking."

Maggie found it difficult to be patient but she forced herself to smile encouragingly at him until he continued.

"She *was* blackmailing him," he said reluctantly. "In a way."

"I don't know a whole lot about blackmail," Maggie said, "but it seems to me if you publicly announce that your intended victim has no money and can't get it up, you've pretty much blown the thing you had to blackmail him with," Maggie said. "Unless there was more."

Olivier made a face. "There was more."

"I'm listening."

He sighed heavily. Maggie saw his shoulders sag with weariness. "When Lanie spoke out publicly at lunch that day, she was giving Monsieur Anderson a message that it was just...a taste of what she *could* reveal if she...I hate talking about her like this. And I'm not convinced she would have gone through with it."

"What did she have on him?"

"It was true that Monsieur Anderson has no money and it is also true that he can't get it up...with women."

"I see."

"I blame myself because it was I who told this fact to Lanie."

"Jim came on to *you*? Because you probably know the rumor is he and Lanie slept together."

Olivier laughed roughly. "It is not true. It is in fact ridiculous."

"Did you tell the police this?"

"*Non*! Of course not. Never."

"But if you could discredit the motive they feel like they have for you..."

"You mean because people think I was jealous of an affair between Lanie and Jim Anderson?"

"Exactly. The police see the so-called affair as a motive for you. It would help your case if Jim's true sexual preference was revealed."

"I know, but I don't want the world to see this side of her," he said miserably. "A blackmailer."

Maggie nodded but didn't speak. Was this love or what? To be willing to go to prison so the world didn't discover some unsavory fact about your dear one? She would definitely have to ask Laurent if he'd do this for her.

As far as putting Jim at the top of her list of suspects, Maggie had already come to the unfortunate conclusion that regardless of how much she personally disliked Desiree—and was absolutely convinced the woman followed her to Nice and stole her purse—the jump drive likely wouldn't have held up as evidence. The recording could have been made at any time of the day and there was no confirmation from any other source that a screaming altercation had happened *at the time of the murder*. It was, in fact, *because* the rooms and hallways had been so silent at the time of the murder that the cops were particularly stymied.

While she knew everything she had discovered was just

gossip and hearsay at this point, she realized the information on Jim was officially the best lead she'd had in the case so far.

Olivier leaned in so closely Maggie could smell the coffee on his breath.

"Please don't let Desiree fool you into thinking she did not want my beloved dead," he said.

"I'm sure she wanted her out of the way," Maggie said gently, "but who can say if she's crazy enough to actually commit murder?"

"She *is* crazy enough."

"I don't like her either, Olivier, but—"

"*Non*, I have proof that she is capable of it."

"What kind of proof?"

"I overheard Randall talking with her when I joined the tour last spring. It was late one night and I was checking on my camera by the bus. They didn't know I was there." He leaned in even closer and Maggie saw his eyes glitter with intensity. "Desiree said she spent the last three years in the *Centre pénitentiaries de Fresnes.*"

Maggie's stomach tensed. "I don't suppose you heard what for?"

"Manslaughter."

∽

GRACE WATCHED the sun drop along the horizon of the vineyard from her bedroom window. She didn't bother looking for Laurent wandering the carefully organized lanes. He still hadn't returned from wherever he'd run off to this morning.

To see Madame Mystery Lady again? Grace had to admit, if Laurent *was* having an affair he didn't spend very much time with his lover. Except for that one very public liaison at Le Canard in St-Buvard—and of course wherever he'd gone off to today—he'd stuck pretty close to home.

The affair was looking more and more like a non-affair. Thank God she hadn't said anything to Maggie about it. The vineyard, on the other hand, was a different matter. Even Grace could tell the grapes were so ripe and juicy they were practically falling off the vines, and yet Laurent had not called in his pickers.

Was it a money issue? She knew handpicking was more expensive than mechanical harvesting, but Laurent and always hired pickers to do his harvest. In fact, now that she thought about it, everyone in Laurent's co-op hired pickers. Usually the little village of St-Buvard was abuzz with excitement by now of the impending harvest—from the influx of immigrant pickers, mostly from Hungary and Romania, to the anticipated inpouring of money to the village—certainly the bar and café.

Why was this year different?

She turned away from her window and smoothed out the nonexistent creases in her lemon yellow Yves Saint Laurent slacks, which she wore with her favorite vintage Charles Jourdan heels—the result of a very pleasant shopping weekend in Nice three years ago. She could still remember the little boutiques that lined the narrow street of the *Vieux Nice* neighborhood. She'd just found out she was pregnant with Zouzou after months of agonizing infertility treatments.

Unavoidably, Grace thought of Windsor. He had been so happy then. They both had. He'd accompanied her that weekend. They'd stashed their four-year-old daughter, Taylor, with the nanny—the only one who could really handle her anyway—and had one last wonderful fling on the French Riviera. She touched the hem of her tunic.

Before it all went to hell.

Her eye fell on her leather carry-on, open on the bed.

Was she really going to do this? Her stomach lurched painfully at the thought. *Shouldn't I pay attention to gut reactions?* She smiled ruefully. *Maggie practically lives by them.*

A light tap at the door made her turn her head. "Come in."

Haley opened the door and Grace felt a comforting warmth infuse her at the sight of her new friend's face.

"Madame Alexandre's grandniece, Margo, is here to help me watch the kids this evening. You okay?" Haley moved into the room and Grace saw her eyes go to the suitcase on the bed. "So you've decided?" Haley asked.

"I don't know. Maybe."

Haley settled herself on the bed next to the bag and lifted out a pale pink silk and lace baby doll camisole. "Pretty."

Grace sat down on the other side of the bag and sighed. "Am I doing the right thing, Haley?" Haley dropped the negligee and reached over the bag to take Grace's hand. "One thing I know is that happiness doesn't go in a straight line. And it's the jagged parts that hurt."

"I feel like I'm slamming the door on my life before today and nailing it shut. There's no going back."

"There's always a way back. If that's what you truly want."

"And if I don't know what I want?"

"Well, I always think trying things on for size, or taking a few steps down a new road, helps to shine a light on what you really want."

"You are a seriously wise woman, Haley."

They both laughed. "Now if I could just use some of that wisdom in my own life," Haley said, the smile dropping slowly away from her face.

"Anything happening lately between you and Ben?"

Haley shook her head. "Nothing bad. Nothing good. Just...nothing."

Grace squeezed Haley's hand and stood up and walked to her dresser. She pulled open a drawer and lifted out a matching bra and panty in black lace. "I guess if I'm going to go down a new road I should start by being honest with myself." She returned to the bed and carefully placed the lingerie in the bag.

"It'll all work out, Grace. Did you ever get back to Windsor about letting your oldest daughter visit you here?"

Grace shrugged. "He said he didn't want to interrupt her school year."

"What about the Christmas holidays?"

"He said it made more sense for me to come back to the States with Zouzou than sending Taylor over here. He's right. It does make more sense. I hate separating the girls."

"Are they close?"

"No. Taylor is hard to love, frankly. She doesn't care at all that Zouzou and I are gone."

"I'm sure that's not true."

Grace smiled at Haley. "All family stories aren't warm and fuzzy."

"I guess I know that better than anyone." Haley stood and walked to the door to leave. She turned and smiled sadly at Grace. "You know I'll take good care of Zouzou while you're gone."

"That means a lot to me, Haley. Thank you."

"And *that* sounds like you've finally made a decision."

"I guess I have."

16

*H*oly crap. Desiree is a convicted murderer? And Randall knows this? And the Nice police know this? How is that not one hundred percent relevant to Lanie's murder?

Maggie sat on top of her carry-on luggage as she waited for Randall to sort out the hotel bill and finish loading the car. Janet stumbled over toward her. With anyone else, Maggie would be tempted to think it was the uneven stones in the sidewalk.

"Did you see her?" Janet asked Maggie without preamble. "Was she just going into surgery?"

Maggie frowned and looked past Janet, where she saw Bob putting his wallet away and walking toward the car. He looked like he'd aged since breakfast.

"She didn't need surgery," Maggie said, standing.

"Is it true Bob had someone lying in wait for her?" Janet dropped her voice to a loud whisper that caused her husband and Desiree—both of whom were standing by the front bumper of the car smoking—to turn toward her. "That he was trying to *assassinate* her?"

"Don't be ridiculous," Maggie said, her eyes on Desiree. When the Frenchwoman saw Bob walking toward them, she tossed her cigarette down and hurried toward him. He put his hand up to forestall any attempts on her part at communication. Nonetheless, Desiree began speaking French to him in a low voice.

Randall put his hand in front of her face, as if to push her away. "I can't frigging understand you so just stop," he said with irritation, moving past her. "Everybody's bags in?" he called out. "Let's get this show on the road."

Janet looked at Maggie. "We're leaving Dee-Dee in Arles?" The smell of wine poured off the older woman's clothes, her hair, her breath.

"I have no idea," Maggie said, picking up her bag and rolling it to the car.

She handed her bag to Randall, who placed it in the trunk without looking at her. Desiree was at his elbow, a pleading look on her face, but she didn't speak.

"May I have a word, Bob?" Maggie asked, her eyes on Desiree.

Without answering, Randall turned and walked away from the group. Maggie followed.

"What happened with the police?" she asked as he lit a cigarette.

"Dee-Dee dropped the charges," he said, sucking in sharply on his cigarette.

"What made her do that?"

Randall narrowed his eyes at her, but Maggie knew he would answer. Whether he was still afraid she might bring up the little matter of his unannounced visit to her room the other night or whether he was just worn down from the day's events, she saw he didn't have it in him this afternoon to play games.

"My producer faxed a contract to the hospital giving her the co-host position or twenty-five g's, my choice. She signed it."

"I'll bet she did. You gonna give her the money?"

"I don't know. Probably."

"Because you still think Desiree's the right one for the job?"

Randall laughed, but it wasn't a nice sound. "Dee-Dee's going to have a seven-inch scar on her calf. She might even walk with a limp."

"So she no longer fits the part."

"Seriously? Gimping around Europe with a big-ass scar up her leg? Wardrobe would never be able to put her in shorts when we do the Italian Riviera. She actually had a decent body before she met El Toro."

Maggie forced her face not to show her revulsion at his insensitivity.

"You're not worried about Desiree's criminal past coming back to bite you on the ass?"

He started and nearly dropped his cigarette. "How the hell did you find out about that? My producer got those files expunged."

"Wow. Your producer really earns his money."

"Besides, there were major extenuating circumstances. It's not like she's a murderer."

"Of course not."

"It was an ex-lover. I told you, she's very passionate."

"Are you still going to hold up her alibi for Lanie's murder?"

Randall tossed the cigarette down and ground it out with his shoe, his patience clearly finally drained. "I believe your chariot awaits, Madame. I promised your husband I'd have you home before you turn into a pumpkin." Without another word, he strode to the car, got into the driver's seat and laid an arm on the horn. Maggie walked to the SUV and climbed into the backseat. Jim and Janet were already there. Desiree sat in the front with Randall.

"Where's Olivier?" Maggie asked, but no one answered her.

It's going to be a seriously tense forty minutes to St-Buvard. Maggie pulled out her phone to see if Laurent had called her back. He hadn't.

"*Chérie,*" Desiree said to Randall, her hand snaking along the top of the back of the front seat to rest on his shoulder. "Do not let us end this way. Please let us finish our adventure in glory, not recriminations and unspoken—"

"What the hell are you talking about?" Randall said in frustration as he fired up the car and began backing out of the parking lot of the hotel.

"Please give me the chance to make it up to you. It's just ten minutes away by car—"

"You cost me twenty-five grand!"

"Je suis désolée!"

"*Désolée* my ass! You're crazy is what you are." He lowered his voice and muttered, "You're all crazy."

"Think of it, *chérie*. If you give the co-anchor slot to me everyone will know there can't be a breath of guilt attached to you over the incident with Lanie."

"How do you figure that?"

"Is it believable that two people so in the public eye could get away with murder and then go on to anchor a major popular television show? It's *incroyable*. No one would ever believe it. Better yet, they'll feel *sympathique* toward you, toward us...and the show."

"I don't need the sympathy vote, Desiree. I'm innocent. Remember?"

Maggie was astounded that the two of them would have this conversation in front of her and the Andersons. It was a testimony to Desiree's desperation, and Randall's callousness.

Desiree responded, her voice wheedling. "But in our business, it's all about perception, no? Let us show the world together that we have nothing to apologize for. Make me your co-anchor."

He hesitated but Maggie could see he was relenting. "You're crazy," he said.

"*Peut-être,*" she said, tentatively touching his arm and trying to catch his gaze, "but I think we can make that work."

Maggie felt the tension in the car build as the silence grew.

Wedged in-between Janet and Jim, she almost felt like she was watching a movie. An irrational part of her was tempted to reach out to try to raise the volume just a tad.

"We need one last presentation," he said quietly, lowering his voice for the first time as though finally aware they had an audience, "so Dee-Dee's isn't the final one."

Desiree put her hand on his neck and leaned toward him. "*Le Abbaye des Martyrs*," she said. "It is ten minutes away. Let me remind you of your faith in me." She dropped her voice. "Just ten minutes away."

∽

LAURENT WORKED the kinks out of his neck as he drove the last curve of the long drive to Domaine St-Buvard. It had been a long day. Even in the growing dark, he could make out the rough outline on the horizon of his vineyard. For the first time in months, he felt his heart lift to see it. His meeting with Adele ensured the continuation of his life here with Maggie and Jem. It wouldn't be the same, true. He and Maggie would have to have a painful heart-to-heart about the foreseeable future of their finances.

But in the end, it would work out.

As he pulled up to the gravel parking lot in front of the house, he saw the shadowy form of Ben Newberry leaning against the front pillar, smoking. Laurent grimaced, but thought in light of the new, positive change of circumstances perhaps the man could be endured for a few days more, at least for Maggie's sake. It would take more energy and drama to throw the *putain* out than to finish the visit. He turned off the car and watched Ben approach him.

Laurent had spent too many years studying people not to have figured out some basic assumptions about unspoken human behavior. After having been caught red-handed last night ransacking Laurent's study, Maggie's brother was apologetic and pleading.

But this evening, Ben's posture as he sauntered to the car told Laurent the man had rebounded. To affect this kind of confidence in the wake of last night's humiliation told Laurent that the snake had replenished his venom. Laurent waited for him to come.

"Care to take a little ride, Laurent?" Ben said smoothly when he reached the car.

Laurent hesitated only a moment and then nodded. "Get in."

They drove in silence back down the long driveway toward the village. Laurent knew it was likely that whatever gambit Ben had up his sleeve was not as potent as the man thought it was. Even so, long years in the trenches had taught Laurent not to assume too much. Better to be prepared for whatever was coming than taken unawares. He drove to the gravel turnaround at the entrance to St-Buvard and pulled onto the verge. He didn't bother turning the car off. And he didn't speak.

"I'll need the light for this little magic trick," Ben said, reaching up to turn on the car's interior light.

Laurent watched him, his eyes missing nothing. There was a stain on the man's shirt from lunch. He reeked of tobacco, so had evidently been attempting his nonchalant welcome home for Laurent for hours. And Ben's fingers trembled as he reached into his jacket pocket, belying his outward presentation of calm and control.

Ben unfolded a copy of the Ordeur contract and placed it on the dashboard. Next, he took a pen out of his pocket and put it on the pages.

He's confident, Laurent thought. *I'll give him that.*

Ben pulled an envelope out of his breast jacket pocket and extricated a photograph. The image was grainy, the background broken up and indistinct. The figure in it, unmistakable.

Laurent said nothing. A photograph of him at a counter of a

jewelry store was evidence of nothing. He couldn't help notice, though, that Ben's envelope was thick.

"A good likeness, don't you think?" Ben said. "I have two others taken seven years ago at two different jewelry stores on the Côte d'Azur."

Ben pulled out the photographs, surveillance camera screen grabs, each showing Laurent in a jewelry store talking with a different man behind the counter. Ben unfolded a text document that was obviously a fax.

"I've got testimony from two of the marks in the photos—that's what you call them, isn't it? Marks?"

Laurent looked at Ben, a slight smile on his lips. "This will not work."

"Oh, no? Well, I have written testimony from a Monsieur Denis Blanc—you probably didn't bother to remember the names of the people you scammed—but Monsieur Blanc remembers you well. He's in prison, you know, doing time for criminal money laundering. A very bitter man, I assure you."

Laurent waited for the rest. Three photos and the ranting of a convicted felon didn't concern him. Yet.

"He said you posed as an attorney in order to collect a phony debt from a corporate client of yours. Ring any bells?"

When Laurent didn't respond, Ben continued pulling sheets out of the envelope. "So when Monsieur Blanc deposited the cheques you sent him, fake, of course—and yes, before you say anything, I know he's a greedy bastard and likely deserved what he got—he was arrested. My little online research did enlighten me that most marks usually fall for a conman's tricks because of their greed or outright larceny. Doesn't change the fact Monsieur Blanc went to jail and *you* walked away with a half a million euros."

Laurent put the car into gear. "You have been busy," he said, turning the car around and pointing it back toward Domaine St-Buvard. The contract on the dashboard fluttered to the floor.

"Well, in all honesty," Ben said, picking up the contract, "I can't take full credit for finding all this. But, yes, it was hours of research. I have more, too. I have documented evidence of rip deals you did up and down the French Riviera: exact dates, testimony from your marks, photographs. You name it."

Laurent didn't know what the bastard had, how damning it was, or if any of it might stand up in a court of law. He did know that if it came to a trial—even if it didn't put him in prison—it would ruin everything he had built at Domaine St-Buvard.

"And all of this just for a signature from me?" he said dryly.

"See, I knew you were smart. Yes, exactly. Sign the contract and I won't go to Interpol with these. *Don't* sign it and you'll lose the vineyard, the house, your freedom, probably your marriage." Ben fumbled on the floor for the pen and held it up. "I have a recording of a telephone conversation between you and a Roger Bentley—he is a confederate of yours, I believe—that I can guarantee a jury will see for exactly what it is: two con men at work."

Laurent drove slowly, his head aching from the long day, Ben's voice droning in his ear. He was tempted to roll down the window for some night air but wasn't sure he wouldn't vomit as soon as he did. What control he had needed to stay firmly in place.

"You *will* go to prison, Laurent," Ben said. "It's that simple. Sign the contract, if for no other reason, then for Jemmy's sake—"

Laurent slammed on the brakes, and was startled because he hadn't realized he was about to. The car sat in the middle of the road, the engine humming, the half moon illuminating the trees that bordered the road like jagged black spears pointing skyward. Laurent looked at his hands as they gripped the steering wheel.

Ben cleared his throat. "Look, my parents may know *theoretically* about your criminal past, but it's a little different seeing it in vivid color. Imagine sitting at the family Thanksgiving table in Atlanta across from John and Elspeth Newberry after they've heard the audio of you posing as a businessman to sell worthless shares to unsuspecting victims. Oh, but what am I saying? It will only be Maggie sitting there. Because you, my criminal friend, will be in prison. For many, many Thanksgiving Days to come."

Laurent turned to look at him, his face impassive.

"Don't blame *me* for this," Ben said, a line of perspiration popping out on his forehead. "You brought this on yourself. There *is* an easy way out."

"Thanks for reminding me," Laurent said as he leaned across Ben and jerked open the passenger side door. "Get out."

"Are you serious? We're at least two miles from—"

Laurent grabbed Ben by his shirtfront and slammed his face into the dashboard. Ben screamed and grabbed his face as blood gushed between his fingers.

"You broke my nose!"

With a hard shove, Laurent toppled Ben out of the car and onto the road.

Too bad we don't have a recording of that, Laurent thought as he put the car into gear, not bothering to look in the rearview mirror but hearing the creature's howls as he drove away.

One thing was certain: the day had suddenly and definitely turned to shit.

17

If it wasn't so creepy, it would be truly beautiful, Maggie thought as she stared up at the towering stone structure of the forbidding Benedictine monastery. *L'Abbaye des Martyrs* perched like an ominous hulk over the D17, a scant ten miles from Arles but visible the minute they broke free of the city limits.

"He saved the best for her," Olivier said in disgust. He and Maggie stood in the dirt car park at the base of the steep walkway that would take them to the abbey. The others had already walked up to the structure but Maggie stayed behind to help Olivier carry his video equipment. He'd arrived by taxi minutes after the group had arrived at the scene.

"I really don't think he knew Desiree would try to hurt Dee-Dee," Maggie said, her eyes going from the tops of the darkened towers across the multiple and variable pitched roofs. For some reason, the word *wicked* formed in her mind and she shivered. "Are you really going to have enough light to shoot? It's nearly dark."

"I'll set up lights inside," he said, hoisting the heavy tripod onto his shoulder. "The acoustics are amazing in there. *Dee-Dee* earned this part of the tour. *She* should be giving the last presentation. You won't need your purse. We'll be done in twenty minutes. Can you grab the camera bag?"

Maggie shouldered Olivier's camera bag and began the long walk up the drive. "Is it deserted?"

He shrugged and squinted up at the facade of the looming stone castle. "They talk about turning it into a museum or something," he said, joining her on the gravel walkway. "But for now, it's just a ruin. It sits on a huge rock that rises out of a former lagoon."

"Not getting any less creepy. How old is it?"

"900 AD?"

Maggie looked at the stark architecture and tried to imagine anyone living here, as the monks must have done for centuries. She tried to imagine anyone feeling warmth or joy within its hostile, cold walls—from life or God Himself.

A sound up ahead made her look up in time to see Randall and Jim coming back down the path supporting Janet between them. She and Olivier stepped off the path to let them pass.

"What happened?" Maggie asked.

"She's drunk," Randall said in disgust. "Gonna let her sleep it off in the car."

"I don't see why I have to come," Jim grumbled. A closer look showed he wasn't really helping to support Janet. His hands were shoved in his pockets. Maggie watched them disappear at the bottom of the path and turn toward the car, now swallowed up by the night.

"Ever hear of the book *Ten Little Indians*?" Maggie said as she turned back to Olivier.

"No. What's it about?"

She trudged up the path. "It's about a group of people who disappear one by one."

Desiree was visible at the top of hill smoking a cigarette. "Bob said to go ahead and set up," she said as Olivier and Maggie walked by. They didn't respond. At the base of the abbey was a small courtyard that led to an opening on top of a series of wide stone steps.

"Kind of anticlimactic," Maggie commented.

"Wait 'til you see inside."

"I take it you've been here before."

She saw him nod in the half-gloom.

"Once. With Lanie."

They mounted the steps, then turned to see if they could see Randall and Jim returning. Maggie assumed Janet must be causing some kind of trouble because they still hadn't returned. She saw a halo of blue smoke curl around Desiree's head, then turned to see that Olivier was holding open the massive wooden door.

Inside, the quiet enveloped them and Maggie was struck by a feeling of unearthly holiness. But the feeling didn't bring with it any sense of peace. Her shoes were rubber soled and made no sounds on the slate floor. The entranceway opened up onto the grand hall—dark, austere, dangerous, unwelcoming. Graceful repetitive arches telescoped within each other in a series of symmetrical doorways that led them onward.

Olivier walked forward and Maggie hurried to stay with him. She had to force herself not to grab on to his sleeve. There was a feeling of death and hopelessness here that engulfed her and made simple breathing difficult.

"Wait for me, please." Her voice sounded calm and reassuring in her ears and she decided that more talking might help chase the ghosts back to their tombs. Olivier set the tripod down and began loosening the bolts to extend each leg. There was a moon tonight and it gave some light to the room through the high, small windows.

She cleared her throat. "Can we put the lights on? I'm not loving the whole creeping around in the dark thing."

Olivier laughed, but he reached in the camera bag and pulled out a heavy flashlight with a large clip on it. He attached it to the base of the tripod. "This is probably not the time to tell you about the crypt beneath where we are standing."

"Very funny, Olivier."

"I am not joking. They're graves of centuries of monks, of starving peasants and villagers slaughtered by the plague, and of course, all the Protestants tortured and murdered here. They sleep now beneath these stones."

"Where are we in the abbey?" Maggie asked, looking around, her flesh crawling and goose-bumping.

"This is the cloister," he said. "It's where the monks prayed. Built in the eleventh century, I think."

"Where *are* Bob and Desiree?" Maggie asked, feeling her heart begin to speed up. The light was almost worse than the darkness, she decided. It accentuated the pockmarks in the ancient stone walls and revealed how high up those walls went, disappearing into the darkness of the ceiling with only a few streaks of moonlight dappling the dark. She tried to hear if anyone was coming. Nothing.

"May I ask you something?" Olivier said.

"Sure." Maggie rubbed her arms through her thin cardigan. It was summer in Provence and she wasn't dressed for icy caverns or stone dungeons.

"I know you are trying to find justice for Lanie, but after all the time we have spent together I still do not know who *you* think killed her."

"Oh, I have my theories."

Olivier snapped the video camera onto the tripod and tightened the screws. "Any you might share with me?"

"Well, for starters I've always believed the paternity of Lanie's baby was the key to who killed her."

"Really?" Olivier took Maggie by the shoulders and gently

moved her in front of the camera. "May I check the white balance on you?"

"Sure," Maggie said. "I mean, I can't help but think that her pregnancy was the catalyst. Without it the murder feels too random."

Olivier didn't speak.

"Did you and Lanie talk about it?" Maggie asked. "The baby?"

"I did not know she was pregnant."

"Oh." *Of course that makes perfect sense, especially if Lanie knew the baby wasn't his.*

"But if I had known," Olivier said, "nothing would have given me more joy."

Maggie nodded. She decided it wasn't worth mentioning that Lanie probably wouldn't have kept the baby. She surely stood no chance at the co-anchor slot with a child.

Olivier looked at Maggie through the viewfinder and she found herself feeling uncomfortable. Was he acting a little strange tonight?

"I've been meaning to ask you," Maggie said. "The keycard the cops found in your wallet. Massar says it's their main piece of evidence against you."

"That's not a question."

"Did Lanie give it to you?"

"Of course. She slipped it under my door that night."

"And then you put it in your wallet."

"That's right."

"So were you planning on visiting her later?"

"*Comment?*"

"Well, she gave you the key to her room, right? Like an invitation?"

"*Oui*, of course. Yes, I was intending on going to her later."

"Only you didn't go?"

"*Non*. I had an errand to run. When I returned, I felt it would be too late to disturb her."

"But if she was expecting you, would you really have been disturbing her?"

"Why all these questions? This is what the police asked me."

"Sorry. It's just that I got the idea that Lanie *wasn't* expecting a visit from you. It was late when she took her bath and she had no makeup on."

"The light sucks here," Olivier said, picking up the tripod and collapsing the legs into one. The flashlight, still attached to it, bounced an erratic beam crazily around the stone room. Maggie's stomach lurched to watch it.

"You want to set up somewhere else?" she asked.

"Where the hell are they?" he said, looking over his shoulder toward the door.

"I was wondering the same thing."

"You are cold, Maggie?"

"Aren't you? It's like a walk-in freezer in here."

"During the Protestant Reformation, the Abbaye was used to imprison suspected Protestants." Olivier replaced the lens cap on the camera, his eyes focused on the task. "It is said that any poor soul left in the abbey's dungeon, even on the hottest day of the year, would perish from the cold within fifteen hours."

"Wow. You really know your history, Olivier. *You* could give the tour."

"I overheard Desiree rehearsing it."

"Really? When was that? Because I thought she only rehearsed alone in her hotel room."

Olivier looked at Maggie and she was struck by how flat his eyes were. For a moment, she wondered if he might be feeling ill. Suddenly, in one swift movement, he unsnapped the light from the tripod and shoved it into her hands. "Wait here," he said, then turned and walked to the main entrance and disappeared around the corner.

Maggie was so startled that she stood holding the light and gaping after him for a full five seconds before breaking into a run to where he had gone. Before she reached the outer hallway leading to the entrance, her ears told her what her mind could not believe.

He had slammed the door behind him.

18

This isn't happening. It can't be.

The door was too heavy for Olivier to have *accidentally* shut it. And it didn't close on its own.

Maggie stood in front of the door, her hands against the heavy wood, her cheek pressed against it.

Why would Olivier shut her in here? Was he about to do something he didn't want her to see? That must be it. She turned to look behind her and flashed the beam of her light upward but the darkness came within feet of her.

Does that make sense? If he doesn't somehow kill or neutralize the others, then there were *five* people out there who knew she was locked in here! Her hands felt damp, and without looking at them she knew they were trembling.

Olivier knew she was in here. Her hand traced the wood grain in the door and felt along the hard iron hinges with her nails.

Olivier had put her in here.

Why? Were they all in on it? What possible reason? Were they all in on Lanie's murder? And somehow I got too close to the truth?

Maggie heard the sound of her own heartbeat thrashing in her ears. She felt a sudden urge to sit down before her legs gave out on her.

Would Laurent miss her yet? And come looking for her? What would they do with her purse? Her bags?

She took a step back from the massive door and tried to breathe slowly to combat the panic. They were either going to come and let her out or they weren't, she reasoned. *If they come back, my problem is solved. If they don't...* She rubbed her free hand against her jeans and was surprised to feel even in the cold that it was damp with perspiration.

If they don't, I'll just have to find another way out.

She directed her light in the direction she'd come and felt the coldness permeate her bones. Something unimaginable, untouchable was urging her to stay back, to go no further. She hesitated. Staying in front of the door wouldn't help her get out. She took two steps toward the cloister, the muffled sounds of her shoes and her pounding heart the only noise in her head.

The camera bag! Olivier had left it behind. There might be a cell phone in it. Maggie hurried back to the cloister. Forcing herself to ignore the ghostly grotto walls that engulfed her, she shone the beam in front of her and ran to the bag. Setting the light down so its beam was directed downward, she threw back the flap of the bag and dug into it. There was an energy bar, a lens cap, and a wad of papers. In frustration, Maggie emptied the bag onto the slate floor, hearing the sounds as the contents hit the ground as eerie preludes to some low-budget horror movie about to inch toward its climax.

There was nothing in the bag that could help her. Maggie felt a wave of nausea thunder through her and she sat on the floor to steady herself until it passed. *This is panic, pure and simple,* she admonished herself. And panic was the enemy to planning and reason. Panic was not going to get her out of here.

When her stomach settled, she stuck the energy bar in her

sweater pocket and picked up the papers. She shined the light on them and saw they were a set of three sheets stapled together and folded into a tri-fold. The words were in French. The title of the pages read, *L'Abbaye des Martyrs*. Scanning the document, she saw it was a description of the abbey. Maggie flipped to the back sheet, where someone had written in an obviously female hand: *remember to stand over the crypt when talking about the hermitage.*

Maggie looked away from the paper. These were Desiree's notes for the presentation. She looked toward the entrance hall. *Unless she's doing it outside, in which case I wouldn't hear her, Desiree is not giving the presentation...but she clearly intended to.* Maggie looked back at the sheet.

Why are Desiree's notes in Olivier's camera bag?

~

MAGGIE SAT in the dark with her back against the north wall of the cloister. She wanted to preserve the light battery for as long as possible. How she wished she wore a watch like in the days before she used her cell phone for telling time. Laurent still wore one because he wasn't tied to his smartphone like she was. She thought back to the moment when Olivier told her she didn't need her purse.

No purse, no cell phone.

She figured she had been in here at least an hour, maybe more. And still Olivier hadn't returned. So he was likely gone with the others. And he wasn't coming back. This wasn't a joke, sick or otherwise. This was Olivier trying to...get rid of her? Kill her?

She glanced at the camera bag. *If Olivier and Desiree are together, does that mean Olivier was in on the attack on Dee-Dee?*

How stupid can I be? Because I liked him—just like Annie—I didn't want to believe he could be guilty.

So did Olivier kill Lanie after all?

She rubbed her hands together, trying to create some kind of friction or warmth. Her teeth chattered. Olivier had said they were in the cloister, whatever that was. Were the cloister and the dungeon the same thing? Did the same warning go for the cloister about not staying here longer than fifteen hours if you didn't want to die a freezie-pop?

She picked up Desiree's notes and snapped the light back on. Waiting for rescue in the cloister was as stupid as waiting for rescue by the door. If Maggie was going to find a way out, she needed to get off her butt and find it.

While there wasn't a map in the notes, Maggie thought the descriptions might help to at least orient her. She read the first page and then looked around where she was sitting. It appeared she was in the north gallery of the cloister. She stood and aimed the light above her head, where she saw leaping traverse arches supported by ornate brackets that were decorated with elaborate carvings.

Weird, she thought, flicking the light over the carvings. Everything from the floor to ten feet up was barren and bald, with all the fancywork happening way over your head where nobody could see it. Except the angels. Her beam caught the carving of a leering maw of a monster and she nearly dropped the light. When she steadied her arm, she saw the monster was devouring a man whole.

Lovely. I'm sure that got everyone in the mood to pray.

Her fingers and toes were tingling painfully and she rubbed her fists against her slacks to relieve them.

Some of the other columns and brackets showed carvings of human heads. Many appeared to be in distress, others were outright screaming in agony.

None of this is helping. She eyed the small window over the arches. *I can't climb up there.* Her eyes flicked to the stone archway that led out of the cloister. It was darkened and she had no idea where it led. But she also knew staying in the cloister wasn't getting her any closer to getting out. She glanced down at the paper in her hand.

Built in 1030, the dungeon in Saint Jean's chapel is the oldest existing part of the abbey. It is situated off the cloister and consists of a narthex with two parallel naves—the older one cut into solid rock and leading to the cemetery.

Maggie felt her scalp prickle. She did not want to go there. If she knew anything, she knew she did *not* want to go there. She looked again at the dark archway. *But a cemetery is usually outside, isn't it?*

She shone the light into the archway and realized the beam had dimmed considerably. She figured if she and Olivier had entered the abbey around nine o'clock, with the summer sun just setting, and she'd been in here another hour, then she had at least seven hours of the darkest part of the night left.

Her light wasn't going to last one more.

A fissure of fear pierced her and the need to hurry fluttered through her chest.

That's panic. Don't pay attention to it. Don't give in to it. She walked to the archway, her wavering light beam weakly piercing the darkness before her, and entered it.

It was a long tunnel of stone. The obviously colder temperature wrapped around her immediately. No matter how far she held her arm out, her light wouldn't reveal an end to her path, just more darkness. Every step she took she found herself imagining she would suddenly come upon a skeleton grinning at her from a cage hanging from the stonewalls.

One of the poor Protestants. She unconsciously crossed herself. *But this is the only passageway from the cloister. The notes say it leads to the dungeon in Saint Jean's chapel.*

Desiree's notes, she reminded herself. Could they have been planted for her to find? And was she now walking right into a trap they'd laid for her?

Stop it. They're not that smart. If you can't trust the stupid notes, you've got nothing.

Careful where she placed her feet but mindful of the minutes she had remaining with the light—*What would I do if it quits on me right now? Feel my way through the tunnel?*—Maggie walked quickly, her shoulder once scraping the wall when she didn't see the tunnel curving around until it opened onto a room flooded with moonlight.

She ran into the room, desperate for the light and space it afforded after the dark, narrow tunnel and felt the chill of a hundred opened graves against her bare skin. An arcade of rounded Romanesque arches rested on columns that seemed to beckon her forward.

Floral designs were carved in the columns at eye-level and the room seemed perfectly round, with no other passageway except the one she'd just taken.

The light was coming from a set of eight high windows that flooded the area with moonlight. She snapped off her light, hoping to save a few precious minutes, and walked to the center of what looked like a rotunda.

What was this place? Could it be the dungeon? Except it had light and space, whereas the cloister was much more forbidding. On the other hand, for whatever reason, it was colder here.

Much colder.

She walked a slow circuit of the room to feel its dimensions and to see if there was any possible exit, but also to warm herself. Her teeth were chattering again.

Maggie knelt in the center of the rotunda and pulled the energy bar from her pocket. She wasn't particularly hungry but had read somewhere that eating helped your body produce warmth. She wasn't sure if that was true but it was worth a try. She forced two bites down and put the rest away. Before she finished chewing, an explosion of nausea gripped her stomach and forced the food back up. She retched it out onto the stone floor.

Her muscles quivered under her sweater as she hunched over the vomit, and even in the cold she felt a light sheen of perspiration form across her forehead. The frustration of failing at even the simple action of fueling herself brought tears to her eyes. She knew she was feeling helpless and weak, cold and tired. And afraid. And any one of those things was enough to derail her best efforts to find a way out of this place.

"Hello!" she called, listening to the sound of her voice ricocheting around the stone room. "I need a hand here! If you're not too busy!"

She listened to the reverberating of her voice as it dissipated into the walls. "Hello," she called softly, her voice pinging back to her in gentle, mocking waves against the hard surfaces. *Screw walking for warmth. That's probably a myth, too.*

She settled down on the hard floor and wrapped her arms around her knees, drawing them to her chest. She could hear her heart pounding through her legs. She closed her eyes and began to sing.

When Jemmy was a newborn, Maggie sang to him. Laurent was delighted at this sign of normal maternity from her, she knew, but she didn't sing because she wanted to provide lullabies for her little lamb—or at least, that wasn't the main reason. She sang because it gave her courage and she could hear it in her voice—the strong tones, the spot-on keys. And she sang because hearing her seemed to confuse Jemmy into silence, at least temporarily.

In fact, Maggie remembered years ago when she rode competitively but suffered from nerves she would sing on horseback before her set. The singing, straight from the diaphragm, always calmed both rider and horse.

Now, she gripped her legs and sang *Amazing Grace*, all three stanzas, slowly and in varying pitches and levels, listening to how her voice reflected back to her—strong and sure. *Little Jemmy.* Maggie missed him so much right now, physically longing to feel his chubby, active little body in her arms. She slapped a hand to her mouth to stifle the sob that would spoil all her good work up to now in keeping the terror at bay.

Why had she left him? Haley looked at her like she was an alien, wondering how a loving mother could leave her adorable child for so long. And why had she?

Maggie looked into the dark realms of the rotunda. Surely a church was as good a place as any to admit she'd felt relief when she drove away from the house and climbed onto the train that took her away from him.

Was she so insecure as a new mother that she'd rather just run away? Is that what she was doing? A cold needle of dread pierced her spine. Is that what she saw in Annie too? Is that why she understood Annie's guilt so well? Because Maggie, too, was a bad mother?

I love my baby, she thought fiercely. *He may deserve a better mother than me, but I'm what he's got.* She rubbed tears from her face that she hadn't realized she'd shed. *Is that what Annie told herself too?*

No. No way. When I get out of here, I'm not leaving that boy until they pry my fingers off his lunch pail on the first day of Kindergarten. I will not be that Mom. I will not be Annie.

She jumped to her feet and pulled out the sheet of paper again. *I am coming back, Jemmy. Mommy's coming back right this damn minute.*

"Where am I?" she said out loud. "The church passage, that *must* be that creepy tunnel, leads to a natural cave, which is the dungeon, which leads to the graveyard." She looked around. "Is this a natural cave? Is it even really a cave?" She glanced once more up at the windows overhead. "Maybe they don't mean *cave* the same way I do. But whatever they call it, it is supposed to lead to a cemetery, by God." She pushed from her mind the other fact she knew about the dungeon: that it was the place a prisoner could die of hypothermia within fifteen hours.

She snapped the light back on, noticing the beam was even weaker, and directed it to the far wall—the most natural place to put a corresponding exit to this maze. She walked closer, feeling the excitement of moving and taking direction, when her foot slid in the vomit on the floor and she dropped the light. As if on roller skates, she careened helplessly across the floor before falling hard against a wall she hadn't seen.

Maggie heard her own scream as she plummeted down, through the floor and past it, plaster and stone and straw and dirt churning up around her as her body flailed in the air, falling, falling...

∽

GRACE WALKED DOWN THE SMOOTH, wide steps to the living room. The taxi would be at the front door momentarily and she was sure she heard Laurent come in. She set her luggage down in the foyer and saw he was seated in the living room facing the French doors and the terrace. He had what looked like a glass of whisky in his hand.

"Howdy, stranger," she said. "I thought I heard you come in. Are you alright?"

Laurent looked up from his obvious distraction and smiled mildly at her. "You are going out?"

"I've got a taxi coming. I'll be gone tonight and possibly tomorrow. Haley has all the details."

"*Bon.*" He turned away from her and back to his thoughts again. That was totally *not* like Laurent. Perhaps now would be a good time to see where it all led.

"Haley went to bed early," Grace said, reaching for his glass and taking a small sip. "She had a headache."

Laurent said nothing. His eyes followed the horizon of his

vineyard—he couldn't see even a quarter of it at this time of night. But, of course, he knew where it was without looking.

"Heard from Maggie today?" she asked. "I thought she was coming home tonight."

Laurent absently patted his shirt pocket. "I left my phone upstairs. The battery was dead. She was supposed to come tonight, but you know Maggie. It might not be until tomorrow."

"I hate missing her but I'll catch up with her on Sunday. Have you seen Ben this evening?"

"I have."

"Well?"

Laurent shrugged. "I believe he's found other living arrangements."

Grace stood in front of Laurent. "I'm not sure how familiar you are with the direct approach."

A corner of his mouth twitched in a near-smile. "I am married to Maggie, no?"

"Good point. So, what's going on, Laurent? What's going on with Ben and what's going on with the vineyard? Spill, darling. I'm not leaving until you do."

"And if your taxi comes?"

"It will wait. What. Is. Going. On?"

Laurent sighed. "I may be making a change of plans."

"What the hell does *that* mean?"

"Where is the young man? Asleep, yes?"

"Jemmy? Yes, he's been in bed for hours. Quit stalling." Grace sat down in front of Laurent and crossed her arms to appear resolute.

"I have thrown Maggie's brother out."

"Bravo. About time. Next?"

"It's possible I broke his nose in the process."

Grace clapped a hand to her mouth to stifle the involuntary and very unladylike guffaw that threatened to erupt. "Oh, dear lord. Well *done*, darling Laurent. But what do you mean 'change of plans?'"

Laurent didn't answer immediately, looking around the room as if trying to memorize certain furnishings. Grace had the sickening, unmistakable feeling that he was saying goodbye.

"You're scaring me, Laurent," she said softly.

"I believe I am in the process of securing Maggie and Jemmy's future," he said. "I feel confident that I am, but tonight a few obstacles were introduced."

"Obstacles how?"

"Maggie's brother works for the corporation that has bought out the village co-op." When Grace looked confused, he said, "Not just our co-op. They have contracted controlling operational shares in co-ops all over France and Spain and Italy."

"Okay." Grace adopted her best *I'm listening and trying to be patient* face.

"Jean-Luc and I are the only ones in St-Buvard who did not sell the rights to our wine production. Jean-Luc, because I asked him not to."

"What do you mean, sell the rights?"

"The right to work it as my own vineyard."

"So if you contract with them you'd still produce wine but the corporation would be in control?"

"*Oui*," Laurent said. "There would be no Domaine St-Buvard label. I would have no control over how the wine was produced or marketed." He stood and walked to the French doors. "Like the others, I was offered a long-term contract with the American conglomerate to lease out pieces of my vineyard to *negociants*."

"That sounds horrible. Can you just not sign?"

"Yes, but I do not own the machinery necessary to crush and process my own grapes. That was the co-op's. Without them..." He lifted his shoulders in a heavy Gallic shrug and then turned back to Grace. "Just this week I found an investor who would work with me and Jean-Luc and a few others to form our own crush operation. It would be hard work, to be sure, and the money...well, we would be poor for a very long time. But I would own my own wine."

"I know there's more to this story," Grace said, "because you still don't look happy."

"Maggie's brother is in trouble back in America. His company is pressuring him to have me sign the contract."

"And so I guess he's pressuring *you,* right?"

Laurent laughed hollowly. "You could say that."

Grace sat quietly and watched Laurent as he reached for a cigarette. She knew he rarely smoked, and never in the house. She waited until he'd expelled the first long draught of smoke.

"I thought you were having an affair," she said.

Laurent snorted. "And I thought I was hallucinating the day I saw you riding a bicycle in the village."

"You saw me? Why didn't you say something?"

He shrugged. "You were so happy to be on your secret spy mission. I had no heart to spoil your fun."

"The woman was one of your investors, I guess?"

"*Oui.*"

"I'm sorry, Laurent. I'm an idiot. I guess I see cheating spouses everywhere these days."

"Windsor did not cheat. *You* left him."

"I know." Grace let the words echo quietly in the air between them. She saw Laurent retreat to his own thoughts again. "Is the thing Ben is trying to pressure you with...your past?" His eyes glittered in the near dark as he glanced at her. She was almost sure she registered a benign amusement in them.

"*Oui,*" he said dryly.

"Does he have anything?" she asked quietly.

"I don't know. *Peut-être.*"

"Oh, Laurent. Sign the contract. That bastard! I hope you did break his nose. Do you think he'll really try to use what he has against you? He wouldn't dare. Maggie would never speak to him again."

"She doesn't really speak to him now."

"His parents will disown him if he does this."

"It doesn't matter," Laurent said, rubbing a hand through his hair. "He says he is attempting to avoid prison himself."

Hearing Laurent use the word *prison* so casually made Grace's fingertips tingle unpleasantly. *Would Laurent really go to prison? Dear God! Maggie would come unglued.*

"What did Ben do to have a possible prison sentence hanging over his head?"

"I do not know the details."

"Laurent, sign the damn contract."

He didn't answer, just brought the cigarette to his lips and stared out the door at his vineyard.

"Screw the vineyard, Laurent," Grace said heatedly. "Maggie doesn't care about that if it means she loses you."

"*I* care that the vineyard is safe for Jean-Michael," Laurent said, using Jemmy's full name. "I will not bequeath to him a *gîte*... a bed and breakfast, when I die."

"I'm probably the last person to give advice on happy, non-dysfunctional families," Grace said, standing and grabbing Laurent by the arm to get his attention, "but I'm almost positive Jemmy would rather have his papa with him *now* than a profitable vineyard when he's fifty."

Laurent grunted but didn't answer. The tip of his cigarette glowed in the gloom of the room. Just when Grace thought he was about to say something, she heard the muffled sound of her taxi's horn outside in the drive.

"Time to go," Laurent said, opening the French doors and flicking his cigarette onto the terrace. "I'll get your bag."

∽

THE DARKNESS WAS THE WORST.

Almost.

Maggie forced herself not to move. The pain vibrated down her arm and her first instinct was to try to shift position to relieve it. She took in a long breath, her eyes closed, and carefully, slowly, moved her left leg and then her right. Thank God she didn't seem to have broken anything. She opened her eyes, but she may as well not have bothered. There was no moonlit window down here. There was no flashlight, feeble beam or not.

Her breath came to her ears in jagged rasps and Maggie fought to accept the fact she could not orient herself by sight. The terror was like another person in the room: malevolent, focused, and always there.

Very slowly, Maggie tried to sit up and then gasped as pain shot through her left hand like a careening thunderbolt. She stopped moving and gingerly touched her left wrist with her hand. It was already swelling up.

A wave of hopelessness crashed down on her shoulders. How far had she fallen? Where was she now? A horrible thought that she was in the crypt slithered quick as a snake into her head. Olivier had said it was beneath the cloister. She began to shake, the cold bone-deep now as if she'd walked into a freezer. She shook harder, involuntarily, and at first it helped so she gave herself over to it. But within seconds it started to feel more like convulsions and she tried to resist the sensation, her teeth chattering loudly in her ears.

Is this retribution? Is God punishing me for trying to escape from my own child?

Her wrist was throbbing now. She could move it so she was sure it was just a sprain. Sitting up among a pile of boards and rock that had fallen from the floor above, she used her other hand to feel behind her. Was she anywhere near a wall? Was she sitting in the middle of a room?

When the tears came, she was almost grateful for their

warmth against her cheeks. Reaching out a little bit further, she touched what felt like the base of a cement statue or obelisk.

Or sarcophagus.

She snatched her hand away. She bent her head. *Dear Lord, if I ever get out of here I promise things will be different. I swear they will.* An image came to her of Laurent's face asking about the cut on her forehead: a picture of him smiling tolerantly—knowingly?—at her while she told the truth, but not the whole truth. And how many times had she done that—lied by omission but refused to call it that?

She had gotten so use to believing that Laurent had secrets and that he would lie to her that, until this moment, it hadn't dawned on her that she lied to him too.

What is the matter with me? I'm telling lies to the person I love most in the world. I'm sitting in a medieval crypt with a broken wrist preparing to freeze to death and everything I've done, every action I've taken, every effort I've made, has pushed me inevitably to this moment.

I made this happen. I made every bit of this happen.

When the tears came, Maggie knew they weren't totally for herself. They were also for the two people in her life, her husband and child, who had the serious misfortune to care for her when she didn't have the sense not to throw her life the hell away—and for what?

For Annie?

Isn't that why I lied to Laurent? Because that's not believable even to me, and it certainly wouldn't pass his bullshit detector. It wasn't for Annie she realized as she leaned back against the cement block. *It was for me, because of what a crap job I felt I was doing at home.*

I swear, God, I swear to you with my life if you give me a chance for a redo, I'll never again create an excuse to keep me from the people I love. I'll stand firm to try to be the person they think I am. I'll try to be deserving of their love.

She bowed her head and wept beyond care or hope of relief, her sobs echoing softly in the dungeon until it sounded as if a chorus of mourners, as if the dead themselves, had awakened to join in her grief.

She didn't know how long she sat there. She must have fallen asleep, which was a surprise in itself, but when she awoke, Maggie felt a little better, a little stronger. She touched her wrist and found it wasn't as hot or tender. She stretched out her legs, groaning as she did since she was still sitting on boards and rocks that had fallen with her. Although she couldn't see for sure, she thought she felt a long gash in her calf through her jeans. The blood felt sticky inside her pant leg.

She pulled her legs back up under her and gripped her left arm tightly to her chest, hoping to stabilize the wrist enough to assuage the constant pain radiating down her arm. When she did, she realized she'd had a dream. Whether she'd been out for fifteen minutes or an hour—and she didn't think it was much longer than an hour—she had experienced a full-blown dream that had taken her a long way away from this cold, evil place. She'd dreamt it was Christmas morning and she was sitting at the top of the stairs in her pajamas with her brother and her sister. In the dream, she remembered the joy and anticipation she'd felt, and the camaraderie with her two older siblings. She could even smell the cinnamon and pine in the air. Somehow there was bacon, too. Her mother must have already been downstairs getting a jump on Christmas breakfast.

She blinked back tears, thinking of Elise gone and dead now these last five years. Murdered by someone who was insane enough to think she was really killing Maggie. Although for all intents and purposes, poor Elise and her addictions had died many years before.

But it was the memory of Ben that was the sharpest. Maggie remembered how as children he was always in charge. As the eldest and the only son, that was hardly surprising. And Maggie had worshipped him. She'd forgotten that. In many ways, Ben was her first crush.

Whoever that boy was all those years ago, he had morphed into someone Maggie had never gotten to know. And the man he became—as foreign as a changeling left by the fairies—was not just someone who didn't share her interests or tax bracket. Maggie, and her parents, too, had refused to see it for way too long now.

I don't know what Olivier's role is in all this, she thought, her shivering faltering and giving away to a static apathy as her core body temperature continued to drop, *but it wasn't his baby.*

Haven't I always known in my gut that it was Ben's?

Ben lied about being with Lanie. Not just on the tour, but knowing her in high school, too. Why would he do that unless he was hiding a bigger, more horrific secret? And Ben was the only one besides Olivier without an alibi. Haley said she'd taken a pill and gone to bed early that night with a headache.

If the baby *was* Ben's, Maggie realized, it was the final, damning piece of evidence that finally triggered the up-to-now missing motive. In her heart, she'd always believed the identity of the murderer hinged on the paternity of Lanie's unborn baby.

Ben's baby.

It was all so clear now. As if pain and fear had sharpened her vision, and the panoply of images showed Ben's true colors in living, breathing high-definition.

If Lanie threatened to go public with the pregnancy, it wasn't just Ben's marriage on the line. It was Ben's whole way of life in Atlanta— his country club, his parish, his circle of friends, his job.

All the pieces finally came together and the picture was ruthlessly clear: Lanie was pregnant with Ben's child. Lanie was a blackmailer. And Ben is a ruthless bastard. For anyone with eyes to see, there was no other way around it.

Ben was Lanie's murderer.

19

In the dream, she was still cold, which was annoying. Strangely, Ben was there, too, all in black, the features of his face hard to distinguish from the ghouls and trolls carved in the stone columns that lined the main hall.

Was she dreaming? Maggie shook her head and felt the sharp pinch of a rock pressing into her thigh.

"I thought the guy said you'd freeze to death down here if you hung around."

Maggie watched the dark form that may or may not be Ben move around the room.

"Ben?" The sound of her voice, ragged and hoarse, was terrifying. It was not her voice. It was not any Earthly sound.

"Since you know you're going to die if you just lay there," the voice said, "why are you just laying there?" A peevish matter-of-factness entered his voice.

Were spirits supposed to be sarcastic?

"I'm cold…and I'm tired," she whimpered.

"You were always whiny, even as a kid."

Maggie hauled herself to a crouching position, ignoring the

broken board she'd been sitting on. She pulled a rock out from under her.

"Are you dead?" she asked. "Am I dead?"

"Don't be an idiot, Maggot," the voice said. "Someone's waiting for you. So please move your ass."

Maggie shook her head and the sensation of dizziness made her reach out for support. Her hand struck the rough wall in front of her. It was wet.

Someone's waiting for you.

A tremor of dread laced through her chest.

Jemmy. I can't not come back to Jemmy.

She held her injured hand to her chest and turned to stare into the darkness but the form was gone.

"Ben?"

Her voice lilted in the room until its echo faded softly away.

I'm not cold any more, she realized suddenly. *That's probably not a good thing.*

She bent her head and closed her eyes. She couldn't see anything anyway. What was it she was hearing? She blocked out all thoughts, pushing the throbbing in her wrist to the recesses of her mind, and concentrated on listening.

It was the sound of water, either moving or lapping or dripping. She felt a sudden, irresistible compulsion.

Go to the water.

She sat perfectly still, one hand on the wall. Her legs wouldn't obey her. The thought of rising from her knees seemed insurmountably impossible. She was so tired. She was cemented to the floor.

Maggot. The voice had called her by Ben's pet name for her as a child. She opened her eyes.

Someone's waiting for you.

She brought Jemmy's face to mind, and when she did he was laughing. He was always laughing. He was the picture of Laurent as a baby, she knew, with his thick brown hair tousled around his cherubic face, his deep set brown eyes squeezed into merriment. That is, if Laurent had been loved as a child. If Laurent's mother had cuddled him and kissed him and read to him at night.

Maggie groaned loudly as she clawed her way from her knees to her feet, leaning heavily against the wall, feeling the slime of whatever coated it against her hand and face. She had been so focused on the wall that when she turned from it, she was surprised to see she was no longer in total darkness. Her eyes adjusted and the terror of seeing her surroundings was replaced with a thought that bulldozed all other fears.

I need to get back to my baby.

She could see now that the walls were not smooth stone but stacked, both on the floor and the sides. She looked up to try to see the hole she'd made when she'd fallen but the ceiling dissolved into blackness and there was only a hint of moonlight from the upstairs room.

She heard a light rustling sound and her stomach twisted. Of course there were probably snakes and spiders down here, she thought, fighting down a building panic. But if that was the case, then there was a way out and in, too. She turned her head to where she thought she heard the sound and, fighting every natural instinct she had, went toward it.

At first she slid along the wall using it for support, but within a few steps she realized she was steady—and that she needed to hurry. With her good hand on the wall, she moved into the darkness until it opened up and let her see the next few steps in front of her. She saw she was in a passageway, not a room. Narrow and curving, *and leading somewhere.* She inched through the hall, stopping twice to rest but too afraid to sit down again for fear she'd never get back up.

Either I go forward and get out, she thought dully, haltingly putting one foot in front of the other, *or I stay here and die.* After what seemed like hours, the sound of water became more distinct. Maggie moved more quickly, walking into the darkness pushing her fear ahead of her into the black void.

When the passageway suddenly opened up to a large underground room, Maggie stumbled into it without realizing at first that light was pouring in from the high windows above. She blinked against the new brightness and tried to listen for the sounds of water again to get her bearings. Her legs quivered and threatened to give way as she listened. She tucked her head to concentrate.

She heard absolutely nothing.

But she smelled the aroma of coffee percolating. Another vision?

Is this the end? Is this what happens when you die? You smell the inside of a Starbucks?

Without knowing she was about to, Maggie opened her mouth and screamed. Her howl was inhuman to her own ears and left her exhausted and trembling.

Jemmy.

"Is somebody down there?" a voice called from the nearest high window. "Can I help you?"

∽

Maggie huddled by the campfire and gripped the cell phone tightly, hoping it might stop her trembling. It was three in the morning.

Milo, an Australian medical student backpacking around Europe before starting his residency in Sydney, sat watching her. His hair was long and uncombed, his eyes searching hers as if he wasn't completely sure she was real. He had hung his hammock and built his campfire near the creek at the base of the abbey—the same creek that fed the indoor wellspring of the abbey, and which Maggie had been listening to and following for nearly half the night.

In the end, there was no door in or out of the dungeon, no obvious way out. Milo climbed down to her from a ground-level window, stepping onto the massive stone tombs that crowded the large room like a macabre, irregular staircase. Maggie had no memory of the climb back up with Milo behind her pushing, and in the end, half carrying her to his campfire.

But she knew that if it hadn't been for the young man's sudden desire for a middle of the night caffeine hit she would still be down in the frozen halls of the ancient dungeon. Only she would probably no longer be walking.

"I guess I'm trying to get used to working weird hours," Milo said, handing Maggie a sandwich. "Or maybe the abbey is haunted, you know? Because I just couldn't fall asleep."

"Thank God for that," Maggie said, reaching for the sandwich. She took a quick bite and then turned to the phone as the line connected. "Laurent? It's me."

"Where the hell are you?" Laurent barked in English. "I've been driving around half the night looking for you. Why are you not answering your phone?"

At the sound of his voice, familiar and close, Maggie's throat closed up and she worked to speak past the lump burning in her throat. "Laurent, I'm sorry," she said, sounding choked even to her ears. "I was locked in a dungeon and I just now got out."

"If you are being sarcastic with me, so help me God—"

"I'm telling the truth. Please come get me but don't kill yourself in the process. I'm okay but I need you and I love you, Laurent. I love you desperately."

"*Bon.* Where exactly?"

Maggie gave him directions and handed the phone back to Milo. "Thanks," she said, sagging onto a blanket next to the fire. She huddled in Milo's rain jacket. He was equipped for a summer backpacking expedition and had not packed anything for warmth.

"Did you break your arm?"

"I think I sprained my wrist," Maggie said, putting the sandwich down. "Oh, my gosh, thank you." She reached for the mug of black coffee he handed her, but her hand shook so much it sloshed down the front of her sweater.

"I cannot believe you spent the night in there. With no blankets or food or water? That's totally hardcore."

Maggie managed a few sips before setting the cup down. "I think I'm going to throw up."

"Over there," Milo said, pointing away from his campfire.

Maggie stood up but her stomach settled down.

"Is that your husband?" Milo called.

Maggie looked up to see Laurent's Renault speeding up the winding road, heading toward the abbey. Warmth radiated throughout her body at the sight of him.

"Please tell me you got here so fast because you were in the area," she said under her breath. She walked to the grassy knoll overlooking the road and waved her good hand. He roared up, slammed into park and bounded out of the car.

She didn't even have to speak. His eyes took it all in and without a word he ran to her and pulled her into his arms. The smell of him was so familiar and safe. She burst into tears.

I kept him. The black night is over and I didn't pay a price for my sins.

"I feel like Scrooge on Christmas morning," she whispered into his chest. Her legs gave way and he lifted her easily in his arms and walked back to the car.

THE ER at Arles looked much the same as it had the day before. Only this time, Maggie sat in the waiting room with Laurent. The room was full from weekend mishaps and a wrist sprain was triaged as not urgent. Laurent procured a couple of ibuprofen for her and a bottle of water. On the ride over, she told him that Olivier left her in the abbey for reasons she could only guess at.

"I didn't have anyone's phone number," he said in frustration. "I didn't think to get one when I dropped you off. And you weren't answering your phone."

"It's still in my purse in the car with them."

Laurent had called the police during the ride into town.

"Why would Olivier lock you in there? Was his intention to kill you?"

"Laurent, I honestly think it was."

"For what purpose?"

"I have no idea. Unless he thought I had evidence against him for Lanie's murder."

"Do you?"

"No."

"I hate to see you in pain, *chérie*. I can't tell you what I thought when I went upstairs to bed and saw your texts and realized you'd tried to contact me all day. But by then you were unreachable."

"Laurent, I am so sorry for all of this. For leaving you and Jem alone, for abandoning you when my brother showed up. For...everything."

"Does 'everything' include the lies?"

Maggie sucked in a quick inhalation of breath, jerking her wrist in the process, which made her wince. "I guess I hoped they weren't really *lies* so much as—"

"So your purse really *was* lost as you told me? Not stolen?"

Maggie sighed. "Okay. But it's because I didn't want you to worry."

"That is another lie. You didn't want me to *interfere*."

Maggie grimaced and looked away.

"What are you afraid of? Do you ever do *anything* I tell you to do?" Laurent's dark eyes bore into hers.

"I try to."

"Yes, unless it is something you want very, very much. Then you just lie to me and do it anyway."

"It's because I don't like to fight with you."

"Fighting would be better than lying to me."

"But how about the time you told me you couldn't promise you wouldn't ever lie to me?"

"That is different."

"How, exactly?"

"My lies would always be for your own good. To protect you. Your lies are for convenience."

"I'm thinking a lie is a lie."

He gave her a baleful look.

"Look, Laurent, I feel like I have good reasons—same as you —for hedging the truth now and then," she said. "But things have been so good between us, I just don't want to ruin it by fighting with you."

"But you must! You must stomp your feet and throw a dish at me. Don't worry. You will not hit me."

"And then you'll just cave in? You'll say, 'Okay, fine, go ahead'?"

"*Pas du tout*. I will fight hard for you not to do something stupid or that may get you hurt. It will be a fight *formidable*. But I don't own you. I will not lock you in the garden shed."

"Fine," she said, "I'll tell you what. I'll risk fighting with you if you'll risk my knowing what you're up to in spite of how little you trust me."

He looked at her with surprise. "I do trust you, *chérie*."

"Well, in that case, we have a deal. No more lies. And let the chips fall."

He narrowed his eyes as he regarded her for a moment. "*Bon*," he said finally. "And after we fight, and have scared the pigeons from the rafters with our shouts, I will take you to bed and we will soothe away all the terrible words with our love."

She grinned. "Works for me."

~

It was late morning by the time they left the hospital with Maggie's wrist wrapped. The police called Laurent back to say Olivier had been taken into custody and was being escorted back to Nice, where he would remain until the trial.

"I guess trying to kill someone is a pretty serious bail violation," Maggie said.

"He told the others that I came and picked you up early," Laurent said.

"I was such an idiot, Laurent. I trusted him. I thought he was a good guy. Do they know why he attacked me?"

"Does it matter?"

"Yes, it matters. What did they say?"

"It's nothing, *chérie*. Just the ramblings from a distraught man."

"Ramblings like what?"

"The detective I spoke to seemed to think Olivier blamed you, well, everyone, but mostly you for—"

"Me? Blamed *me*? For what?"

"Evidently your friend Lanie said some things to him about you."

Maggie stared at Laurent and then slowly redirected her gaze to the road ahead.

"Maggie. Please do not upset yourself. These people aren't rational."

"I know," she said quietly. "It's just…Lanie hated me. I never knew that."

"You still don't know that," Laurent said firmly.

They drove in silence for several minutes. At one point, Laurent reached over and gave her knee a squeeze. "How are you feeling?"

"It doesn't hurt as much."

"Good. We need to talk about some things."

Maggie twisted in her seat to look at him and yelped as the motion pulled against her sling. "I thought we got all that sorted out. The lying and stuff."

"This is something different."

"Oh, God, don't tell me you want a divorce. Today's not a good day for me to hear that."

"I will never understand your humor."

"Just tell me, please."

"We are about to go into a dry spell," he said. Maggie knew Laurent was proud of his grasp of American idiom so she nodded as if she understood him and waited for the other shoe to fall on her head.

"We are going to be poor for a little bit," he said and then shrugged. "Perhaps longer."

"I knew there was something going on! It's the vineyard, isn't? I thought we had a bumper crop this year."

"We do. This is a very good year for us," Laurent said, never taking his eyes off the road. "But the co-op I use to crush and bottle my grapes has sold out to an American corporation."

"What? Everyone in it? They all sold? Jean-Luc, too?"

"No, not Jean-Luc."

"Well, didn't this company offer to buy your interests too?"

Laurent smiled wryly. "The terms were not favorable."

Maggie frowned and bit her lip. "Okay, so we have grapes but no way to get them turned into wine?"

"No, we do. I have recently made arrangements to form what is called a studio winemaking operation. A few other vintners and an investor will join with me in getting our grapes crushed and bottled."

"Great. Well, then problem solved."

"Yes, but it will be expensive for awhile, I'm afraid."

"So that's why you said we'll be poor."

"*Si.*"

"*Poor* as in no more weekend trips to Paris or *poor* as in no trips back to the States?"

"*Oui, chérie.* All of that. I am sorry, Maggie. It is just until the new business finds its legs."

Maggie turned to look out the window. She looked down at the jeans she'd crawled around a medieval dungeon in. The ER physician had had to cut a section of the pant leg away to clean and bandage the cut on her leg. The cut wasn't deep and Maggie was relieved she hadn't needed stitches. She turned her face to the sun and felt its strong rays caress her cheek through the car window.

"Laurent," she said, still not looking at him, "the main thing is you and me and Jemmy. As long as we three are together, that's all that matters."

Laurent seemed to hesitate and Maggie turned to see why, but all he said was, "I am glad, *chérie.*"

"So that's it? *That's* what's been bothering you? I have to say I was worried, Laurent. This is no big deal. But a little communication next time, please."

"*Je sais, chérie.* I should have told you sooner. Oh, but you're right, there is something else you probably should know."

"What?"

"I might have broken your brother's nose."

MAGGIE WASN'T SURPRISED when Laurent pulled into the parking lot of the little restaurant before they reached St-Buvard. In his mind, any and all ills, whether physical or emotional, were best dealt with on a full stomach. Food ranked very high with him as aphrodisiac, panacea, and balm. The parking space was dirt and parallel to the country road just off the D17.

At first glance the restaurant looked like a gas station to

Maggie except for the striped awnings over the windows. After washing her face at the hospital and having her wrist bandaged, she was amazed to realize she was hungry. Laurent helped her out of the car and, holding her good elbow, guided her into the *brasserie*.

Tin ceiling tiles stamped with ornate patterns and hardwood floors, polished to a gleam, gave the inside of the little bistro an immediate, cozy feel. Heavy toile café curtains hung against the large windows facing the street, and the gilded antique frames and mirrors on the dark walls presented a touch of understated elegance along with a feel of *en famille*. Maggie instantly felt cosseted and pampered.

Of course, she thought, tears welling up in her eyes, *that was Laurent's intention.*

A waiter greeted them and sat them in a booth overlooking the parking lot. It was still warm outside but even now, in late August, Maggie could see evidence of the mistral and the coming autumn in the swirling, miniature cyclones of dead leaves in the street. She relaxed into her chair while Laurent ordered for them both.

If you'd have told me six hours ago that I'd be sipping a Pinot Noir and waiting for a hot lunch, I would've worried a whole lot less about being attacked by the spirits of crazed monks. The waiter brought the wine and poured their glasses.

"One glass won't hurt," Laurent said.

"You mean because of the drugs?" Maggie said. "They didn't give me any. I'm only on ibuprofen."

Laurent gave her a strange look as if he was about to say something and then thought better of it. He raised his glass.

Maggie reached for her glass and then looked at Laurent.

"You think I'm pregnant," she said suddenly.

He raised his eyebrows and grinned. "Don't you?"

The waiter came and set a tureen of potato and leek soup in

front of Maggie and placed a large, silver soupspoon by her napkin. Someone else came with a basket of fresh baked bread.

She waited for the server to leave and then, unable to hide the tears stinging in her eyes, smiled at Laurent. "How in the world did you know? I wasn't completely sure myself."

"There is no one I know so well as you, *chérie*," he said, reaching for his own soupspoon. "I have made an art of studying you in all your forms and incarnations. The one where you are carrying my baby is one of my very favorites."

"Oh my God, Laurent, we're going to have another baby. That'll make two."

"Your mathematical abilities continue to astound me, *chérie*," Laurent said with a smile, his eyes shining.

Maggie ate her soup and enjoyed every drop of her wine, vowing it would almost certainly be the very last she drank until the baby was born. She ate several pieces of bread and every bite of the luscious and creamy Quiche Lorraine that was served after the soup. She and Laurent talked of their children and their future until Maggie thought her happiness could not be more complete. Finally, she dropped her napkin on the table and groaned. "I ate too much."

Laurent signaled to the waiter for the bill.

"How in the world did you find this place? They act like they know you."

"They are trained to act that way with everyone," Laurent said.

"Ben was sleeping with Lanie."

"*Comment?*" Laurent looked at her and frowned.

"My brother, Ben. He lied about not being with Lanie."

The waiter delivered the bill and walked away. Before Laurent opened his wallet, he said, "Is this important information if Olivier is the murderer?"

"I don't think Olivier *is* the murderer."

"That surprises me, *chérie*."

"I think Ben got Lanie pregnant—inconveniently pregnant."

Laurent pulled bills out of his wallet and tucked them into the folder with the bill.

"You have reasons for thinking this?"

"Remember at dinner a couple nights ago Ben said he didn't really know Lanie in school?"

Laurent nodded slowly.

"It's true they were in different grades," Maggie said. "Ben graduated by the time Lanie and I were there, but it was a lie that he didn't know her."

"She may not have made an impression on him."

"He took her to prom his senior year."

Laurent's eyebrows shot up.

"At the time I thought Ben was trying to downplay it for Haley's benefit, you know? But I'm sure she knew about it. So why lie?"

Laurent stood and held a hand out to help Maggie from her chair. "Is that all?"

"When I was all alone and so cold last night and wishing desperately I had your warm arms around me—"

"I must remind you that you would not have been cold and sleeping in a viper-infested medieval castle if I had been with you last night."

"Okay, but the point is when I was really miserable last night, I remembered Ben saying when I first came to Nice that he had no idea which hotel room was Lanie's."

"And now you think he did?"

"One of the maids told me that Ben went to Lanie's bedroom. At night. More than once."

"*Pas bon.*"

"Yeah, *pas bon* at all. Why would he lie about not knowing which room was hers?"

"*Évidement* he was not supposed to be in her room, *chérie*. A married man? It is not *difficile* to comprehend."

"I *get* that he lied to Haley about cheating on her, Laurent. But he lied to the *police*."

"You think *your brother* might have killed Lanie?" The look on Laurent's face clearly showed he didn't share this theory.

"I know Lanie was pregnant with someone's baby and it *wasn't* her boyfriend. Don't you think the cops should do a DNA analysis of every man on the tour?"

"What are the odds that will happen?"

"Zero," Maggie admitted. "The homicide detective in Nice told me they wouldn't spend any money collecting DNA to prove paternity. They barely have the resources to check it at the crime scene. The only reason they have it on Olivier is his defense team paid to have it done."

Laurent handed her into the car and secured her seatbelt around her.

"What time is it in the States?" she asked, reaching for his phone in the console.

"You are calling your parents?"

"No, I have to find out about something that's been bugging me all night—when I wasn't quaking in fear for my life." She dialed the number from memory and waited until Annie picked up while Laurent climbed into the car.

"Hello?"

"Hey, Annie I know it's early. Sorry about that."

"Oh, Maggie, dear! That's fine. I am always glad to hear from you."

"I just have one quick question and then you can go back to sleep. Lanie had her high school reunion this year. Do you happen to know if she went to it?" Maggie looked at Laurent, who was nodding his head.

"Of course, dear," Annie said. "Can you imagine our girl missing it? She posted all about it on Facebook. I wasn't in direct contact with her at the time, but I read about it."

"Okay, thanks, Annie. That's all I needed. Go back to sleep and I'll talk to you later, okay?"

"All right, dear. I hope I helped."

Maggie hung up the phone and then leaned her head against Laurent's shoulder. "Take me home, Laurent. I have to ask my brother a very big question."

20

Maggie didn't wait for Laurent to get her door when he parked the car at Domaine St-Buvard. She jerked the door open with her good hand and ran up the slate steps to the front door.

"*Faites attention, chérie,*" Laurent called to her.

But she couldn't be careful, or wait another moment. The front door was unlocked and Maggie jerked it open and ran inside. "Jemmy?" she called. "Jemmy, Mommy's home!"

"*Maman!*"

Maggie pivoted on her heel and saw the baby sitting in his high chair in the kitchen. Haley stood next to him, a spoon poised in her hand, her eyes wide with surprise. "Maggie, what happened to you?" Haley gasped.

Maggie went to the baby and crouched in front of him. She put her good arm around him and kissed his cheek, then nuzzled his neck. "Hello, little man," she said softly. "I missed you so much."

"Go sit down," Haley said, unlatching the tray on the high chair, "I'll bring him to you. What in the world happened?"

Maggie knew she must look a sight: filthy, bruised and

battered. She settled on a dining room chair and held her good arm out as Haley set the baby on her lap. Maggie kissed his head.

"Haley, I'll never be able to thank you enough for taking care of him while I was gone."

"It was my pleasure, Maggie. Is everything okay? What's going on?"

Maggie lifted her head to see Laurent enter the room. There was an electric charge when he did. She could feel it. And Haley's reaction to Laurent was immediate and palpable.

"Where is Zouzou?" he asked, looking around the kitchen.

"She's napping," Haley said stiffly, crossing her arms, not looking at Laurent.

Laurent held out his arms for the baby and Maggie relinquished him. Her arm was hurting and she was afraid he might slip off her lap. She smiled as she watched Laurent absently kiss his son on his head.

"Is Ben here?" Maggie asked.

"That's a very good question," Haley said acidly. "In fact, you might want to ask your *husband* why your only brother spent the night in the emergency room in Aix. He came home early this morning after I informed him that Laurent was gone, and then only to pack his things and leave again."

"Where is he?" Maggie asked as she stood next to Laurent and took the baby's hand in hers.

"He's staying in Aix," Haley said.

Maggie touched Laurent's arm. "I'm going to take a shower and lie down for an hour."

Laurent nodded and turned to Haley. "Where in Aix?"

∽

TWO HOURS LATER, Ben walked into the living room at Domaine St-Buvard. He had a large white piece of medical tape across his nose. Both eyes were blackened. Frankly, Maggie was surprised someone hadn't punched her brother in the face before now. Probably had.

Many times.

She sat on the couch, an afghan wrapped around her legs, a large cup of tea in front of her. Haley was putting the children down for their nap. After arriving home with Ben, Laurent had gone straight to his study.

When she saw Ben, Maggie held up a hand before he could speak. "Don't tell me. I don't care."

"I would at least like to tell my side of things."

"It doesn't matter. I only have one question for you. After that, you can leave, drop dead, join the Peace Corps…I don't care."

Obviously the process of attempting to roll his eyes was painful, if not slightly dizzying, as she watched Ben put a hand to his head and wince. "What's your question?" he asked.

"Was the baby yours?"

Ben looked at her and for a moment she thought he'd deny it. His face softened and he glanced upstairs, listening for sounds of Haley and the children.

"When did you find out about it?" Maggie asked.

"In Nice."

"No wonder you've been out of sorts."

He pointed to his face. "You know your husband did this, right? Broke my nose?"

While Laurent *had* mentioned it, the reason *why* hadn't been immediately forthcoming during the car ride back. Maggie assumed her brother stepped over the line once too often. Seeing the extent of the damage on her brother's face this morning set off alarm bells in her mind. Laurent had more power of self-control than the Pope. If he hadn't been able to endure Ben for *two days*—worse, had been driven to create this kind of physical damage—something serious must have happened between them.

And Maggie had no earthly idea what that was.

She put the thought from her mind and forced herself to

focus on the task at hand. The one terrible, heartbreaking thing that she had wrestled with half the night and was most afraid of in the world—*that her own brother was capable of cold-blooded murder*—was on the table in front of her right now. Would he lie? Would she be able to tell if he did?

"Lanie was blackmailing you," she said.

He looked down to his hands. A very un-Ben-like gesture, and an admission tantamount to an announcement over a public address system.

Maggie took a breath and dove in. "I can only imagine how she phrased it. Did she remind you of your position in the community? Did she talk about your being a respected member of your parish and on the board of Catholic Charities? I know Lanie. She wouldn't have held anything back."

He didn't speak.

"Tell me I'm wrong. Tell me she didn't threaten to tell the world about your happy event."

He grunted and then spoke softly, as if afraid he'd be overheard. "She said she'd send out baby announcements."

Maggie let the silence grow between them for a moment. "There's no way she would have kept the baby," she said finally.

"I couldn't take the chance," he said, his eyes on his knuckles, his fingers moving relentlessly, rubbing an imaginary stain off his hands.

"So. Did you do it?"

He looked at Maggie with tears shimmering in his eyes. His silent admission prompted a fresh wave of nausea in Maggie. She'd known it, been expecting it, but the reality of knowing for sure was as shocking as a punch to the gut. "You killed her and your own child?" Maggie felt her skin tighten and grow cold.

"Hardly a child," Ben said bitterly, but he looked away as he said it.

Maggie stood. She was pretty sure she was about to vomit up her lunch and she didn't want to do it in the living room.

Out of the corner of her eye she saw Ben reach out for her, and then seemed to notice for the first time that she was wearing a sling and drew his hand back. He instantly recoiled and Maggie realized Laurent must have come into the room behind her. She took a long breath to steady her stomach and felt Laurent's hand on her good shoulder.

"Ça va, chérie?" he murmured to her.

She felt his strength and calm seep into her and she stood a little taller. "I'm fine, Laurent. Would you mind calling the police, though? My brother needs to talk to them." She turned and Laurent brought her gently into his arms, his hand on the back of her head. She heard Ben get to his feet.

"That won't be necessary," Ben said, his voice hoarse. "But if I could get a ride to Nice, we'll just do this thing properly."

Maggie turned in Laurent's arms and faced her brother. For the first time since she'd seen him this trip, he looked almost...relaxed.

"You are giving yourself up?" Laurent asked him.

"I am. And I'd be grateful if, as your last official act as my brother-in-law," Ben said stiffly, "you would deliver me."

∼

WATCHING the sunset on the vineyard, Maggie felt a new, gut-level connection to the view. Somehow, after her conversation with Laurent, she felt differently about the vineyard. Always before it had been Laurent's vineyard, Laurent's project, Laurent's obsession. This evening, for the first time, Maggie saw it as theirs. Whether that was because it was at risk or because it was now the source of their future (hopefully temporary) poverty, the vineyard now appeared to her as something joint, something integral to their marriage and their lives here in France.

Now when she looked at the sun setting on the vineyard—the

splashes of violet and red seeping down into the fields of grapes—she felt like she was looking at *her* inheritance too.

"Go *fish, Tante* Maggie!" Zouzou said next to her, her chubby little fists gripping a handful of cards—most of which were upside down and face cards showing outward.

Maggie shifted Jemmy in her good arm, the feeling of him solid and comforting against her, and pulled a card from the deck on the coffee table.

"Got any *trois*?" she said to the little girl.

"Which one are them?" Zouzou asked, frowning.

Haley leaned over the back of the couch and plucked a card out of Zouzou's hand. "They look like this, sweetie," she said.

Zouzou squealed happily and flung the card at Maggie.

"Having fun, Maggie?" Haley asked, then laughed.

Maggie was glad Haley was in a better mood. Her affect had noticeably lifted when Ben came back with Laurent and, since she was smiling, Maggie had to assume Ben had *not* filled her in on the details of why he and Laurent were driving to Nice. But whatever explanation Ben *had* given seemed to satisfy her. It wasn't Maggie's place to tell her what was going on.

It would all come out sooner or later.

Maggie worked to push the thought of her brother—and what he had done—away. She wanted to enjoy her baby tonight, and the feeling of being clean and unafraid, warm and secure. A flickering thought of Olivier came to her and she chased it away, too. He was being dealt with and whatever she had thought about him—*and how wrong she had been about him*—was history now. Except for the conversation she still needed to have with Annie about him. But there was time enough for all that.

Tonight was for her and for Jemmy.

"You know," Maggie said, "it occurs to me that just because I don't enjoy endless hours of watching *Sponge Head Square Pox* with little people who can't yet tie their shoes, it doesn't mean I don't adore these little creatures."

Haley sat down on the couch. "We're all different, Maggie. Some of us are cut out to teach pre-K and some of us definitely not." She leaned over Zouzou's shoulder and pointed to a card in the child's hand. "Ask Aunt Maggie if she has any of those. Do you know what that is?"

Zouzou frowned and looked up at Haley, looking for the answer.

"Come on, Zouzou," Haley said. "You know it."

"Um...a two?"

"Yes! Well done! *Yes*, it's a two."

Zouzou beamed at Haley while Maggie cheered and made Jemmy's little fist pump. "Good job, Zouzou," she said. "Mummy will be so impressed when she gets home. Speaking of which..." She looked at Haley. "Where exactly did Grace go today? And shouldn't she be back by now? It's after six."

"I'm pretty sure she's not coming home tonight," Haley said.

Maggie looked at her in surprise. "Why not? Where is she?" Maggie had tried calling Grace a couple of times but the calls went straight to voicemail.

"She'll be back in the morning."

"Where is she?"

Haley sighed and lifted a curl off Zouzou's forehead. "Honestly, I'm not sure I'm at liberty to say. She told me in confidence."

"Are you kidding me? Grace is my best friend."

"Well, if that's so, wouldn't you know where she is tonight? I'm sorry, Maggie. I hope that didn't come out too harsh."

Maggie stared at her. Haley looked apologetically at her over Zouzou's blonde head.

Was Grace mad at her? Had something happened? All of a sudden, Maggie remembered a phone conversation—or two— where Grace said she needed to talk to Maggie about something. Maggie also remembered the evening she'd deliberately sent an incoming call from Grace to voicemail because she'd been too tired to talk.

She cleared her throat. "She asked you not to tell me?"

"Not in so many words, no," Haley said. "But she didn't say I could and it's definitely a secret. Come on, Zouzou, let's wash our hands for supper, okay? Aunt Haley made cornbread just for you."

JEMMY'S EYES began to close long before his supper was finished and Maggie watched Haley pick him up and detach him from his bib. "This little guy's done for the day," Haley said. "Aren't you, angel?"

Maggie felt a stab of envy that Haley was able to handle her son so easily. She felt like taking him from her but the steady throb in her wrist reminded her not to.

"You look pretty beat, too, Maggie," Haley said. "Let me give the little ones their baths. Why don't you go on to bed?"

"I'll wait for Laurent," Maggie said.

Haley hesitated and gave her a strange look. "He may be awhile."

Does that mean Ben told her the truth after all? Impossible. She doesn't act upset. But why does she think Laurent will be late?

"In any case," Haley said, standing at the foot of the stairs with the children, "at least lie down on the couch. You look dead on your feet."

Maggie had to admit she was exhausted. As much as she wanted to put Jemmy to bed, she reminded herself that she had several years of bedtimes ahead of her to do that. The short nap she'd taken before Laurent and Ben came in from Aix had done little to touch the bone-deep exhaustion and mental anguish of her night at the abbey. For at least this one night, she probably needed to take care of herself.

"I think I will, Haley," she said, walking to the stairs and kissing Jem on the cheek. "I owe you forever for all the help you've been."

A thought came to Maggie that Haley was going to be all on her own soon, although of course the family would help her as much as they could. Ben would surely go to prison. Perhaps that would be the best thing for Haley—to start over without someone abusing her on a daily basis.

Maggie went to the couch, turned off the lamp and pulled the afghan over her, the sounds of Jem's cooing and Zouzou's singsong voice drifting in and out of her consciousness.

MAGGIE HAD NEVER SLEPT MORE DEEPLY. Her dreams were fretful and dark, and when she awoke she didn't feel refreshed. She felt on guard. She pushed herself up to a sitting position on the couch, moaning because she'd been sleeping on her wrist. She heard Haley in the kitchen, humming and moving pans on and off the stove.

Maggie's mouth was dry. The ER physician had told her to drink plenty of water, but somehow in all the excitement of the homecoming and talking to Ben...

Ben. A feeling of unease settled on her shoulders. She rubbed her face with her good hand. What will her poor parents say? This was going to absolutely kill them.

"You awake, Maggie?" Haley called from the kitchen. "I heated up the beef dish Laurent made. Why don't you guys have a microwave? How can you live without it?"

Maggie licked her lips and stood. She eased the stiffness out of her back and realized it was a souvenir of the night before, when she had slept on broken bricks and boards. She was covered with bruises and scratches. When she'd taken her shower earlier she'd removed the bandage from the cut on her calf and forgotten to put on another one. She limped to the kitchen, blinking against the bright overhead light.

"Can you hand me a juice from the fridge?" she said, suddenly tired again. *Is it the baby making me feel so lousy?* she wondered. Her good hand involuntarily moved to rest on her still-flat abdomen.

"Sure, sweetie," Haley said opening the fridge and then handing a juice bottle to Maggie. "Need a glass?"

Maggie shook her head and drank it down from the bottle. It was quenching and sweet and she felt instantly revived. "I can't believe I slept so long. Did Laurent call? What time is it?"

"Just a little after nine," Haley said. She picked up two large bowls full of Laurent's *boeuf en daube* and moved past Maggie to set them on the dining room table. "Do you feel like a glass of wine?" she asked over her shoulder.

Actually, a glass of wine sounded pretty good. It would probably put her right back to sleep but, come to think of it, why not sleep? Why not sleep for hours and hours and hours? She'd had a hell of a night and anything Laurent had to tell her, he could tell her in the morning.

"I'll get it," Maggie said. "You sit down. You're going to make me feel guilty, taking care of the kids and then waiting on me."

Haley laughed. "Well, all right," she said, settling down onto one of the dining room chairs.

Maggie walked to the door of the *cave* on the other side of the kitchen. "Any preferences?"

"I like any of Laurent's."

"He has others down there, too," Maggie said. "He likes for us to drink wines other than just the ones we make. A Côtes du Rhône, or a nice Rosé maybe?"

"*Anything* but a Côtes du Rhône."

Maggie laughed and snapped on the light over the stairs leading to the basement. "You came to Provence and won't drink a Côtes du Rhône? I think it's practically a mandate here."

"Well, certain ones affect me worse than others. I can't stand a Château Saint Cosmo for example. It gives me a terrible headache."

"Saint Cosmo? That's a new one on me. God, the French will make anyone a saint." They both laughed.

Maggie went to the *cave* intending to fetch a bottle of whatever caught her eye, but something nagged at her in the far recesses of her mind. Like a searing bolt from the depths of her memory, an electric light briefly illuminated in her head—flashing an idea, a memory—and then went dark again, leaving behind a feeling of dread.

Must be the basement. She never stepped into it without a feeling of dread creeping up her back. It was a small room with a series of high, ground-level windows, and was the only room in the house that was air conditioned, although Maggie was sure so deep in the ground it was probably plenty cold enough all by itself.

Laurent had erected shelving and racks on both sides of the longest part of the room. She knew he had some method of organization, but since he normally fetched the wines from the cellar she had no idea what it was. She shivered and looked at the long rows and triple-stacked shelves of bottles, punt-side facing outward.

Laurent need never know they drank a white with his *boeuf en daube*, she thought. She started to pull a bottle free from its slot, when she hesitated, aware that she was still feeling unsettled. Driven by an urge she couldn't immediately understand, Maggie pried her smartphone out of her jeans pocket and scrolled to the notes she kept on it. The second she realized what she was doing, a light sweat popped out on her forehead.

"You okay down there? Didn't miss a step, did you?" Haley called. Maggie could tell Haley was no longer in the dining room. Her voice sounded like it was coming from the kitchen now.

"No, I'm fine," Maggie called back, hearing the artificial lightness in her own voice.

In the time it took to recognize what she was doing, Maggie

knew—before she ever found the entry on her phone—what her notes would say.

After her conversation with the concierge, she'd jotted down the name of the wine that was sent up to Lanie that night—the name of the bottle of Côtes du Rhône that had gone missing from Lanie's room.

The bottle that had killed her.

A Château de Saint Cosme.

CHAPTER 21

The proprietor of the restaurant led the way to a table by the window. Laurent had been there once or twice before. A few miles from Nice, *Le Matin* had a very evolved menu, but mainly it featured a lack of the high prices typically found in a restaurant so close to Nice.

He knew Ben was surprised when they pulled off the A8 and into the unassuming little parking lot. He probably thought Laurent intended to cut his throat for his earlier behavior. Laurent shrugged as he picked up the menu.

People must eat.

The bistro was small and undiscovered, the way Laurent preferred it. He ordered for both of them. Maggie's brother knew no French; it was easier this way. After the waiter took their order, Laurent regarded Ben across the table. They had spoken not a single word in the two-hour drive from Domaine St-Buvard.

Ben watched him closely and then cleared his throat. "I imagine you were surprised when I asked you to escort me."

Laurent raised an eyebrow but said nothing.

The waiter brought a bottle of wine, which Laurent approved without tasting. The server poured their glasses and disappeared.

Ben cleared his throat again, and this time reached into his jacket pocket and extricated the same thick envelope he had shown Laurent earlier. He touched the bandage across his nose and laid the envelope on the table in front of Laurent.

"Before I forget or before the police take all my personal belongings," Ben said, his voice nasal and thick, "I wanted to make sure you had these." He fanned out the sheaf of papers and photographs onto the starched white tablecloth between them. "I won't be needing them where I'm going."

Laurent didn't speak.

"I'm not going to apologize for how things went down," Ben said, staring out the window at the parking lot. "You wouldn't believe it anyway and there's no point. Suffice to say, things got out of hand." He touched his bandaged nose again and laughed. "Frankly, I think I went a little mad. It actually feels a relief to just let everything...happen now."

The waiter brought their starters, two plates of golden fried calamari with mini-bowls of red pepper and feta dipping sauce.

"You didn't kill Lanie," Laurent said, reaching for his wine.

Ben sipped his own wine and Laurent was impressed that the man was so relaxed.

"I'll tell you," Ben said, "but only if you promise not to turn around and drive us back to St-Buvard once I do."

"I am surprised you think me incapable of lying to you."

"Whatever happened to honor among thieves?"

"It's a myth."

They ate in silence. Laurent knew Ben would tell him in his own time.

"I love my wife," Ben said. "There's probably nobody in the world who's ever seen us together who would believe that, but I do. And I am about to do the one thing in my life that doesn't make me want to retch. After two years of feeling hunted, guilty and like the biggest prick on the planet, can you imagine how great that feels?"

Chapter 21

"It *won't* once you're inside," Laurent remarked dryly.

"I know," Ben said quietly. "But at this moment I know I'm doing the right thing. And I can't ever remember feeling better."

The server came with their *moules frites* and they focused on their meal without further conversation. Laurent paid the bill, and picked up the envelope of incriminating photos. As they walked to the car, Ben stopped to take in a big breath of fresh air.

"I think I'm always going to remember this moment," Ben said. "This moment on a perfect summer night in the south of France where I did a noble thing."

Laurent grunted and slid into the driver's seat.

"There are no other copies," Ben said as he buckled his seatbelt and Laurent pulled back onto the A8, heading once more toward Nice. "I don't know whether it was seeing all the cute pictures of Jem on Facebook that Maggie posted or hearing my parents gush about how his was the most significant birth since Jesus, but Haley became obsessed with him right after he was born."

Laurent felt a tingling in the back of his neck, as if he were forgetting something. Was it something Ben said? He gripped the steering wheel tighter. Hadn't everything fallen into place now? He had Ben's evidence against him, the vineyard was saved...

"I mean, I knew she was doing Internet research," Ben said as he watched the scenery fly by, "but I thought it was about Provence, you know? I didn't know it was about you until we got to France. By then, she'd hired private investigators to help find the bits she couldn't."

"To what end?" Laurent asked.

"Because of this whole infertility business, she's become obsessed about who does and doesn't deserve to have kids. She was convinced you were a bad influence on Jemmy."

"Her intention was to have Maggie raise Jemmy alone?"

"I hate to say it because it really makes her sound bat-shit crazy, but I think she had some idea that *we* would somehow end up with Jemmy."

"In order to do that, wouldn't she also need to get rid of Maggie?" There was that feeling again, only now it was an agitated flush that crept up the back of his neck and made him want to punch something.

"Don't be ridiculous."

Laurent slowed down, glancing at the sign that indicated the next exit was ten kilometers away, Nice twelve.

"Your wife has already killed once," Laurent said. "Give me your cell phone."

Ben handed him his phone. "You're wrong, Laurent. Haley thinks Maggie doesn't *want* Jemmy. With you gone, she thinks Maggie will be happy to give him up."

"Your wife is indeed insane. The call went to voicemail." Laurent swerved the car into the median and climbed over the cement curb to reach the other side of A8 heading west.

They were at least two hours from St-Buvard. One, if he hurried.

∼

Maggie grabbed the bottle of wine. Her hands were shaking so much she knew there was a very distinct possibility she was going to drop it. She clutched the bottle to her chest.

Haley knew the name of the wine bottle that had been used to club Lanie to death. Not even the police knew that. Only Maggie, the concierge—and Lanie's murderer knew it.

"What is taking so long, Maggie?" Haley called from the top of the stairs.

Maggie saw Haley backlit against the kitchen light. For a moment, Maggie was reminded of her night in the abbey. The frigidity of the *cave*, the light coming from way up high...the feeling of building dread.

Ben never really confessed. He never actually said he did it. He just let me think he did.

Every piece of evidence Maggie had against Ben worked for Haley, too. *In some cases, better.*

She took a deep breath and began to climb up the stairs. Haley took a step backward, and Maggie prayed she wouldn't see her hands tremble.

All she has to do is shut the door on me. The thought of being trapped again in darkness and the cold made Maggie run the last few steps up the stairs.

"I hope it's the blood of Christ or something for as long as you took picking it out," Haley said.

Maggie noticed Haley didn't smile when she said that. Did she normally smile at her own jokes?

"I just can't tell you how much I appreciate your taking care of the kids," Maggie said, feeling a swelling of relief to be back in the well-lit kitchen.

"You already said that," Haley said, frowning. "I did it for the kids and, really, for myself."

What if Haley found out about Lanie's pregnancy? Wouldn't that be all it took? Or the fact that Lanie was trying to blackmail Ben?

Maggie stood in the kitchen facing Haley, her breath coming in quick pants.

It's true Ben doesn't have an alibi for that night...but of course neither does Haley.

"What's the matter with you, Maggie? You look like you saw a ghost down there. Was it your friend Connor?"

Maggie dropped the wine bottle and it smashed into hundreds of shards across the hard tile floor of the kitchen. The rich Bordeaux wine splashed onto her slacks.

"Jesus, Maggie!" Haley jumped away from the mess and grabbed a handful of the cloth towels Laurent kept in a stack on the counter. "I can't believe you just did that."

"How...how did you know about Connor?" Maggie asked, her eyes on Haley.

"What? Well, your parents were here when it happened, weren't they? You don't think they're not scarred for life when someone is murdered on the floor below them on Thanksgiving Day? You don't think they don't still talk about it?"

"Well...I don't appreciate the ghost reference," Maggie said haltingly. "Connor was a friend and it was horrible."

Haley scraped up the bigger pieces of glass and dumped the wine-soaked towels in the kitchen garbage. Maggie's eyes went to the sight of the broken glass on the kitchen floor sitting in a brown and red puddle.

"Well, excuse me," Haley said sarcastically. "I had no idea you took it so hard. That's hardly the impression we hear of you back home. Do you want *me* to go down and get the damn wine?"

"I'm out of the mood for wine," Maggie said, bringing her lips together tersely to keep them from trembling. "And I shouldn't be drinking anyway."

She shouldn't have said that. She knew as soon as the words were out of her mouth that she shouldn't have said that. The look on Haley's face was one of shock, then revelation and finally... hatred. The evolution of expressions chilled Maggie, and when she looked down at Haley's hands she saw she gripped a large shard of broken bottle.

"You're pregnant?" Haley said, her eyes wide and boring a hole in Maggie's midriff.

"I...no," Maggie said, hurriedly. "No, but we're trying again. So I shouldn't be drinking."

"You *are* pregnant," Haley said. "I can see it in your face. You're lying to me." Suddenly her face opened up and she narrowed her eyes. "Did Ben tell you about Lanie?"

Oh, this isn't good. Maggie's eyes darted again to the shard in Haley's hand. *This is not what I want to happen right now.*

"He told you, didn't he? That I killed her? That slut? Well, did he also tell you that he screwed her the night of my reunion? Did he happen to leave that little bit out? *And* that she got pregnant by him?"

It was the one piece of evidence that never fit, Maggie realized, the one piece she had deliberately chosen to ignore—the fact the killer had written *slut* on Lanie's forehead. There was no way Ben would have done that. He didn't have that kind of passion.

"You wrote on her," Maggie said, her eye on the large shard still in Haley's hand. Suddenly, she became aware that there was something different about the house. Something she'd noticed in the back of her mind but couldn't put her finger on. Something stridently wrong—*wrong in-her-bones wrong*—that she couldn't place.

"I did," Haley said. "There's nothing like old-fashioned cursive to get your point across. Lanie was always the master of the snarky text, the ace of the bon mot. It wouldn't have been right not to give her the last word. So I did." She shrugged. Maggie watched in horror as blood dripped from Haley's hand onto the floor and she realized Haley was squeezing the shard in her fury...and didn't even feel it.

Haley noticed where Maggie was looking and glanced down at her hand. She looked back at Maggie. "I don't know what you think you're doing, Maggie," she said. "Getting pregnant again. You can't even take care of the child you have. Plus, you'll be a single mother. And *that* is a scary thought."

Maggie felt a strong chill invade her chest. "What are you talking about?"

Haley affected a patient tone, but Maggie saw the gleam in her eye that showed her excitement. "I've got proof that shows Laurent was a conman operating on the Côte d'Azur," Haley said. "Your husband is going to prison."

Was she lying...or crazy?

Maggie licked her lips. *I'm going to go with crazy.*

Haley idly scraped her foot in what was left of the glass and wine puddle on the floor. It made a loud and discordant grating sound that seemed to echo through the kitchen. The second Maggie heard it, she realized what was wrong. The house was too quiet. She looked in the direction of the baby monitor.

The power light wasn't on.

Fear ratcheted up her spine until she was sure it was showing in her face. The monitor was always on. Haley was anal about it being on so she could hear every gurgle, every cough, every potential call.

What reason would she have for deliberately turning it off? Because there could be no doubt it was deliberate.

Haley still held the bloody shard. There was also no doubt in Maggie's mind that was deliberate, too.

Maggie forced herself to appear calm. She stood with her back to the dining room, facing Haley, who stood with her back to the open *cave* door. Between them on the floor were the remaining bits of glass from the broken bottle. Maggie forced herself not to telegraph her intentions by looking at the *cave* door.

Her sling kept her arm pressed tightly to her chest and she leaned a hip against the counter to help support her.

"You're wrong, Haley. Ben confessed," Maggie said. "He's turning himself in for Lanie's murder as we speak."

Haley jerked her head back. "You're lying," she said in a high voice. Her eyes flicked away from Maggie for a moment as if trying to digest this. The second she looked away, Maggie pushed herself off the counter and shoved Haley hard in the chest. Haley shrieked and grabbed for Maggie but she was off balance and went easily through the *cave* door, falling backward down the first few steps.

Maggie slammed the door shut, knowing she only had seconds before Haley would be up and wrenching at the doorknob. Even if Maggie had two working arms, Haley—a tennis player—was much stronger. Maggie grabbed the latch, her fingers slick with sweat and her injured wrist screaming in pain. She slid the latch shut just as she felt the door jar under her hands.

"You bitch! Open this door! I'll kill you, Maggie! Open it!"

Maggie backed away, watching the door vibrate and jump with every blow from inside, then turned and ran up the stairs. She fell once on the smooth, slippery stairs and instinctively put out her injured hand to catch her fall. The pain shot up her arm and she cried out. The pounding on the door behind her was growing louder.

Dear God, don't let her have hurt him. Please God, kill me now but please don't let her have hurt him.

The door to Jemmy's bedroom was shut but not locked and Maggie flung it open and ran inside. It was dark, but moonlight peeked in through his curtains providing a shaft of light that dimly lit the room. Downstairs, she heard the distinct sounds of wood splintering as Haley battered at the door with her shoulder or whatever she was finding in the basement.

Maggie ran to Jemmy's crib, fighting to keep her sobs of terror from overtaking her, trying to think of where she would go, how she would get him and Zouzou out and away. She jerked back the covers.

The crib was empty.

CHAPTER 22

Maggie flung the covers out of the crib, her mind was racing, refusing to accept what her eyes were seeing.

The baby monitor was off to hide the fact that there was no baby upstairs. She looked around the room in building hysteria, knowing he wasn't there.

This can't be happening. He has to be here. He has to be.

A half empty bottle of Maggie's allergy medicine, diphenhydramine, sat on the nightstand. Her skin crawled as she turned and ran out the door and down the hall toward Zouzou's room. As she ran, she realized she wasn't hearing any noises from downstairs.

Maggie tore open the bedroom door and froze.

Haley straightened up over the small bed with Zouzou in her arms...and an eight-inch chef's knife pressed to the baby's neck.

Maggie's heart pounded. Zouzou was still half-asleep, providing no resistance, thank God. Maggie scanned the room in case...

"He's not here," Haley said calmly.

"Where is he? What have you done with him?" Maggie's voice sounded strong and menacing. Not at all how she felt.

"Let's just say he's safe...for now."

"What did you do with him?" Maggie took a step toward her and Haley pressed the knife against Zouzou, pinching the child until she whimpered and tried to shake her head and move away from the knife.

"You don't need to know that," Haley said, shifting the weight of the child in her arms, but keeping the knife to the child's throat. "All you need to know is that he'll die if I don't get back to him soon."

"Why are you doing this?"

"You really don't know? God, I knew you were clueless in high school."

"I don't know what you think you're doing, Haley—"

"I'm righting a few wrongs here, Maggie, okay? A few *life* wrongs. A few universe wrongs. You think you can break the law and then enjoy a charmed life after that? Is that fair?"

"What in the world are you talking about?"

"Your husband. He's a felon and thanks to me, he's going to jail. And you? God, where do I start? You don't deserve Jemmy. Until your little performance today I was half convinced you'd let me just take him, but okay, so you want the world to think you're a loving mother. Whatever. It won't do you any good. You know that, right?"

"I know you're going to let Ben go to prison for what you did."

Haley made a snorting sound of derision. "Ben is going to prison one way or the other."

"Is this payback for how he's hurt you?"

Haley grinned. "I love that. Everyone thinks he hits me. That's hysterical."

"You...your black eye when you came last week..."

"I got that wrestling with Lanie before I bashed her brains in. Ben's never raised a hand to me. God, you don't know him at all do you?"

Chapter 22

Maggie's mind raced, but all she could see in her mind's eye was Jemmy sleeping...somewhere in the dark.

"Why did he confess?"

"I don't know. He loves me? Go into the hallway, Maggie. I'd like to get this over with. As I said, Jemmy doesn't have unlimited time where he is and I need to get to him soon."

"Please, Haley. For the love of God, you acted like you cared for him. I'm begging you—"

"I *do* care for him," Haley said fiercely. Zouzou, now fully awake, squealed in Haley's arms. The knife had made a bloody line on the baby's throat. "More than *you* do. I'm ten times the mother you are. In fact, if you really want to help him, you'll do what's necessary to keep him alive."

"Anything. Tell me." Maggie watched Zouzou arch her back; her whines were full-blown cries now.

Haley pointed to the top of the stairs. "Stand over there. And do not think about charging me. I will kill Zouzou and you'll never, and I mean *never,* find Jemmy and then he'll die too. Is that what you want?"

Maggie backed away, her hands up, and walked slowly to the top of the stairs. The bottle of diphenhydramine had to mean Haley drugged Jem to keep him quiet. Calling for him would be futile.

"You're not afraid Zouzou will tell everyone you cut her with a knife?"

"Nobody believes children. I'll say she was upset and got it all wrong. Stop right there," Haley said as Maggie went to the top of the stairs. "Okay, so here's how this next part goes. I can personally name three people who will swear that you habitually leave laundry baskets at the top of the stairs just waiting to be tripped over. Believe me, it will not be a surprise to anyone who knows you."

"You're going to push me down the stairs?"

"I'm hoping I won't have to touch you. See, there's only one way for you to save Jemmy and that's by killing yourself, Maggie. You should be glad you have such a wonderful way to prove how much you love him."

Maggie could hardly hear Haley over Zouzou's screams. She watched the child wriggle to get away from the knife but Haley held her firmly, her eyes glued to Maggie's face.

"You'll have the accident that nobody will be surprised happened, and with Laurent in prison, I'll end up with Jemmy." She laughed. "Think of it; I'll have everything you have. And believe me, I'll do a better job with it than you ever could."

"I'm surprised you don't want to steal my husband. You're going after everything else I have."

"The last thing I want is another husband. I'll settle for your house, your life, your child and your best friend—oh yeah, and your parents. With you, Ben and Elise gone, I'm looking pretty good. A far cry from where we were in high school, huh, when you weren't interested in being pals."

"What are you talking about? You were popular."

"I was *lonely*. Turn around. I hear forensics these days are pretty good about being able to tell which way you were facing when you fell, even in a backwater like France I imagine. I don't want them saying you were pushed."

Maggie turned to face the foyer, her arms by her side. The stairs were slick and steep. She stared down them, her mind whirling in frantic circles. An unbidden flash of memory came to her of Ben, her and Elise sitting at the top of the stairs on Christmas morning. She could hear her brother and sister whispering and laughing. She could smell the pine needles of the Christmas tree in the living room below.

"Oh," Haley said, "I forgot the clothes basket. It's right there off to your right, but I need your fingerprints on it, Maggie, especially since I haven't seen you touch the basket in a few days. So if you would kindly do the honors."

Chapter 22

Maggie turned to see the laundry basket a couple feet from her. "You want me to..."

"You know what I want you to do," Haley said, impatiently. "May I remind you it is not very comfortable where Jemmy is and the longer you wait—stop it!" Haley shook Zouzou, who was in the process of throwing a full-blown tantrum, the knife slipping out of position for the few seconds Haley needed to reposition the squirming child.

A few seconds were all Maggie needed.

She hurled herself at Haley, grabbing for the knife and pushing Zouzou away at the same time. The child shrieked and fell from Haley's grasp but Maggie didn't have time to see if she was hurt.

"Cut me," Maggie panted as she grappled with Haley's knife hand, "and nobody will believe it was an accident.."

Maggie fought to push past the pain of her injured wrist. An image of Jemmy crying, afraid, came roaring into her head and the outrage it triggered blazed through Maggie like wildfire. *How dare you hurt my child!*

She gave one last surge of strength and wrenched the knife out of Haley's hands. Haley stared at her empty hand and then at Maggie with astonishment.

"Where is he?" Maggie screamed, holding the knife as if ready to bring it down on Haley.

"Go ahead and kill me!" Haley yelled, her face twisted into a visage of pain and grief. "He'll die without me!" Haley turned and bolted for the stairs.

"Don't you do it!" Maggie yelled, grabbing Haley's arm. But Maggie's uninjured hand was holding the knife, and Haley easily twisted free.

The front door flung open, crashing with a loud bang against the foyer wall. Laurent filled the doorway and Maggie watched him look toward the living room before seeing movement at the top of the stairs.

He charged for the stairs just as Haley launched into the air. Maggie watched in horror as she plummeted, arms windmilling desperately as if she'd changed her mind, as if to stop her terrible plunge. She fell in slow motion, graceful and macabre, her scream aborted harshly when she hit the ancient tiles of the lower steps with a sickening thud that reverberated through the bare halls of the house.

"Haley, no!" Ben screamed, pushing past Laurent. Haley lay halfway down, her legs twisted behind her on the higher steps.

Laurent looked up at Maggie on the upper landing and she saw his face flush with relief. Ben pulled Haley's broken body into his arms, making soft, guttural noises. Sounds Maggie never heard her brother make before.

"Laurent," Maggie said urgently, "she's taken Jemmy and put him somewhere." She knelt next to Zouzou, who was curled up on the floor, her thumb in her mouth but finally silent.

"Call an ambulance!" Ben screamed at them. "For the love of God."

Laurent bounded up the steps, touching Maggie on the shoulder to confirm she was all in one piece and then scooped up Zouzou. Maggie watched the child wrap her arms around his neck and bury her face in his chest. He looked at Maggie. She had never seen such fear in his eyes before, and for a moment it robbed her of her strength before she felt the beginnings of an unholy fury descend upon her.

"She said it's some place where he can't stay for long," Maggie said as she hurried down the steps and crouched near Ben. She ignored her brother's anguished face and focused on Haley. Ben had pulled her around so that her head and shoulders rested against his chest, but the blood where she had lain was pooled and thick. Maggie saw that Haley was unconscious.

Just as well. She wouldn't tell me anyway.

Maggie picked up Haley's hands. They were bloody from the wine bottle shard she'd held in the kitchen, and from Zouzou's scratches. She looked at Haley's fingernails. Polished, with bits of skin under them.

Likely mine, Maggie thought, standing and looking at the body, forcing herself to take her time, not to rush, *to think*. She was aware of Laurent behind her on the stairs. He was breathing hard, his body radiating an energy that seemed to vibrate in the air around him but she couldn't look at him. She needed to focus on what Haley could tell her.

She knelt down again and touched Haley's knee. A bloody, white bone pierced free of the linen slacks she wore.

"Leave her alone! Don't touch her!" Ben snarled, trying to push Maggie away. "Somebody call an ambulance!"

"I was asleep for two hours," Maggie said. "And when I awoke, Haley was heating up dinner in the kitchen." She reran the scene in her mind, trying to block out Ben's words, Zouzou's renewed whimpering, and the ever-present temptation to break down at the thought of never seeing her child again.

Maggie fast-forwarded to the moment when she knew Haley was Lanie's killer. She saw the broken bits of green wine bottle and the wet mess surrounding it on the kitchen floor. Not just purple as it should have been in Laurent's spotless kitchen, but dark brown. Among the spilled wine were bits of mud. Maggie grabbed one of Haley's feet, ignoring Ben's protests.

The tread of the shoe had a thin layer of mud on it.

"She took him outside," Maggie said, standing up. "She drugged him so he wouldn't cry, and took him outside."

"The well," Laurent said, turning and rocketing out of the room through the French doors. Maggie ran behind him, stopping only long enough to snatch up the flashlight they kept by the door for when she let Petit Four out.

As soon as she ran through the door, Maggie saw it was raining. Hard. She directed the beam of light in front of Laurent. He still carried Zouzou in his arms, his long legs pulling farther and farther ahead of her.

Maggie saw the well come into view at the edge of the vineyard, a ghostly dark stump in the gloom of night.

How long ago had she put him there? Three hours ago? The well would fill up after every rainfall. *Did Haley know that? Is that why she said he only had a short time until he died?*

Laurent was at the well now. She watched him set Zouzou on the ground and begin to pry the boards off the top. She ran to him, breathless and drenched from the rain.

"Jemmy! Jemmy!" she screamed as she picked up Zouzou, the child shivering in the rain even though the night was warm.

She stepped back as Laurent threw boards behind him until he had a big enough hole to peer into.

"Jean-Michael!" he called, his voice frantic with fear.

Maggie pulled him away from the hatch and shoved Zouzou into his arms. "I can fit through the opening," she said, shining the flashlight down into the dark well. The bottom wasn't visible but she could hear water falling on water. It was filling up. She handed Laurent the flashlight and he boosted her to the lip of the well. His hand squeezed her upper arm, as if he might change his mind and pull her back, but she didn't wait. She stuck her feet against the slick sides of the aged cistern, her hands resting on the rim, and shot down, her feet and hands sliding down the sides.

"Light, Laurent!" she called, but the interior was illuminated before she finished speaking.

Would that madwoman really have put a baby in here? She fell the final ten feet to the bottom, her hands serving only to check her descent. When her feet touched the floor, the water was up to her knees. An icy fear raced up her spine. *If he was in the well....* She forced herself not to finish the thought, instead dropping to her knees to feel the rough floor of the well with shaking hands.

"He's not here!" she yelled up to Laurent. The rain sluiced down her face, plastering her hair to her head and neck. She bowed her head and screamed a long howl of despair and frustration.

The long minutes ticked by as she waited for Laurent to come back with a rope. She closed her eyes to the dark and the cold—it was freezing fifteen feet into the ground—and prayed.

When Laurent finally returned and threw the rope down to her, she secured it around her waist and let him haul her up, using her feet along the sides of the wall to try to walk her way up. Once out, she lay panting at the foot of the well while he wrapped a towel around her shoulders.

As soon as he touched her, she began to cry, her strength seeping out of her. Her shoulders shook convulsively with her sobs as he gathered her into his arms and held her tightly. She knew he wanted to go, to do anything but sit here when Jem was in danger somewhere. She forced herself to push Laurent away.

Plenty of time later to grieve if it comes to that, she thought bitterly.

"We are not finished yet," he said in her ear as he helped her to her feet.

"*Oncle* Laurent," Zouzou whimpered, wrapping her arms around his leg. "Zouzou's cold. I don't like this game."

Laurent lifted her up and spoke to her in French, all the while his eyes searching the vineyard, the gardens, even the roof of the house.

Jemmy could be anywhere.

"Aunt Haley said we can't play the game in the rain," Zouzou sniffled. "And I'm hungry. I want my cocoa."

"What game?" Maggie said, snapping her head in Zouzou's direction. "What game of Aunt Haley's?"

"She only does it with Jemmy," Zouzou said. "She says I'm too big."

"Where, *mon chou*?" Laurent asked her. "Where do they play the game?"

"*Tu sait*," Zouzou said. "In the swing in the orchard. The bough? I know the song real good but she says I'm too big."

"Bring her!" Maggie called over her shoulder as she dropped the towel and sprinted for the orchard. Laurent had built a swing for Zouzou there, but just possibly...

The orchard looked eerie and unwelcoming in the dark and the rain. Maggie never came here. The apples were sour and the trees themselves only good for making fragrant kindling in the fireplace on winter evenings. She knew where Laurent had hung the swing. It was the prettiest part of the orchard, affording a view back down the hill of the house and the first quadrant of the vineyard. Maggie found the swing and stopped. She turned back to Laurent and Zouzou.

"Where do they play the game, Zouzou?"

The little girl pointed past Maggie to a pair of apple trees, off the path and far back from where anyone might take a pleasant after-dinner stroll. Maggie ran to the trees and flashed her light at them. The rain was coming down harder now and it served as a greater impasse to clear vision than even the night did. She saw nothing.

In frustration, she raked the light from one side of the two trees to the other.

"Dammit!" she said. "I don't see anything!"

Laurent strode past Maggie to the larger of the two trees. The trunk forked in a deformed display of branch and leaves. Maggie watched Zouzou turn to Laurent and talk but she couldn't hear her words. And then she saw Zouzou point to the saddle of the forked trunk.

Maggie ran.

She pushed past Laurent and ran to the crux of where the two trunks split at chest height and saw a cardboard wine cask. It was dark and hidden by the leaves and the night. Dropping the flashlight, she grabbed the box and lifted it away from the tree, hearing water slosh around inside as the sodden sides began to collapse in her hands.

Inside, his face just inches above the water collected in the bottom, Jemmy opened his eyes and blinked as the rain hit him in the face. He opened his mouth wide and began to cry.

EPILOGUE

The crunch of the gravel beneath her shoes always felt so satisfying, Maggie thought as she walked to the car parked in the driveway. She shifted Jemmy to her other hip and opened the car door. Grace followed her. She wore a long, flowing dressing gown—like something from the forties, Maggie thought, with her hair piled loosely on the top of her head and naturally still gorgeous with not a speck of makeup on. Grace held a coffee cup to her lips and watched Maggie tuck the baby into his car seat.

"I still cannot believe I missed all the excitement," Grace said. "Zouzou can't stop talking about it."

"I'm just glad she's not damaged for life," Maggie said, stopping to kiss Jemmy on the nose.

Grace walked to the passenger side and slipped inside, setting her coffee on the dashboard. Maggie put her seatbelt on and looked at her expectedly.

"It's just that we didn't really get a chance to talk," Grace said, not looking at her.

"Grace, it's okay. I'm not pissed. If anything, I owe you an apology."

"She totally had me fooled."

"She had us all fooled."

"It's because she was so damn helpful all the time."

"I know. I hate it when people do that."

"No, seriously. You know kids can be relentless and they want every single piece of you all the time. It was just so nice to...to hand Zouzou off for just a little break."

"I'm sure it doesn't mean every person who offers to relieve you is a sociopath," Maggie said dryly.

"Good thing, since I obviously can't tell the difference." Grace sipped her coffee before speaking again. "So it turns out all the people on the tour were just your basic not-very-nice but non-murderous people?"

"Pretty much," Maggie said. "I mean Olivier is a total nut job. He loved Lanie and blamed me and Dee-Dee and Randall for what happened to her."

"Why did he blame you?"

"Well, she told him I betrayed her in high school."

"Goodness. How?"

"I have no idea and I probably never will. But she got it in her head that I'd let her down and she carried it with her. Olivier seemed to think he was honoring her in death or something by trying to hurt me."

"And Dee-Dee?"

Maggie shrugged. "He just knew Lanie hated her and so he added her to his list."

"But he was sleeping with Desiree?"

"Apparently. He was in on the raging bull attack with Desiree. But I'm sure he would've gotten around to taking care of Desiree eventually, too."

"Has he been released?"

"No. He was cleared of the murder charge, but he's still on the hook for what he tried to do to me."

"I still can't believe you spent six hours in a medieval dungeon, darling. I miss all the fun."

"Yeah, trust me, you do," Maggie said dryly.

Maggie watched the leaves scuttle across the gravel driveway and wondered if it was a precursor to the famed *mistral* heading their way.

"What will happen to Haley now?" Grace asked quietly.

"I guess she'll push for an insanity plea," Maggie said. "Take it from me, there's nobody more qualified for it."

"You want her punished."

"I honestly try not to feel that way. She caused so much pain, but I know she's sick."

"By the way, Laurent told me the good news."

"Oh! Grace, I'm sorry. I wanted to tell you."

"Don't be sorry. It's amazing and I'm delighted. You and Laurent are the best parents I know. There should be more kids on the receiving end of all that."

Maggie shook her head. "I don't feel very good about the kind of mother I was. But I know I adore Jemmy beyond reason."

"Well, that's a good start," Grace said, patting her hand. "Unless, of course, you start shoving people down stairs as a result of it."

"Who's the guy, by the way?"

"Oh. My weekend in Aix? Turned out to be nothing," Grace said, picking up her cup and opening her car door. "Will you be home for dinner?"

"Are you going to tell me about it?"

"Of course. By and by. I'm sorry we misconnected, Maggie. You know nobody can take your place, don't you?"

Maggie smiled. "I do. But it's nice to hear."

ON A DAY LIKE TODAY—SUNNY and bright but with a special spice in the air—Maggie could feel the coming autumn in her bones. In her mind, as desirable as summer was to the tourists and anybody else who liked a warm clime, blue seas and ever-present ice cream cones, surely it was the autumn in Provence that was the most beautiful.

She glanced in the rearview mirror at Jemmy. He seemed to be watching the scenery, his little face frowning as if attempting to process the images as they spun by.

Dear God, will I ever stop cherishing the fact that I still have him? She drove down the main road that led to the village but that also bordered the far reaches of their vineyard. The pickers, if they had vehicles, would park along the road and along the verge of their property. As she approached, she saw a scattering of tents erected along the perimeter of their property.

It felt nice to know what was going on with the vineyard. Always before, she knew they were harvesting because strange people would show up at her door asking for water. Now, Laurent sat down with her and explained why he was doing what he was doing. And although he hadn't gone so far as to ask her for an opinion—nor would she have an intelligent one to give on harvesting techniques—it was still nice to be included. In fact, even though she had already felt the pinch of the purse strings tightening in just the two weeks since he'd told her about the co-op situation, amazingly, the air of communication and sharing between them had more than made up for it.

If we're going to be poor, at least we'll be poor together, she thought as she pulled up onto the verge.

"Dada?" Jemmy said from the backseat. A quick glance at him showed the baby pointing out the window. When she followed his gaze, she saw Laurent, taller than all the other men in the field, walking toward them, his stride purposeful, his face serious and bronzed from the sun.

"Yep, that's your daddy," Maggie said, rolling down the passenger side window and waving to Laurent as he approached the car.

"You are on your way to Arles?" he asked, reaching into the car to give Jemmy's foot a squeeze.

"I am. You forgot your lunch." She pointed to the box on the seat next to her.

"Ah, *bon*," he said, reaching in and plucking it out of the car.

"Things going okay? Good pickers this year?"

He shrugged. "As long as I watch them," he said, turning to regard the field. She knew he loved harvest time, loved the sun, the hard outdoor work, the baskets and baskets of grapes every evening loaded on the flatbed back of the tractor. He turned to her. "You have not forgotten about tonight, *chérie*?"

His investor, Adele, along with some of the other vintners in their new business, was coming over for dinner and drinks. Maggie was delighted that Laurent had set up a mini-*degustation* at their house instead of meeting with his new associates in the village café as they so easily might have done.

"I'll be back in plenty of time," she assured him. "Don't lose track of time, yourself," she said. "Will Jean-Luc and Danielle come?" She hadn't seen their elderly neighbors in several weeks and was anxious to catch up with Danielle.

"*Bien sûr*," he said, clapping a hand on the car as if to release her. "Drive safe, *chérie*. Tell your brother hello." She watched him smile a wry smile and felt a flood of affection in his direction.

Dear God, will I ever stop cherishing the fact that I still have him?

IT WOULD TAKE NEARLY an hour to reach Arles. She selected a playlist of French songs on Jemmy's music player and turned the volume down so he could hear but she could talk on the phone.

"Ready, champ?" she said to him, glancing again in the rearview mirror. "Off on an adventure with Mommy?"

Jemmy grinned and stuck a pacifier in his mouth as the first few notes of the songs began to play.

Maggie turned her attention back to the road and punched in

Annie's phone number. She'd texted her earlier in the day to expect her call, so she wasn't surprised when Annie picked up on the second ring.

"Hello, darling!" Annie said. "I was waiting for your call."

"You sound good," Maggie said with surprise. Although she'd already spoken to Annie several times about the turn of events in the murder case—and especially the news about Olivier and his involvement—she was amazed to hear the energy and interest in the older woman's voice.

"I am much better every day that goes by," Annie said. "Do you have an update for me?"

"Well, I heard that Bob Randall is closing down production on his television series," Maggie said. "I forget the actual wording he used in the public relations release, but it doesn't matter since I'm sure it probably wasn't the truth anyway."

"Oh, my."

"I also heard that Desiree assaulted a waitress in Cannes over something and is facing deportation."

"Deportation?"

"Yeah, it seems the quintessential Frenchwoman isn't French at all. She's Swiss."

"Goodness."

"I don't have any information on Janet and Jim, and you're up to speed on my crazy sister-in-law. Or at least as up to speed as I am."

"And Olivier?"

Maggie took in a long breath and glanced at Jem in the backseat. She watched his eyes slowly close as he fought sleep.

"I guess you could say he loved Lanie to a fault," Maggie said.

"I still feel sorry for the boy," Annie said quietly.

Maggie cleared her throat. "Annie, I need to say something to you and I hope you can hear me and that you won't take it wrong but I really need to say it."

"What in the world, dear?"

"I...I hope you can give some thought to the idea of forgiving yourself for whatever you think you did or didn't do to Lanie."

Maggie heard a quick inhalation of breath, but Annie didn't respond.

"There were some things wrong with Lanie," Maggie said, "and I mean some really serious things wrong with her, but I don't think those things were your fault."

Maggie let the silence rest between them until she heard a sigh emit from Annie's end.

"Thank you, dear," she said quietly, her voice over the line coming to Maggie wavering but strong.

∼

AN HOUR LATER, Maggie sat on one of the curving benches in the park tucked into the Boulevard des Lices in Arles. Gigantic cedars fanned out overhead, shading her and Jemmy from the worst of the late summer sun. She chose this park because it seemed less hectic than most of the children's playgrounds she and Grace visited in Aix and Arles.

Jem reached for the can of orange soda on the bench next to them and she positioned the straw for him.

So much for Mother of the Year.

"Thanks for coming."

He must have walked up from behind because she didn't see him until he spoke, right before he slid onto the bench next her.

"Sure," she said, scooting over to give him more room than he needed. She hadn't seen her brother since the night the ambulance had taken him and Haley to Aix. She'd spoken with him on the phone a few times but, amazingly, Laurent had talked to him more than she had. This meeting was also Laurent's idea, although Maggie wasn't sure whether or not Ben had put him up to it.

It didn't really sound like something her brother would do.

"When will they move Haley back to Atlanta?" Maggie couldn't bring herself to ask how Haley was doing. She reminded herself to feel bad about that later.

"Not sure. As soon as she's stable."

"They expect her to recover?"

Ben looked at Maggie, trying to determine her motive behind the question. Finally, he said, "Probably won't walk again. And there might be some...brain damage."

"I see. Enough to keep her from standing trial."

"You do know she's mentally ill, right? I'm not trying to make excuses for her."

"She killed someone. She tried to kill me."

"I know. Who would know better than me?"

He looked like hell, Maggie thought. He had shaved and his clothes were clean but he clearly hadn't spent any more attention than that on his appearance. Probably hadn't slept. He looked like he'd aged ten years.

"You really didn't know Haley killed Lanie?" she asked him.

"I swear I didn't. Not until the night before...she tried to hurt you."

Jem squealed at the sight of a squirrel and pointed excitedly. Maggie bounced him on her knee to distract him.

"We had a fight that morning when you and Laurent were gone and it came out," Ben said. "I was totally freaked. I had no idea she was that...that.... Anyway, then when you came home and accused me of it, I thought...I don't know."

"You thought this was your chance to be a hero."

"Thank you for making it sound so lame. I figured I was heading to prison anyway and this was what I should do. What Dad would do. Step in and fix it."

"How did it go down with Haley and Lanie? It'll be years before I get the facts from the police."

Ben sighed heavily and rubbed his face with a large hand. "It was stupid. And all my fault."

"I'm listening."

"You already know I hooked up with Lanie in the girls' bathroom at the school reunion."

"Really charming, by the way."

"I haven't been punished enough?"

"Do you think you have? Are you feeling sorry for yourself?"

"Never mind."

"Continue. And Haley found out?"

"No, I confessed. Told you it was stupid. But she forgave me. Or seemed to. And I had so much on my plate with this damn Ordeur mess—"

"What with needing to come over here and extort Laurent's livelihood out of him."

"I can only tell one story at a time, Maggie. Which one do you want to hear?"

"The murder."

He grimaced at her bald statement, but before he could respond Jem reached out and grabbed at Ben's shirt and laughed. Maggie was surprised and began to pull him away when Ben held out his hands.

"May I?" he asked.

"Are you serious?" But she handed the baby to him and watched her brother as he tucked Jem into the crook of his arm and smoothed down the baby's hair.

"You know how many times I looked at this little guy and thought of what might have been?"

"You mean with Lanie's baby?"

Ben nodded miserably. "I had no idea she would be on the tour. That was a serious shock, but worse was the text message I got from her as soon as I arrived telling me she was pregnant and wanted money."

"I'll bet."

Ben turned to glance at her. "You're going to think I'm crazy, but I didn't think it was the worse thing that could happen. I really didn't."

"Getting a one-night-stand pregnant when you're married?"

He shrugged. "Alright. It was bad."

"Another confession to Haley?"

He shook his head. "No. I was pretty sure she couldn't handle it. We'd been trying so hard to get pregnant. But she stumbled onto the text that Lanie sent me." He grimaced. "Thank you, Cloud."

"Oh, snap."

"I guess when she saw that I was still in contact with Lanie—and worse, that she was pregnant—she just cracked."

"How did she get in Lanie's room?"

"Lanie had given me a key. Haley found it, used it, then slipped it under Olivier's door when she…when she was finished. He must have found it and put it in his wallet thinking Lanie had slipped it under the door."

"That's the main reason Olivier was arrested," Maggie said. "The cops pinpointed it was *that* keycard used at the time of the murder."

"I know."

"And by slipping it under his door it shows Haley deliberately tried to pin it on Olivier."

"She's sick, Maggie."

"And Lanie's dead."

"I'm not saying it's fair. It's a damn mess is what it is."

"Okay, now you can tell me about Laurent."

"He hasn't told you?"

"I want to hear it from you."

"Ordeur hired me because they knew I was in trouble. They helped me dig in a little deeper, not that I'm trying to dodge the blame. I did it to myself. But then they offered me a way out: go to France and convince Laurent Dernier—by any means necessary

—to fall in step with the rest of the vintners in the co-op they'd just purchased."

"And they knew they could ask you because they'd specifically recruited someone who knew Laurent's family."

"Yes."

"And because you didn't *really* know Laurent, it wasn't that hard for you to lie to him and try to manipulate him."

"It was never not hard, Maggie."

"Poor you."

"I was desperate. I'm glad for you, little sister, if you've never felt like that before."

"I've felt in fear for my life and for the life of my child. Does that count?"

"I'll never be able to make that up to you. Never."

"You're right."

He looked at her as she reached over and took Jemmy back.

"And then when you couldn't trick Laurent into signing, you pulled out the big guns."

"That was all Haley," Ben said. "She'd started obsessing about you last winter when Jem was born."

"It *wasn't* all Haley," Maggie said, smoothing Jemmy's hair and licking a finger to force his cowlick in place. "You knew where she kept the documents—"

"Yes, alright. I suck. I don't deserve your forgiveness."

"Do you want it?"

He looked at her in surprise. "What? Of course I do. I've apologized to Laurent and he seems ready to move past it."

"So that just leaves me."

"Yeah. Just you."

"Aside from what your crazy wife did, you tried to sabotage my life and put my husband in prison."

"As I said, I'm aware I don't deserve your forgiveness."

They didn't speak for a moment.

"I need to get back," Maggie said, standing. "When does your train come? Are you flying out of Marseille?"

"I won't stop trying to get it," he said quietly. "I am so, so sorry, Maggie. I beg you to forgive me, no matter how long it takes. And if you never do, I swear I'll understand."

"Okay, well, I do forgive you, Ben."

"You do?"

"Of course. I have to. You're my only brother and I love you. I'd just as soon not see you for a while though, which I imagine won't be tricky since you're always a no-show at family gatherings."

"I'll be at Mom and Dad's this Thanksgiving," he said. "And Christmas too," he added quickly.

"Oh. Well, that will be nice for them. I'm afraid I can't make it this year, but you going is a step in the right direction."

"Thank you, Maggie."

"You're welcome, Ben."

JEMMY FELL ASLEEP the minute Maggie buckled him into his car seat for the drive back to Domaine St-Buvard. She found a soothing classic musical station on the radio and relaxed in the driver's seat as she pulled onto the entrance ramp of the D17 toward home.

As far as closure went, she had to admit the afternoon had been a very good idea. *Whoever's* idea it was, she decided with a smile, she fully intended to reward her big, handsome husband for its happy outcome.

As she accelerated, she heard her cell phone vibrating in the console and glanced at the screen. It was Laurent.

"Hi, lover," she said into the speaker. "I'm on my way home right now."

"*Bon.* Everything okay?"

"Good as gold, darling. Are you cooking tonight?"

"*Bien sûr*. Nothing big, just a few *amuse-bouche*. You and Grace and I will eat later after our guests have gone."

"Or not. I still don't have all the pregnancy weight off me from Jemmy, Laurent."

"I forbid you to diet."

"And I forbid you to use that word again."

"Forbid or diet?"

"Both of them, now that I think of it. Besides, you're just trying to keep me fat so no one else will want me."

"Impossible. I am beating your suitors off daily with sticks. Don't rush back, *chérie*, but get here as soon as you can. I must now go watch my *gratin dauphinois*."

"Of course you must. Oh, wait, Laurent, I've been meaning to ask you something, and with our new policy of total disclosure I thought this would be a good time."

"*Oui, chérie?*" he said impatiently.

"Did you really have half a million euros when I met you?"

RECIPE FOR SALADE NIÇOISE

Laurent whips this Provençal staple up at least once a week. It's an easy way to make sure everyone gets their vegetables in the most delicious way possible. Please note, however, that if your tomatoes are not stellar, you should probably make something else.

Otherwise, you will need:
3 TB Fresh lemon juice
2 pound Tuna steaks (canned tuna will do)
5-6 Small potatoes
½ pound Green beans
3 Cups Romaine lettuce
3 Cups Raw spinach leaves
3 very good, very red tomatoes, cut into wedges
3 Eggs, hard-boiled
1 Pepper, green or yellow
½ cup Niçoise olives
2 TB Capers
6 Anchovy fillets

Marinate tuna with the lemon juice for 30 minutes in the fridge. Toss the lemon juice and get the grill ready (if using steaks.) Cook 3-4 minutes each side until medium-well.

Steam the potatoes for 2 minutes, then add the green beans and continue to steam another 7-8 minutes.

Arrange lettuce and spinach on a platter. Place tuna, green beans, tomatoes, potatoes, eggs and the pepper on top. Finish off with olives, capers and anchovy fillets. Drizzle any kind of garlic-basil vinaigrette on top.

Laurent's Garlic-Basil Vinaigrette: Combine 1 tablespoon chopped fresh basil, 1 tablespoon extra-virgin olive oil, 1 tablespoon fresh lemon juice, 1 tablespoon red wine vinegar, 1 teaspoon Dijon mustard and 3 garlic cloves, crushed. Season to taste with salt and pepper.

ABOUT THE AUTHOR

Susan Kiernan-Lewis is the author of the bestselling *Maggie Newberry Mysteries,* the post-apocalyptic thriller series *The Irish End Games, The Mia Kazmaroff Mysteries,* and *The Stranded in Provence Mysteries.* If you enjoyed *Murder in Nice,* please leave a review saying so on your purchase site.

To see sneak previews and giveaways as they happen, be sure and go my website at susankiernanlewis.com or my Author Facebook Page.

Printed in Great Britain
by Amazon